THE CHIEF'S WILD PROMISE

HIGHLAND SCANDAL: BOOK THREE

JAYNE CASTEL

All characters and situations in this publication are fictitious, and any resemblance to living persons is purely coincidental.

The Chief's Wild Promise by Jayne Castel

Copyright © 2025 by Jayne Castel. All rights reserved. No part of this publication may be reproduced, stored in a retrieval system, or transmitted in any form or by any means—electronic, mechanical, recording, or otherwise—without the prior written permission of the author.

NO AI TRAINING: Without in any way limiting the author's exclusive rights under copyright, any use of this publication to "train" generative artificial intelligence (AI) technologies to generate text is expressly prohibited. The author reserves all rights to license uses of this work for generative AI training and development of machine learning language models.

Published by Winter Mist Press

Edited by Tim Burton
Cover design by Winter Mist Press

Visit Jayne's website: **www.jaynecastel.com**

It started with a knife to the throat …

When a young clan-chief travels to meet his bride-to-be, their violent first encounter ignites a tempestuous relationship—one that risks ending in tragedy. High stakes collide with epic romance in Medieval Scotland.

Makenna MacGregor is about to slit a man's throat, when she discovers he's not one of the hated Campbells but her betrothed.

Unfortunately, Bran Mackinnon isn't quick to forgive and forget.

Worse still, her husband-to-be is prickly, proud, and dislikes the idea of having a warrior wife.

But Makenna won't put down her sword. Not for any man, especially with the enemy baying at her clan's borders.

Their marriage risks becoming a battlefield—until a vicious attack brings them together against a common foe.

Suddenly, they must both face what's really worth living, and dying, for.

Full of impossible choices, forbidden love, and steam, Jayne Castel's new series, HIGHLAND SCANDAL, is set on Medieval Isle of Mull and follows three unconventional sisters, and the men who put everything on the line for them.

CONTENT WARNINGS

THE CHIEF'S WILD PROMISE is a steamy Historical Romance intended for mature (18+) readers. Here is a list of content that some readers may find triggering:

Graphic sex
Beheading
Violence and murder

To all of us who want to be loved ... just as we are.

This novel is also dedicated to Historic Environment Scotland, which preserves Scotland's unique cultural heritage for generations to come.

MAPS

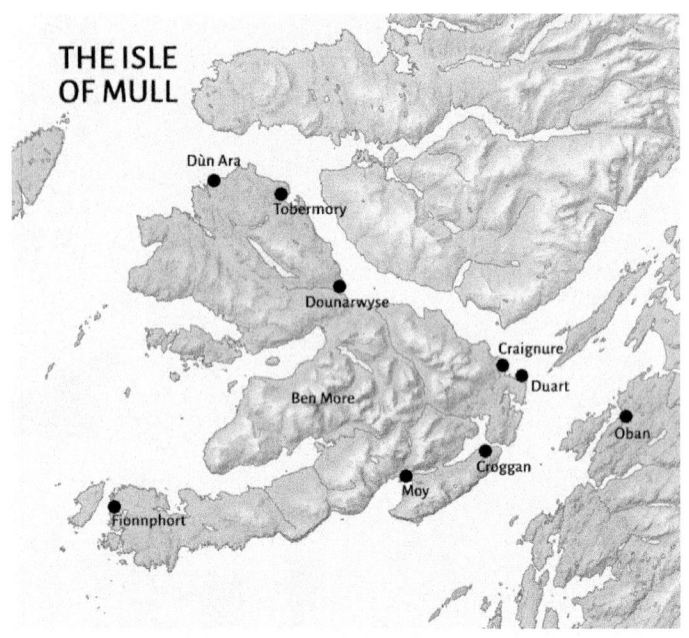

"I love you not only for what you are,
but for what I am when I am with you."
—**Elizabeth Barrett Browning**

1: A KNIFE TO THE THROAT

Southwest of Meggernie Castle
Perthshire, Scotland

Late April, 1319

THE JOURNEY HAD been uneventful—until they were within three miles of their destination.

It was close to dusk. The last of the sun was filtering through the woodland of sycamore, beech, and oak, and the sky above had turned indigo. Bran rode at the head of the company of forty men he'd brought from Dùn Ara. It was unseasonably cold, so he'd pulled his fur-lined cloak close. And as his horse traveled the narrow path between a thick press of trees and a tangle of hawthorn and elder, he silently cursed his father for making an agreement he'd felt obliged to keep.

Surely, a clan-chief could choose his own bride? However, just under four years earlier, Kendric Mackinnon made a pact with the MacGregor clan-chief. And now, here his son was, about to be shackled to a woman he'd never met.

Bran's belly tightened then, frustration clutching hard. His old man was still controlling him—even from beyond the grave. He hated that his life wasn't his own. He was nothing but a pawn.

Nonetheless, he'd done his best to delay this moment. He'd left his arrival as late as possible. It was now the eve of Bealtunn. His plan was to marry the woman with a minimum of fuss and depart for home as soon as possible.

He didn't want to linger at Meggernie.

The snapping of twigs underfoot yanked Bran from his brooding.

His chin jerked up as a host of warriors burst onto the path ahead of him.

Dirks gleaming in the gloaming, they rushed at Bran and his men.

"To arms!" he bellowed, swinging down from his courser and drawing his dirk. No sooner had he done so, when their attackers were on them.

The clash of steel rang through the shadowy woodland, followed by curses.

Fury ignited in Bran's gut.

What devilry is this? They were within striking distance of Meggernie and should have been safe in its shadow. Instead, this wild mob had appeared. And a feral-looking warband they were, with long tangled hair, worn leathers, and weather-stained cloaks. God's teeth, there were dozens of the bastards, rushing from the trees on all sides.

Teeth gritted, Bran ducked the swipe of a blade and kicked the feet out from under his attacker. Chaos had erupted on the path through the woods. The wagons following his men, drawn by feather-footed garrons, lurched to a halt. Meanwhile, the horses he and his men had been riding squealed, leaping out of the way of the struggling figures.

A hiss of pain cut through the air behind him—whether it was friend or foe, he wasn't sure. An agonized grunt followed, although Bran was too busy fighting to risk a glance over his shoulder. He brought his dirk up sharply then, just in time to prevent a blade to the belly.

Hades, these bastards were out for blood.

Ducking under his attacker's guard he jabbed hard, slicing open his arm. The warrior grunted a curse and reeled back. Bran spun on his heel then, to see that one of his men had indeed been felled and lay groaning a few feet away. He couldn't stop to help him. Instead, he swung left, just as a cloaked figure rushed at him, longsword thrusting.

He side-stepped swiftly, wishing there had been time for him to unstrap his heavy claidheamh-mòr from behind the saddle. A dirk was all well and good in close quarters, but his attacker's slender, lethal longsword made their fight decidedly one-sided. It was all he could do to fend off the slashing blade.

The warrior was smaller than him, their face hidden by a deep cowl, yet they fought viciously. Their duel continued, and the cloaked figure lunged.

Bran leaped backward, and as he did so, his foot caught on a tree root. The next thing he knew, he was lying flat on his back, looking up at the trees and the darkening sky.

The following moment, he found the cold, sharp tip of a blade at his throat.

"Don't breathe … if ye know what's good for ye."

Bran went rigid, not just because of the threat, but because the voice that had growled it was female. And as he stared up at his attacker, she raised her free hand and pushed back her hood. Cool moss-green eyes raked over him—and then she froze when her gaze reached his chest.

Staring up at her, Bran took in a strong-featured face, stubborn jaw, and full lips. She was young, no older than him, he reckoned, and under other circumstances, he might have found her comely.

But since this lass had just bested him, humiliation bit hard.

"Ye're a Mackinnon." Her words sounded more like an accusation than an observation. Of course, she'd just spied his plaid clan sash—a cross-hatching of red, blue, green, purple, and white. Earlier, it hadn't been visible, for he'd wrapped his cloak about him to ward off the chill.

"Aye," he ground out, anger simmering. "Ye have yer blade at the *clan-chief's* gullet."

Horror bloomed in those green eyes. "Cods." The curse came out in a wheeze. An instant later, she glanced around her. "Cease!" she shouted roughly. "It's Bran Mackinnon and his men."

Around him, the clang of steel and grunts of fighting faded away. Someone rasped a curse, while a few groans followed, but Bran paid the injured on either side little heed. Instead, he was too focused on glaring up at the lass who hadn't shifted the tip of her sword from his windpipe.

He was close to letting his temper get the better of him. "Aye, so ye know who I am now." He bit out each word, fury simmering. "Tell me who *ye* are."

The young woman swallowed, her expression strained. Then, abruptly, she withdrew her sword and took a step back from him. "Makenna MacGregor, daughter to the clan-chief," she replied curtly as she sheathed her sword at her side. "Yer *betrothed*."

What have ye done?

Makenna moved farther back from the man she'd just bested. The Mackinnon clan-chief still lay on his back, his silver-grey eyes glinting dangerously. Her blood was up, and her palm itched to redraw her sword, yet she stilled the impulse. She'd done enough damage. It was time to stand down now.

Even so, she didn't offer him her hand. She could tell he didn't want it anyway.

The Mackinnon rolled smoothly to his feet and unfolded his lanky frame, rising to his full height. He then brushed the leaves and dirt off his fine fur-lined cloak, his mouth pursed now as if he'd just tasted something foul.

Shaggy flame-red hair framed a lean, youthful face. Freckles dusted the bridge of his nose, although the bullish set of his jaw made anxiety flutter under her ribs.

He was vexed, and she couldn't blame him. Around them, warriors on both sides were injured, although the worst of the wounds appeared to belong to one of the Mackinnons. The man lay bleeding out on the ground nearby. Her chest constricted as she listened to his groans. He sounded in a bad way.

Da will be rabid.

She cleared her throat then, rallying. "We thought ye were Campbells."

"Aye, well, if ye had waited, ye would have seen our clan sashes," Mackinnon growled. "Why the devil would yer enemies stray this close to Meggernie?"

"They've grown bold of late," she replied stiffly, even as fire burned in the pit of her belly. His thinly veiled disdain rubbed her up the wrong way, making her momentarily forget her concern for his injured warrior. He had no idea how bad things were between the MacGregors and the Campbells. They'd long harried her clan, driving them out of the lands around Loch Awe so that her people had been pushed south. Those MacGregors who'd remained in the north had become Campbell tenants and were treated cruelly by all accounts. Now, to make matters worse, the Campbells of Breadalbane, whose lands lay south of her father's, had started to stir up trouble too.

The feuding with their neighbors was one of the reasons why her father had made so many alliances with powerful clans through marriage. It was why she'd been promised to Bran Mackinnon.

Quietly simmering, she watched as the clan-chief turned from her and went to the fallen man, crouching next to him. "How are ye holding up, Tadhg?" he asked roughly.

"Bleeding like a stuck pig," the big man grunted.

"We need to get him back to Meggernie," Makenna said, forcing a briskness into her voice she didn't feel. Guilt quickened her pulse and turned her palms clammy. "There's a healer there."

"I'm sure there is," Mackinnon replied between gritted teeth. His gaze swung around, piercing her like an arrow. "But Tadhg wouldn't need assistance if ye hadn't come at us like rabid dogs."

Makenna's gaze narrowed, even as heat washed over her once more. *Rabid dogs?* "Ye are speaking of the Meggernie *Guard*, Mackinnon," she ground out.

The clan-chief stood up once more, surveying the men—some of them nursing injuries—who'd gathered behind

Makenna. His lip then curled. "Maybe, but ye look like a band of cutthroats to me."

Bran quietly fumed as he followed the MacGregors northwest. He'd been in a foul mood before the attack, but he was *furious* now.

Not for the first time that day, he cursed Kendric Mackinnon. The devil roast his father in hell. The bastard's scheming and selfishness had landed him in this mess. He had few fond memories of the man who'd sired him. Indeed, whenever he recalled the oppressive environment he'd grown up in, a dull ache rose under his ribs. Even as a bairn, he'd been lonely. Life at Dùn Ara would have been unbearable had it not been for his sister.

Tara. Heat washed over Bran then. She'd been the one person he thought he could count on, and yet she'd betrayed not only her clan, but her own brother.

Gut clenching, he shoved his sister from his thoughts and shifted his focus from kin back to the company of Mackinnons surrounding him. Following the attack—many of them bloodied and grimacing from their injuries—they'd warily mounted their horses and continued their journey.

However, there was no conversation, no banter. Tadhg wasn't in a good state. They'd managed to get him into the saddle, although the warrior now sat slumped, one arm cradling his midsection. His head hung, and when his horse had moved off, he grunted in pain.

The mood was understandably tense, and a few of his warriors now wore mutinous expressions.

Bran wondered if any of them blamed him for this situation. After all, they wouldn't be in Perthshire if he hadn't ridden here to keep his dead father's promise.

Teeth gritted, Bran urged his mount forward. That was his problem in a nutshell. His sense of honor was a weakness, not a strength. He didn't owe his father, or the MacGregors, anything. Yet, here he was, like an obedient dog.

His attention swung then to the small figure that marched ahead of him on the track. Like the others of her band, she traveled on foot.

Eyes still upon the hellcat who'd nearly severed his windpipe, Bran's gaze narrowed.

Makenna MacGregor carried herself proudly. Despite that mud splattered the hem of her cloak, he could see that it was of fine weave.

Her boots, too, were well made, and when she'd moved back from him earlier and her cloak parted, he'd seen that she wasn't dressed like the grizzled warriors surrounding her. Instead, she wore a long leather surcote over a pine-green woolen kirtle. Both garments were split at the sides for ease of movement, and as she'd stepped away from him, he caught a glimpse of the thick leather chausses she wore underneath.

Aye, the woman was a warrior, but there was no mistaking that she was high-born.

Somehow though, she held onto her femininity. Her brown hair, threaded with auburn highlights, tumbled becomingly down her back, although she'd made another concession to practicality by braiding the sides and pulling them back into slender plaits so her hair didn't fall in her face when fighting. And when she'd stood over him, Bran had breathed in the scent of an expensive perfume: rose, moss, and musk.

The lady was the greatest contradiction he'd ever encountered.

Bran's lips compressed then. He'd been expecting a sweet, biddable, gently-bred bride-to-be—and patient too, he'd made her wait long enough—not a vicious shrew.

Ahead, the bower of sycamores drew apart then, making him drag his glare away from between Makenna MacGregor's shoulder blades.

2: A MAN OF HONOR

MEGGERNIE CASTLE ROSE before them: a mighty tower house with mossy ramparts brushing the cobalt sky. Bran didn't want to be impressed, but he was. There was no denying it, the seat of the MacGregors of Perthshire was fine indeed, and he found himself comparing it to Dùn Ara. He'd always been proud of his home, but now insecurity wreathed up.

Perched on the north banks of a meandering river, Meggernie's lofty sandstone walls glowed in the gloaming. The last of the light was leaching from the world now, and Bran spied figures on the ramparts, lighting braziers. There were also sentries—many of them—keeping watch. Meggernie was well-defended, and it needed to be if they were expecting enemies on their doorstep.

Bran scowled. Even if the lass *had* been telling the truth, Makenna and her rabble should have made sure they were dealing with Campbells before attacking.

Unlike his fortress, which perched upon a crag, this castle sat on the flat valley floor of Glen Lyon, in the heart of Breadalbane. From this distance, it appeared larger than Dùn Ara—big enough to house an orchard, garden, and a small community. It had a settled look, as if it had always been part of the land.

Indeed, Meggernie hadn't been an easy stronghold to reach, for sprawling mountains surrounded it to the north and south, providing a natural defense from outsiders.

Bran fought a grimace. Dùn Ara's setting was more remote and far less bucolic. Would his bride be disappointed when she set eyes on it?

Anger spiked through him then, although this time, it wasn't directed at the MacGregors, his father, or at the woman who'd just tried to kill him. No, he was vexed with himself. Why was he comparing his fortress to this one? His crippling self-doubt galled him.

Ye're a Mackinnon of Mull, he reminded himself as his fingers tightened around the reins. *And equal to any other clan-chief in Scotland.*

Yanking himself from his brooding, he caught sight of a huge mound of branches and twigs upon the wide meadow that stretched between the river and the woodland to the south. Of course, it was the eve of Bealtunn, and the locals had built a bonfire for tonight's celebrations. After dark, the folk of Meggernie would guise themselves and gather around the fire, dancing, drinking, and singing as they welcomed the summer.

Bran hoped he wouldn't be expected to join them.

The party of MacGregors and Mackinnons eventually clattered over the bridge spanning the river and passed through the large stone arch that led into the bailey beyond.

The heavy stone walls swallowed them whole, and tension curled like an adder about to strike under Bran's ribs.

Drawing up his horse in the cobbled bailey, he cast a suspicious eye around. Ire continued to churn in his gut. The fingers of his right hand itched to close around the hilt of his dirk.

Steady, man, he reminded himself as he swung down from the sturdy courser who'd carried him all the way from Oban. *MacGregor didn't invite ye here with murder on his mind.*

Perhaps not, but after his betrothed's behavior, he'd keep his guard up.

Behind him, the warriors he'd brought with him clattered into the bailey. The carts of weapons and supplies—most of which would be given to the MacGregor as part of their arrangement—followed. They rumbled under the portcullis, drawn by the heavyset ponies.

Two large archways spanned opposite sides of the bailey. Through one, Bran spied apple and pear trees that were newly in leaf, while through the other, he caught sight of neatly tended vegetable plots. Aye, Meggernie was a thriving community, and he found himself wishing Dùn Ara had orchards within its walls. Maybe he should—

He cut his thoughts off savagely. Cods. What was the matter with him this evening?

"Mackinnon!" A loud, hearty voice boomed off stone. Bran's chin kicked up, his gaze swinging right to where a broad, stocky figure bounded down the steps of the tower house.

Bruce MacGregor was well into his fifth decade now, and running to fat these days, but he moved like a man half his age.

Clad in chamois braies, a snowy lèine, and a leather vest, which his gut strained against, he had ruddy cheeks and a thick head of brown hair shot through with silver.

Bran's jaw set as he met the older man's gaze.

The MacGregor clan-chief's moss-green eyes were warm. He grinned then, two deep dimples forming on either side of a wide mouth. "Och, I'd forgotten how bright yer hair is, lad. Ye'll have no need to carry a torch when ye travel at night."

This comment drew snorts of laughter from the other MacGregors around them, although the Mackinnon men knew better than to snigger.

Bran didn't answer. He couldn't care less what the clan-chief had to say about his hair. Flame-red, it ran through his family. What *did* vex him though was MacGregor's use of 'lad'.

Bran was three and twenty. He'd fought in battles and ruled northern Mull ever since his father's death. He was a clan-chief too, of the same rank as MacGregor—and he'd had the integrity to make good on his father's promise. It was bad enough that he'd started to doubt himself as he approached Meggernie; he didn't appreciate being talked down to by this paunchy laird.

It was time he made things clear.

"That must be why yer daughter and her *rabble* spied us so easily," he replied, his tone wintry. "Right before they attacked us."

That wiped the broad smile off MacGregor's face.

A few yards away, Makenna shifted her weight from one foot to the other, even as her chin rose. She was readying herself for a storm, and Bran hoped it would be a vicious one.

Bruce MacGregor studied Bran for a long moment, his green eyes—the same mossy shade as his daughter's—hardening.

Then he shifted his attention to his daughter. "What's this, Makenna?" His voice was still jovial, yet there was an edge to it now.

She cleared her throat. "We thought they were Campbells."

"We were riding through the woods, upon the road that heads straight for Meggernie," Bran replied. "Our weapons were sheathed, and we were minding our own business."

"None of us saw their clan sashes!" Makenna gasped out the words. The lass wasn't so sure of herself now. She'd been defiant with Bran but was less so with her father. A nerve flickered in her cheek, and he was pleased to see that a faint sheen of sweat shone on her brow. "We were on our way back from Fortingall. The Campbells of Breadalbane raided the village yesterday." Her voice faltered then, yet she pushed on. "They killed most of the men and took the women and bairns." She cut Bran a glare. "We thought more of them were scouting around Meggernie."

"Whoresons!" the MacGregor clan-chief growled. "How *dare* they?"

A strained silence fell in the bailey. Bran's gaze flicked between father and daughter. Of course, he knew of the feuding between the MacGregors and the Campbells—everyone in the Highlands did—but Makenna hadn't told him that one of their villages had just been attacked.

He'd had no idea the feuding between the clans had gotten this bad. It was no wonder the MacGregor wished to strengthen his relationship with the Mackinnons of Dùn Ara, and requested Bran bring a company of his finest warriors with him to Perthshire, half of whom would remain at Meggernie.

He needed allies to push back against the Campbells.

"Yer neighbors grow bold," he noted, shattering the tension.

"Aye," MacGregor said roughly. "Duncan Campbell accused us of stealing his cattle a few years back. The shitweasel has harried us ever since."

Bran raised an eyebrow. "And *did* ye steal Campbell's cattle?"

MacGregor scowled. "Maybe one or two ... but Black Duncan uses that as an excuse ... what he really wants is to drive us out of this glen and take Meggernie for his own."

Bran considered the clan-chief's words. He'd never met 'Black' Duncan Campbell but had heard how ruthless and shrewd the chieftain was. He wasn't keen to become embroiled in this feud either. He had his own defenses to worry about, his own problems. Ever since becoming clan-chief, he'd struggled to win his people's respect. To many of them, he was the whelp who surrendered to the Macleans—and they couldn't forgive him for that.

In return, he resented them for making him their scapegoat.

They forgot he was a man of flesh and blood, and one who'd worked hard to do right by them.

The MacGregor clan-chief roused himself then, tearing his focus from the hated Campbells. "Apologies, Mackinnon," he muttered. "My daughter acted hastily." He cast Makenna a glare that could have soured milk before his attention shifted to the men who filled the bailey behind Bran. "I trust no one was hurt?"

"Some of my men will need to be stitched up ... and one of them has a deep wound on his flank," Bran replied, gesturing to where Tadhg hadn't yet dismounted from his horse. The man's face was now worryingly ashen.

Makenna cleared her throat. "A number of our warriors have injuries that require looking at as well," she informed her father huskily.

The clan chief's strong jaw bunched. He then glanced over his shoulder at a balding warrior with piercing blue eyes, wearing a quilted gambeson and leather braies, who stood to his right. "Walker ... tell the healer to ready the infirmary."

The man nodded before moving away.

MacGregor then focused on Bran once more. "Ye have received a poor welcome ... but we shall remedy things. Leave yer horses with my men and join me shortly in the great hall." He halted then, his attention flicking to where Makenna stood, unspeaking. The woman still held herself as proudly as before, yet her expression had shadowed. "Makenna ... I shall speak to ye upstairs ... alone."

Anger now smoldered in the clan-chief's eyes, and vindication ignited in Bran's belly.

Good.

3: MACGREGOR'S DAUGHTERS

"WHAT THE DEVIL did ye think ye were doing?" The MacGregor's voice boomed through the solar high in Meggernie's tower house. "I sent ye out on patrol ... not to make an attempt on Bran Mackinnon's life."

Makenna swallowed. "Da, I—" she began, but her father cut her off.

"Was it deliberate, lass?"

She gasped at the accusation, even as heat rolled over her. After the fuss she'd made of late about her impending marriage, she shouldn't have been surprised her father would draw such a conclusion. However, he was wrong. "No!"

"Oh, aye?" The MacGregor folded his beefy arms across his chest and viewed her down his long blade-like nose.

She'd inherited that nose. His mouth and eyes too. And his stubbornness.

"So, ye thought the Black Duncan's warriors had actually dared venture so close to Meggernie?"

"Aye! Ye didn't see the mess they made of Fortingall," she countered, her own temper rising now, even as her belly twisted. "They *razed* it, Da."

Indeed, the smoking ruin of the village had haunted her all the way home—it would do so for a long while. The only survivors of the raid had been a handful of elderly, too sick or feeble to pose a threat and not valuable enough to carry off. Makenna's chest had ached when they'd told her what happened, and she'd sworn then and there that she'd have reckoning.

MacGregor muttered a salty curse under his breath and turned from her. He then started to stalk around his rectangular solar, his large hands clenching and unclenching at his sides. A hearth burned up one end of the chamber, where two slender deerhounds lay gnawing mutton bones. It was dark outdoors now, and the sacking had been rolled down over the narrow slitted windows to keep out the draft. Weapons hung from the rough stone walls—poleaxes, claidheamh-mòrs, and shields—while sheepskins covered most of the wooden floor. The air in here smelled of leather, woodsmoke—and dog.

"We can't let them get away with it," Makenna said as she watched him circle the floor. It was a relief to shift the focus away from what she'd done and back on the Campbells. Her heart started to thud against her ribs then. "Give the word, and we shall travel to Finlarig and pay them back."

Her father halted abruptly and swiveled on his heel, fixing her with a glare that nearly made her wither. "Ye shall do no such thing!"

Makenna choked back a curse. "But we must respond!"

"And *we* will," he shot back. "Once ye are wedded and Mackinnon takes ye back to Mull, Captain Walker and I will come up with a solid plan on how to deal with the Campbells. Meanwhile, *ye* will put down yer sword for the remainder of yer time at Meggernie, sweeten yer tongue, and mend the mess ye have made."

Panic washed over Makenna, making her breathing come fast and shallow. Put down her sword? Never! Her father was denying her the reckoning she craved—the worst punishment of all. She didn't want to focus on Mackinnon. Especially not now. Her *people* were what mattered. "It was an honest mistake," she said, cursing as her voice caught. "I told ye, we—"

"I heard ye the first time," he cut her off once more. "I may be getting old, but I'm not yet demented."

Bran hadn't thought his arrival at Meggernie could get any more awkward or unpleasant—but that was before he stepped into the castle's great hall.

Although MacGregor had insisted his men would take care of the horses, Bran had gone into the stables to ensure everything was in order. Some of his men would be bedding down in there, and he wished to make sure there was, indeed, space for them. After the welcome he'd received, he'd take nothing as a given.

Nonetheless, when he walked into the large rectangular hall afterward, his boots crunching on fresh rushes, and his gaze alighted on those already seated at the clan-chief's table at the far end, his belly dropped to his boots.

What are they doing here?

Just a few yards away reclined a tall blond man with roguish good looks. And at his elbow sat a broad-shouldered warrior with short dark-auburn hair.

The devil smite them. Alec Rankin and Rae Maclean were at Meggernie too.

Bran's step slowed. His pulse started to thunder in his ears, and crimson now stained his vision. This was too much. Did MacGregor really expect him to break bread with the man who'd slain his father? Or the chieftain who'd bested him in battle? He was surprised that Loch Maclean wasn't here too—to make his humiliation complete.

A familiar burn began in the pit of his gut. He forced himself to keep walking, to cross the wide floor, down the aisle between rows of trestle tables, where his men now took their places with Maclean and MacGregor warriors.

Both Rankin and Maclean watched him closely as he approached.

Stubbornness rose within Bran then. If either of those whoresons wanted a reaction, they wouldn't get one.

Mastering himself, he schooled his features into the blankest expression he could manage. On the inside though, he was raging.

At least, they didn't bring Tara.

The burn in his belly grew hotter then.

His sister's betrayal was like a scab—best left well alone, yet he could never resist picking at it.

Ye adored her once, a voice whispered to him then, reminding him of happier days.

Tara had once been his ally, his confidant, and the softness to counterbalance his father's harsh temperament and unyielding demands. Life had turned bleak without her.

A hollow sensation filled him. He'd been alone in the world for a while now yet never felt it quite as keenly as he did at this moment. Soon, he'd be wed surrounded by MacGregors and Macleans, with no kin by his side. His parents were dead, and he had no siblings except for a sister he'd disowned.

As he drew near to the clan-chief's table, both Rankin and Maclean rose to their feet. Their female companions did the same. In truth, Bran had been too focused on seeing his enemies here to take note of much else—but he did now.

Rankin's companion was a dark-haired, golden-skinned beauty with strong features and night-brown eyes. She wore a wine-red surcote that clung to her shapely form, and she surveyed him with interest. The woman with Maclean also observed him keenly. She too had strong, proud features, but her beauty was gentler. Her thick oak-colored hair was swept up into an elaborate braid.

There was a similar cast to both their features—and they reminded him of someone else. However, before he had time to make the connection, Maclean spoke. "Good evening, Mackinnon."

Next to him, Rankin favored Bran with a nod, his sea-blue gaze veiled. "Mackinnon."

Bran managed a tight nod of his own. He didn't trust himself to speak.

"May I present my wife, Kylie." Rae motioned to the woman beside him. He then gestured to the two young lads seated next to the woman—one auburn-haired, the other dark. "And these two are my sons, Ailean and Lyle."

Bran's gaze narrowed. He knew he should respond, but the words stuck in his throat.

"And I'm Liza ... laird of Moy." The dark-haired woman spoke then, not waiting for anyone to introduce her.

Bran stiffened, and he looked upon her with renewed interest, putting his rancor aside for a moment.

Of course. He should have made the connection. Aye, he'd heard of Liza Maclean. The tale about how her husband, the former chieftain of Moy, had tried to murder her by tying her up and leaving her on a rock in the Sound of Mull had circulated the isle the year before. She'd been rescued by pirates and had hired them to slay her husband and take his place. Shockingly, Loch Maclean had pardoned her and allowed her to rule as lady laird until her son came of age.

Suddenly, everything fell into place. Bran hadn't realized that the pirate who'd saved Liza had been Alec Rankin, or that she'd married him. Still chewing over this scandalous tidbit, he noted that a lad of around six or seven sat next to Liza. He was dark like his mother yet with a solemn face.

Marking the direction of Bran's gaze, Liza smiled. "This is my son, Craeg."

He managed to summon the manners to incline his head to them both.

He had no quarrel with this woman or her son, even if her first husband had fought against him at Dounarwysc. Even so, it was hard to remain civil. He felt cornered. Tricked. MacGregor would have known he wouldn't want to see Maclean and Rankin, and yet he'd invited them to the wedding, nonetheless.

"I see ye have been reacquainted with auld pals," a hearty male voice boomed behind him. "And met two of my bonnie daughters."

Bran stiffened. *His daughters?*

He turned then, his gaze alighting on where the clan-chief approached, a woman on his arm. Two other couples followed, with Makenna sullenly bringing up the rear.

And when his gaze swept over the newcomers, he realized why Maclean and Rankin were here. They were married to MacGregor women.

MacGregor's wife was an older, plumper version of Liza—a comely woman indeed, with a thick mane of greying hair that would have once been the color of jet. Despite that they'd just emerged from a bitter winter and wet spring, and everybody else was pasty white, Lady MacGregor's skin was tanned light gold.

"I won't expect ye to remember everyone's names right away, lad … but allow me to introduce the rest of my family." MacGregor went on. He seemed to have recovered from the news that one of his villages had been attacked—and the shock of learning that his daughter had tried to kill her betrothed—and his hearty manner was firmly back in place. Nonetheless, to Bran, it seemed a little strained, as if he was trying to force an atmosphere of good cheer.

"This is my bonnie wife, Carmen." He gestured next to the two sets of couples behind him. A group of bairns followed them—the eldest of whom looked around twelve summers, the youngest around four or five. "And here are my two other daughters … Sonia and Alma … their husbands, Connor MacFarlane and Rory Lamont … and their broods."

Bran fought the urge to frown.

Sonia. That name tugged at a memory. It reminded him of something he just couldn't place. A moment later though, it came to him.

His father had mentioned that name. He remembered other details too then. Hadn't he been promised to the *eldest* of the daughters ... to a lass named 'Sonia'? Not Makenna. That didn't make sense—but maybe he'd misheard his father. Both Sonia and Alma looked at least a decade older than him and were clearly wedded. Indeed, after meeting all five of MacGregor's daughters, it was obvious that Makenna was the youngest of the brood.

Something strange was afoot here.

Bran's skin prickled then.

Fortunately, he had a document in his baggage, one that his father and MacGregor had both signed. Since his father had explained the agreement he'd made to him, Bran had never bothered to glance at it over the years. In truth, he'd been loath to touch the cursed thing that bound him to a woman he'd never met. But as soon as he had a moment alone, he'd make sure to refamiliarize himself with the terms of their agreement.

His pulse quickened. Had he just discovered a way out of this marriage?

"And, of course ... ye have already met Makenna." The clan-chief's dry tone caused an explosion of smothered coughs and smiles from around them.

Bran didn't share their amusement. And neither did Makenna. His betrothed's cheeks were flushed, her jaw set. She didn't look any happier than him.

The lass had changed clothing since he'd seen her last though and tidied herself up. She now wore a becoming dark-blue surcote over a sky-blue kirtle. The garments fitted her small, compact form perfectly, accentuating the swell of her hips and the dip of her waist. Her hair was unbound, falling over her shoulders in glistening waves.

Aye, his betrothed was comely enough, although right now, Bran would have preferred to have wed the Bean Nighe herself.

They all seated themselves around the clan-chief's table—a tight squeeze with so many present. Servants had added a trestle table at each end to accommodate everyone.

Once again, a familiar emptiness tugged at Bran's insides. What would it have been like to have grown up with such a big family? All the same, he wasn't sure he'd have wanted five sisters. Tara had been enough.

Trying to focus, he took the seat he was directed to. Unfortunately, he was between the clan-chief and his betrothed. Nonetheless, he was relieved to be seated far from Maclean and Rankin. He had nothing to say to either of them.

Serving lads appeared then, carrying huge tureens of what smelled like venison stew and baskets of oaten bread.

The aroma was delicious, and Bran's belly rumbled. Nonetheless, he couldn't focus on the food. Not after the events of the past couple of hours.

And meanwhile, that agreement was sitting in his bag upstairs, waiting to be read. He itched to get his hands on it.

"Yer warriors have had their injuries dressed, Mackinnon ... and our healer is taking good care of Tadhg." Carmen MacGregor met his gaze from where she sat on the clan-chief's other side.

Her voice was warm and heavily accented. Bran recognized the inflection, for he'd met a few foreign merchants who docked at Tobermory and Dùn Ara over the years. He'd wager the woman was Iberian. "All he needs now is time."

Bran nodded, forcing himself to soften his expression a little. The woman was gracious, and he couldn't bring himself to be rude to her. "Let us hope he'll rally."

"Och, he will, laddie." MacGregor slapped him on the back, with such force that Bran nearly splattered hot stew over himself. "No hard feelings, eh?"

Bran bit the inside of his cheek to prevent himself from snarling at the clan-chief. The man was laying it on thick now. *Laddie*. Did MacGregor think he was a swaddled bairn?

And as for 'no hard feelings?' "Aye, well, we'll see," he muttered.

"How about a smile, eh?" MacGregor boomed in his ear. "This is no place for such a miserable face. Ye are about to wed my bonnie daughter!"

"Yer 'bonnie daughter' attacked me," Bran shot back. "Why should I rejoice about our union?"

MacGregor snorted, brushing his comment aside. "It was but a misunderstanding … one Makenna is very sorry for."

Bran had to hand it to him. MacGregor was doing a fine job of trying to blether his way out of a tense situation. It wouldn't work though. He wasn't appeased.

"She doesn't appear sorry," he answered coldly. It was true. The lass didn't look remotely contrite. Instead, she sat next to him, her chin tilted at a defiant angle, her eyes slightly narrowed.

"Of course she is. Come, lad. Put it behind ye now."

Bran glared at the clan-chief. His gut was in knots, killing his appetite. Farther down the table, he caught Alec Rankin's smirk, and his temper flared bright once more.

"Does something amuse ye, Rankin?" he growled.

To his ire, the pirate's smile merely widened.

4: FORGIVE AND FORGET

"THE WEDDING SHALL take place three days from today," Makenna's father announced, holding his goblet aloft. "Let us toast to that."

Murmurs went through the hall as those present raised their drinks high.

Makenna followed suit, even as her pulse throbbed in her ears.

Three days. It wouldn't matter if it were three months. Or three *years.* She didn't want to marry Mackinnon.

She also didn't want to be sitting here, lingering over a fine supper, as if the Campbells hadn't just dealt them a savage blow. The memory of the smoldering ruin of Fortingall made it difficult to relax. How could she when there was reckoning to be had? And how could her father deny her something so important?

She took a gulp of wine and set down her cup before reluctantly picking up her spoon.

She then dug it into the rich stew and stirred, watching as steam wreathed up.

Queasiness rolled over her. Indeed, she had no wish to remain here, eating her supper next to her surly husband-to-be. However, after her poor judgment today, her father wouldn't suffer any more trouble from her. Reaching for the bread, she tore a chunk off and dipped it carefully into the hot stew. Around her, conversation flowed, as did the excellent Iberian wine her mother always served.

The mood inside the great hall was too buoyant for Makenna's liking. Everyone was excited about the forthcoming wedding, yet it was also Bealtunn—and the people of Meggernie were looking forward to celebrating the transition between spring and summer. Nonetheless, her mind kept returning to what had happened at Fortingall. Those seated around her hadn't witnessed the ruin. They didn't realize just how brutal the Campbells had been.

Meanwhile, her betrothed's pale, pinched face and smoldering silvery eyes all made his mood clear, as did his acerbic responses.

Makenna took care not to look his way as she focused now on getting through her meal. There was little space at the clan-chief's table this evening—not with so many guests present—and she was sitting so close to her husband-to-be that their elbows kept bumping.

Unfortunately, the man seemed to favor his left hand, while she used her right, which meant they were getting in each other's way. They sat *so* close that she could smell him: a blend of leather, horse, and a spicy undertone that was purely masculine. Curse him, it wasn't at all unpleasant.

If only her father would cease his ribbing. He continued to engage the younger man, meeting each growled answer with a grin or a back slap.

Makenna's pulse quickened. He needed to leave Mackinnon be. He clearly thought that if he talked his ear off and plied him with food and drink, he'd forgive and forget.

But with each passing moment, her betrothed looked increasingly vexed.

Raising her gaze, she met Kylie's eye across the table.

A few months earlier, when Makenna had been at Dounarwyse broch with her sister, they'd talked often of this union—in truth, they'd argued about it. Initially, Kylie had been dismissive of her worries and complaints. After weathering an unhappy first marriage, her sister didn't see why her younger sister should wriggle out of her obligations. However, her attitude had eventually softened, and the shadows in Kylie's oak-colored eyes hinted that she was now worried for her sister.

Makenna tore her attention from Kylie then and stole a glance at her betrothed. Mackinnon gripped his wooden spoon so tightly that she wondered if he was imagining driving it into her father's eye.

Tara had said her brother had a fiery temper, and she hadn't been wrong. At the same time though, the man was holding himself on a leash. How long before it snapped?

An unexpected jolt of sympathy for her betrothed stabbed her then. How humiliating this evening must be for him. Attacked by his bride-to-be and forced to break bread with his enemies. It was a lot to stomach.

Seemingly oblivious, the MacGregor continued to boom in his ear.

Makenna frowned. Her father was never usually *this* garrulous. Her pulse quickened then. Of course, he'd be worried too that the Mackinnon chief might discover his ruse. He'd been uncharacteristically nervous about his arrival. This alliance was important for their clan, and he couldn't afford to have anything put it at risk.

He was now regaling her betrothed with tales of his youth and the adventures he'd had. "I broke with tradition by wedding the daughter of an Iberian wine merchant," the clan-chief admitted before reaching over and squeezing his wife's arm. "One glance at the raven-haired beauty and I was smitten."

Carmen MacGregor waved him away, even as her night-brown eyes glowed with pleasure. "Ye do talk rot, man. If I recall, ye were too busy driving a hard bargain with my father."

Their banter continued. Meanwhile, Mackinnon had subsided into stony silence. His lips compressed into a thin, hard line.

Heat washed over Makenna. She was used to her parents' ways and usually didn't mind their boisterous exchanges or unabashed affection for each other. But this evening, she found herself embarrassed by it—and not a little resentful.

Aye, her father had broken with tradition, yet she wasn't permitted to.

All Makenna wanted, right down to the depths of her soul, was to continue serving in her father's Guard, to keep her clan safe. Instead, she was about to be shackled to a man she didn't want. Soon she'd be living far from her beloved Meggernie.

Her throat tightened then, and she swallowed a mouthful of stew with difficulty.

At the other end of the table, Sonia and Alma animatedly chatted together, ignoring their dour-faced husbands. Those two marriages weren't particularly happy ones, yet her sisters didn't appear to mind much. However, when Makenna's attention shifted farther down the table to where Rae gazed into Kylie's eyes, her chest constricted.

Aye, she knew her sister had weathered years of unhappiness and loneliness when she'd been wed to Errol Grant. If anyone deserved love, it was her. Rae raised a tender hand then and brushed a stray strand of hair from her cheek. Makenna looked away, her attention alighting on Liza and Alec. And curse them both, there was no doubt they were in love either. They were teasing each other, and Alec had slung a protective arm around Liza's shoulders.

Anger stabbed her in the belly then. *How can they all carry on like this, when our people have been murdered?*

She deliberately put down her spoon and reached for her goblet of wine instead.

Enough food. What she needed tonight was wine. Lots of it. This would be a long evening, for once they finished eating and drinking, they'd venture beyond the castle walls and join the people of Meggernie at the Bealtunn bonfire. This year though, her father had instructed more of his Guard than usual to keep a close watch on the festivities. After Fortingall, they had to be vigilant.

Usually at Bealtunn, Makenna prepared a guise, but not this year. She just couldn't get into the spirit of things. Draining her goblet, she then reached for the ewer in front of her and topped it up. To the brim.

She felt a gaze upon her then and glanced right to find Mackinnon watching her.

And it wasn't a friendly look either. His eyes were narrowed, his lean jaw bunched in an expression of stern disapproval. Clearly, he thought she was consuming too much wine.

God's troth. The man was too young to have the demeanor of a censorious priest. The sympathy she'd felt for him earlier drained away, annoyance replacing it.

Eyeballing him, Makenna lifted the goblet to her lips and took a deep, thoroughly unladylike, draft. *How do ye like that, then?*

The shrill notes of a Highland pipe rang through the crisp night air.

Bairns chased each other around the fire. In contrast, the adults were a little more subdued. News of the massacre at Fortingall had now spread throughout the castle, and many of those who stood near the bonfire, cups of apple wine in hand, wore worried expressions as they huddled together. Some of them shot veiled glances to where, on the perimeters of the celebrations, shadowy figures stood watch over the road and the edge of the woodlands.

It was a reminder of the dangers that lurked beyond the sturdy walls of their castle—dangers that had been growing for a while now.

Of course, the children were largely oblivious. Craeg, Ailean, and Lyle were amongst the bairns, their faces ruddy with excitement. The trio was far from home, and this journey to Perthshire was an adventure for them all.

Moths danced above the licking flames, some of them immolated when they dived too close. Makenna watched them. Standing amongst her kin, she felt detached from her surroundings, as if she were viewing Bealtunn from above.

"Have ye had a chance to mend things with Mackinnon yet?" Liza's voice intruded then, dragging her back to earth.

Makenna cut her sister an irritated look. She usually loved spending time with Liza and Kylie. Of all her sisters, she was the closest to them. But this evening, they were both rubbing her up the wrong way. "No." She was aware then that Kylie had moved closer and was watching her intensely. "He'd bite my head off if I tried."

She focused properly on her sisters then. Unlike her, Liza and Kylie had guised themselves for Bealtunn. Kylie had painted her face white and her mouth blood red and clad herself in a becoming low-cut green kirtle so she resembled one of the Baobhan Sith—beautiful vampiric fairies known for seducing men and then draining their blood. Liza was also dressed in green, although she wore a headdress with straw-colored hair and goat horns upon her head. She'd guised herself as a Glaistig, the mythological 'green maiden'.

Both Kylie and Liza looked arresting, if a little intimidating.

"He certainly appears to be in a foul temper this eve," Kylie noted. "I'd have thought he'd have calmed down by now … especially after some MacGregor hospitality."

"Aye, well, it doesn't help that Da continues to goad him."

Liza cocked an eyebrow. "I thought he was trying to cheer him up?"

Makenna snorted, even as her annoyance swelled. Her sisters were trying to lighten the mood, yet she didn't want it lightened.

Instead, she shifted her attention across the crowd to where her husband-to-be stood with her father and Captain Walker. MacGregor was talking volubly, red in the face after a surfeit of ale. Mackinnon replied with a curled lip.

One didn't need to hear their conversation to know he still wasn't appeased.

"I'm sure he'll warm to ye." Makenna flashed Kylie a withering look at this comment, but her sister pressed on. "It was an unfortunate start ... but ye just need time to get to know one another."

Makenna cursed under her breath and took a large gulp from her cup. Meanwhile, both her sisters raised their eyebrows. Aye, it was a salty curse—one many of the guards she served alongside used regularly. Had their mother been within earshot, she'd have boxed her youngest daughter's ears for using such language. However, Carmen was gossiping with friends a few yards distant and didn't hear her. "He won't 'warm up'," she growled. "And neither will I."

It was fine for Kylie to make such comments. She was wed to a man who'd healed her cynical heart. She now believed in love again.

A hot and prickly sensation washed over her then. Christ's blood. She wished she could run away from all of this, but that wasn't her way. Her throat grew tight, and the back of her eyelids started to sting. Curse it, she'd drunk far too much wine throughout the evening. She'd done it largely to spite Mackinnon but regretted it now. The wine had brought her emotions to the surface.

Clearing her throat, she focused on the roaring bonfire once more. The piper had struck up another rousing tune, and men and women danced alongside the bairns. The scent of woodsmoke filled the night air.

Makenna wished she could enjoy it, but she couldn't.

Squeezing her eyes shut, she silently counted to ten, mastering herself.

Drawing in a deep breath, she glanced her sisters' way once more, to find them both frowning, concern shadowing their eyes. Her irritation toward them faded. She didn't want them fretting over her. "Don't fash yerselves," she said huskily. "I shall rally." She broke off then, dredging up a brittle smile. "And ye are right … perhaps things will improve tomorrow." *Lord, if only it were that easy.* "Maybe Mackinnon and I can start again."

5: IN YER OWN HAND

ALONE IN HIS bedchamber, Bran crossed to the leather satchels the servants had carried upstairs.

Finally.

He dug around inside one of them until he found the scroll he'd brought with him. The urge to rip it open thrummed through him. But, making himself wait, he poured himself a large cup of wine first. He'd refrained from drowning himself in the stuff during supper and the Bealtunn celebrations.

He was already close to storming from Meggernie, and it would take little to persuade him. All evening, the MacGregor clan-chief had shouted in his ear. The man had a hide like a boar too. He'd been *deliberately* impervious to every accusation Bran hurled his way. The man was desperate to make this alliance work; that much was clear.

Makenna hadn't been as restrained with the wine.

The lass had downed cups like an alehouse slattern. And by the time her sisters had escorted her back to the castle, her cheeks were apple-red, and she'd stumbled over her feet.

Taking a much-needed gulp of the rich, peppery wine, Bran crossed to where a log of pine smoldered in the hearth. MacGregor had given him a chamber that was comfortable enough, although right now, it felt like a cage. The urge to saddle his horse and gallop away into the night seized him once more, yet he quashed it. Mackinnons didn't run from their enemies.

Face screwing up, he took another slug of wine. Aye, Macleans surrounded him here, and his father's killer was sleeping under the same roof. Bran's grip on his cup tightened. The pirate had been laughing at him tonight. Did he think him a fazart? Maybe he should challenge Rankin to a fight to the death.

Aye, that would help, he chastised himself. *As if ye don't have enough to contend with.*

Of course, such behavior would just make him look rash, young and foolish—as would his continued angry outbursts. He had to change focus.

Draining the rest of his cup, Bran untied the leather tie that had been wrapped around the scroll, unfurled the parchment, and lowered himself onto a stool.

He then read the agreement his father had made with Bruce MacGregor.

It hadn't been written by his father, for he'd have recognized Kendric Mackinnon's spiky hand anywhere. Instead, the lettering was neater and written with care.

The document outlined the force the MacGregors would bring to their aid: three twenty-oar birlinns and one hundred warriors. It had been generous—especially since Meggernie was landlocked and MacGregor had bought those birlinns especially for the campaign—but not without its price. In return, Kendric Mackinnon promised the hand of his son, Bran, to Sonia—MacGregor's eldest daughter.

His pulse took off at a gallop. *Sonia.* There it was. He hadn't been mistaken.

Bran's fingers tightened around the parchment, his stomach swooping. Suddenly, it was as if the door to his cage had just swung open. For the first time in four years, he could see daylight.

God's teeth, he was a lucky bastard.

Indeed, he'd just found a way out of this marriage.

His gaze traveled down then, to where his father had signed *his* name next to Bruce MacGregor's, at the bottom of the agreement. Heart still pounding, his mind traveled back to a past he'd tried hard to forget.

His father hadn't been himself in those final days. His lust for power and drive to dominate the Macleans, to crush them into dust, had blinded him to all else. And after Tara's disappearance, his already quick temper had become dangerously volatile. He'd been impatient. Reckless.

Despite his exhilaration from his discovery, the lingering taste of wine turned sour in Bran's mouth.

He'd have signed his son's *life* away to get him what he craved. As it was, Bran had only dared to complain once about the arrangement. The words had barely left his mouth when the clan-chief lashed out at him.

He'd ended up lying on the floor, winded, while his father stood over him, hand fisted to strike again. "What was that, son?" he'd asked, his casual tone at odds with the anger burning in his eyes.

Bran swallowed, bitter memories tightening his throat.

He'd had no say in this marriage, but he was no longer a callow youth ruled over by a tyrannical father. *He* was clan-chief now and wouldn't be manipulated any longer.

Instead, it was his turn to take control—and this letter would give him the means.

Re-rolling the document and securing its leather tie, Bran placed it upon the mantelpiece. "Tomorrow, MacGregor," he spoke aloud to the empty chamber, "ye and I shall have a chat."

"It is written here … in yer own hand, I'd wager."

A quiet vindication curled through Bran as he watched the clan-chief's features tighten. Of course, when he'd brought up the subject, the clan-chief had tried to bluff and bluster his way out of it.

But Bran had held fast—and now that he unrolled the document upon the table in the solar, his finger tracing the line in question, the clan-chief couldn't pretend he was making things up. MacGregor now eyed the document warily, as if he expected it to bite him.

Silence fell in the solar then. Bran made no move to shatter it. No, he'd let MacGregor think about how he'd answer him. For the first time since his arrival, he had the upper hand.

As he waited though, he cast a glance at the woman standing by the hearth.

Arms folded across her chest, Makenna was scowling. Nonetheless, her eyes were shadowed.

Bran's heart kicked hard. *She knew.*

He'd made a point of insisting the clan-chief call his daughter in before raising the matter. After all, this agreement affected them both. All the same, he'd expected this to be news to her—and that she'd fly into a temper and refuse to marry him.

But she'd done no such thing.

When Makenna had stridden into the solar earlier, she'd brought the scent of rose and fresh air with her. Her cheeks were still pink from being up on the walls. He'd expected her eyes to be bloodshot, and her expression pinched after all the wine she'd downed the eve before, yet she looked annoyingly fresh. She still carried a dirk at one hip, although managed to look ladylike, all the same. Perhaps it was her well-brushed hair, with neat, slender braids at the sides, or the well-cut surcote and kirtle. Even the leather chausses she wore underneath her skirts, and her supple boots, didn't detract from her appeal.

Bran caught himself then.

Appeal? What in Hades was he doing?

Makenna met his eye, her chin rising in a silent challenge. Bran answered it, his gaze narrowing as their stare drew out.

Eventually, MacGregor cleared his throat, intruding on their silent combat. Tearing his attention back to the clan-chief, Bran noted the older man now wore a pained expression.

"Aye … yer father insisted that he wished for my eldest daughter's hand," he said, his voice gruff, "and so I agreed." Reaching up, he rubbed at his shaven chin.

"I tried to offer my youngest instead, but he wasn't interested. He never asked me if Sonia was already wed though ... and I didn't put him right."

Bran scowled. "And why not?"

MacGregor's wide mouth lifted at the corners in a rueful smile. He then gestured to the document that lay between them. "It's all written there. Not only did yer father promise to unite our families in marriage ... but he promised ongoing support. Warriors. Weapons." The clan-chief paused then. "And until now, I have asked for nothing."

Bran pulled a face. "Aye, I read it ... but he promised those things believing that he'd take Dounarwyse." Heat kindled in his belly. "When the tide turned against us, our allies deserted us. Ye and the MacNabs couldn't retreat fast enough. Ye left us at the mercy of the Macleans."

The accusation fell heavily in the warm, smoky air. That was the crux of it. He didn't want to marry a woman not of his choosing—and especially not one who'd tried to kill him—but his bitterness wasn't just at his father. He resented *this* clan-chief as well. When the Mackinnons needed them, the MacGregors had let them down.

MacGregor eventually shattered the brittle silence. A deep groove had etched between his coarse eyebrows, and his green eyes had hardened. "That's the nature of war, *lad*. Mackinnon bought our loyalty ... but that didn't mean we intended to go to the grave with him should the battle not go his way. He knew that too. If the tables had been turned, yer father would have done the same."

The heat in Bran's belly started to pulse. The bastard wasn't even embarrassed, or contrite.

Stepping back from the table, he folded his arms across his chest. "The fact remains that ye *lied*, MacGregor."

The clan-chief snorted. "A wee falsehood … and one that hurts no one. Yer father insulted *me*, by rejecting my offer of Makenna's hand." He gestured to the lass in question then, who'd held her tongue during the exchange yet was now looking decidedly uncomfortable. "My youngest daughter has as much value as my eldest. Had yer father lived, he would have come around to the idea. Makenna is bonnie and sturdy … she will make ye a fine wife."

She made a soft choking sound at this. Bran didn't blame her. MacGregor had just spoken of her as if she were a carthorse.

Bran didn't look her way though. "If ye won't honor yer promises, why should I?"

Freedom was close now. Soon he'd be riding away from Perthshire, never to return.

Anger sparked in MacGregor's eyes. Aye, the brash fool who'd welcomed him to Meggernie was but a ruse. "I fought the Macleans in good faith," the clan-chief ground out. "And lost fifty of my warriors during that battle. We limped home, bloodied and defeated. *Fifty* men, Mackinnon … warriors who should be defending my borders from the Campbells. Instead, they died for a cause they didn't even believe in."

"Aye, so that ye could get the alliance ye craved," Bran shot back. "Don't make it sound as if ye did it out of friendship for my father."

"The agreement I made with him still stands," MacGregor growled, his large hands curling into fists at his sides. "Ye *will* wed my daughter … or make an enemy of the MacGregors."

Makenna's soft gasp followed these words. Danger crackled through the air now, and Bran was aware that they were all teetering on the brink.

Everything depended on Bran's response.

His blood roared in his ears. God, how he wanted to just turn and walk away from all of this. He had the chance. The door was open. All he had to do was go through it. The night before, he'd lain abed, imagining this moment, savoring the shock and anger on MacGregor's face.

But now that the moment was upon him, he couldn't do it. His damn honor wouldn't let him. What he needed MacGregor to do was get angry enough to *release* him from his bond.

Leaning forward, he placed his hands on the table between them, his gaze seizing the older man's. MacGregor's heavy features had gone taut now, red flushing across his cheekbones. "Aye ... I'll wed yer *feral* daughter ... and ye can have the warriors and weapons that were part of the deal," he ground out, even as his gut clenched. "Unlike ye, I'm a man of my word." He paused then before going for the throat. "But it ends there. I care not if the Campbells bay at yer door like wolves ... I won't come to yer aid."

MacGregor stared back at him a moment before growling, "Ye offend me, Mackinnon."

"As ye have done *me* ... and now we are even," Bran replied coldly. "Be grateful that I am honoring yer devious agreement at all."

Christ's bones. If Mackinnon didn't stop yapping, he'd soon find his teeth scattered over the floor.

Makenna could see her father's temper rising in a crimson tide.

The young clan-chief had insulted his honor, provoked him, and was now changing the terms of the agreement he and Kendric Mackinnon had struck. Their argument had now escalated to threats.

Blood was about to be spilled.

"Why would I give my precious daughter to a man who won't name himself my ally?" Her father said finally, each word vibrating with fury. His fingers flexed at his side then, their tips brushing the grip of his dirk.

Makenna tensed, dropping her arms to her sides. She needed to be ready to respond too.

"Don't then," Mackinnon shot back, his tone goading now. His lean face was taut, his silver eyes glittering with dislike. Makenna's gaze narrowed. Sly bastard. He'd been waiting for this moment. Discovering that he'd been lied to was the excuse he'd needed. "And I shall pack up today … and take *all* my warriors and the weapons ye need back to Mull."

"That's what ye want, isn't it?" Her father countered. Like his daughter, he was no fool. "To worm yer way out of this marriage? Ye think if ye vex me enough, I'll lose my temper and cast ye out of my castle?"

Makenna's pulse leaped into a gallop.

How she wanted her father to do just that. She longed to be rid of Mackinnon. The vile-tempered man hadn't even been here a full day, and already she wished they'd never met.

But she had to be practical. She had to think about her clan's welfare.

They needed those twenty warriors and the cartloads of fine weapons the Mackinnons had hauled all the way from Dùn Ara. Things with the Campbells of Breadalbane had reached a tipping point, and those resources would make the difference.

"I am willing to keep my part of the bargain," she blurted out before she lost her nerve. If only her voice didn't sound so strangled.

Both men's gazes swiveled to her, pinning her to the spot, but she held fast, meeting her betrothed's glittering stare now. "Ye were promised a MacGregor bride, Mackinnon … and ye shall have one. I urge ye to rethink yer hasty words … and to remember that an alliance between our clans doesn't just benefit my father but *ye* too."

Mackinnon's lip curled. His response made her long to leap at him and punch the sneer off his beautifully molded mouth, yet she throttled it. Instead, she kept her clan's future planted firmly in her mind.

"Our feuding with our neighbors has taken its toll on us … but *ye* still haven't rallied from yer defeat against the Macleans. Ye need allies too, or have ye forgotten that?" Color rose to his high cheekbones at this, but she pressed on. "Aye, news of how difficult things have been for ye of late has reached us. Ye are alone in the north of Mull. Yer people resent ye for kneeling to Loch Maclean … and ye have struggled to rebuild yer strength."

Moving forward, she grabbed the document off the table and waved it aloft.

What are ye doing? She was starting to feel a little lightheaded and sick. But now she'd started on this course, she wouldn't halt. This was for her people. Her father wouldn't be happy that she'd interceded, yet he'd thank her afterward. *Ye hope.*

"This parchment has caused enough dissension between our clans." With that, before either man could stop her, she crossed to the hearth and threw the document upon it.

The dry parchment went up like a torch, burning bright for a few instants before crumbling to ash. Turning from the hearth, Makenna found both her father and Mackinnon looking at her as if she'd just lost her wits. "It's time to write a new one."

"Makenna—" her father began roughly, his eyes dark with censure.

"We need each other," she cut him off, irritation surging through her. These men were like two stags in rutting season. Anger had made them both lose sight of what really mattered. "While we waste time arguing over this marriage, the Campbells bay like wolves at our door ... and the Mackinnons of Dùn Ara are but a shadow of what they used to be. It's time to take a fresh sheet of parchment and make a new accord ... one that benefits us *equally*."

"And how exactly?" her father rumbled. However, some of the anger had leeched from his voice. He, at least, was listening to her. Meanwhile, Bran MacKinnon's glower could have cut through granite.

Drawing in a deep breath, Makenna thought swiftly. "The MacGregors will send four lads to foster at Dùn Ara each year, and the Mackinnons will do the same. We will also start trading between us. The MacGregors will provide mutton and wool ... three times a year ... while the Mackinnons will supply us with salted cod, smoked herrings, and oak." She paused then, an odd excitement quickening in her breast. She'd never led a discussion like this before.

"And we shall see it written down that each clan shall promise to come to their ally's aid 'without question', should either of us ever call for assistance."

Mackinnon made a disgusted sound in the back of his throat. "Enough of this rot, woman," he muttered. "My father already—"

"This agreement, *ye* shall sign," she interrupted him, her pulse racing now. "In yer own blood if that's what it takes ... as shall my father." She drew herself up then to her full height, which unfortunately was considerably less than his, and eyeballed him. "And *I* shall bear witness to it."

6: A FORCE OF NATURE

BRAN LEFT THE clan-chief's solar in a daze.

Numbly, he descended the steps to the ground level of the tower house, before he emerged, blinking, into the bailey. It was a bright morning, and the warm breeze carried the sweet scent of summer.

Halting on the cobbles, he watched the men sparring with wooden practice swords a few yards away. It was difficult to focus on them though, for he was still reeling from his meeting with the clan-chief and his daughter.

He'd heard of the MacGregors and their rebellious nature—but dealing with them was like trying to net the wind. He'd met Bruce and Makenna early, just after breaking his fast, but now noon was nearing.

Where had the time gone … but more importantly, what had he agreed to?

Reaching up, Bran dragged a hand over his face.

He felt as if he'd just downed a horn of strong mead and then been clobbered over the back of the head.

He'd been so close to freedom—whatever the cost—yet Makenna MacGregor had ripped it from him. And as she'd done so, she'd pointed out the humiliating truth.

The Mackinnons of Dùn Ara were no longer a force to be reckoned with. He wouldn't be remembered as a strong clan-chief, but one who'd lost the respect of his people. Bran needed allies as much as the MacGregors did. He needed to prove himself.

Both he and her father had stood, poleaxed, as Makenna grabbed a fresh sheet of parchment, settled herself at the clan-chief's desk, and helped herself to a quill. Then, dipping its nib in ink, she'd begun to write.

And now, a while later, he'd agreed to many things—including allowing one of their sons, should they have any, to foster at Meggernie. And damn him to Hades, he'd eventually picked up the quill and signed his name at the bottom of two duplicate agreements, next to Bruce MacGregor's.

And now, in the aftermath, he felt sick.

Was the woman a witch? It was as if she'd woven an enchantment around him.

The MacGregor had also been stunned by Makenna's efficiency, yet he'd made no move to stop her.

Bran's gut clenched then, and he growled a curse. He was now locked into an agreement by his own hand. And he had the scroll tucked away inside his gambeson to prove it. He couldn't even blame his father for this.

He would marry Makenna MacGregor, and the Mackinnons and the MacGregors would henceforth trade, share warriors, and send young men, including their own kin, to foster at each other's strongholds. And should either clan require military support, they would travel to their aid.

Makenna had insisted both men sign, not with ink, but using their own blood.

The sting on the fleshy pad of his thumb now bore testament to what he'd done.

Scowling deeply, Bran turned right and made his way across the bailey to a small low-slung building next to the stables. The infirmary. Upon leaving the clan-chief's solar, he'd asked a servant to direct him to it. He needed to think about something else for a short while, to distract himself from what had just transpired.

Ducking under the low lintel, he entered the dimly lit space. The pungent scent of herbs tickled his nose as he straightened up, his gaze traveling over rows of empty pallets to where Tadhg sat, propped up by a nest of pillows.

In one hand, he gripped a steaming cup of what was likely broth.

The woman sat at his side was nodding at something the warrior had just said. Carmen MacGregor, the clan-chief's wife.

Bran's step faltered. He didn't want to see any of that family right now.

Hearing the thump of his boots on the wooden floorboards, both Tadhg and Carmen glanced his way. A moment later, Tadhg grimaced. There were dark shadows under the warrior's eyes, and his face was slightly strained. Nonetheless, he looked much better than the eve before. "Mackinnon," he grunted.

"Tadhg." Bran made his way down the aisle between pallets, halting at the foot of the warrior's bed. "On the mend?"

"I hope so."

"The healer's applied woundwort and wrapped his ribs with fresh bandages." The clan-chief's wife flashed Bran a reassuring smile. "He *is* on the mend."

Bran nodded, uncomfortable now. An awkward silence then settled inside the infirmary.

Sensing his mood, the lady rose, a trifle stiffly, to her feet and pushed a curl of greying dark hair from her eyes. "I shall let ye lads talk without my flapping tongue intruding."

Warmth rolled over Bran. God's bones, where were his manners these days? "I'm sorry, Lady MacGregor," he muttered. "I—"

"Don't fash yerself." She moved into the aisle and placed a motherly hand on his arm. "I know when I'm not wanted." She eyed him then, curiosity lighting in her dark-brown gaze. Bran braced himself to be questioned, but instead, she nodded to Tadhg. "I shall be back later ... and if Cook's in a good mood, there may be some shortbread in the afternoon."

Tadhg blinked. "Shortbread?"

"Aye ... the best ye've had too." With that, Lady MacGregor departed in a cloud of rose and musk perfume—the same scent her youngest daughter wore.

Alone with his warrior, Bran folded his arms across his chest. "They're treating ye all right then?"

Tadhg gave a soft snort. "Aye ... when they aren't sticking me with a dirk." He raised the cup to his lips and took a sip before sighing. "Good broth this."

Bran muttered an oath under his breath in reply, aware that the warrior—a man he'd grown up with at Dùn Ara—was now eyeing him over the rim of the steaming cup. "Something's amiss?"

"Aye … ye could say that."

Tadhg raised a dark eyebrow, inviting him to elaborate.

Frustration boiled over then, and Bran kicked at the stool next to him, sending it clattering to the floor. "I've nothing but shit between my ears!" he snarled.

Tadhg didn't flinch. "Oh, aye?"

"By the saints … ye should have been born a man." Makenna's father crossed to the sideboard and poured two large goblets of wine.

She didn't reply—in truth, she didn't know what to say. She wasn't sure whether to be flattered or insulted by such a comment. And that meeting left her exhausted.

Picking up the goblets, he turned and made his way back to where Makenna stood in front of the fire. Like Mackinnon, who'd walked from the solar bewildered, her father wore a slightly glazed look on his face. He handed Makenna her drink before shaking his head. "I've never seen the like, lass … but such a victory deserves a toast." He then held his goblet aloft, his green eyes glinting. "To brazen, quick-witted daughters … ye have no need of a dirk or a sword, Makenna. Yer mind is sharper than any blade."

There was respect in his voice, and surprise—for although her father had allowed her to serve in the Meggernie Guard, he'd done it as an indulgence. He'd always underestimated his younger daughter, but he wouldn't any longer.

Forcing a smile, she raised the goblet to her lips and took a sip. Wine was the last thing she wanted right now. She was still queasy from over-indulging the night before.

What have I done?

She'd been so caught up in salvaging the agreement her father had made, in putting Mackinnon in his place and securing the support her clan needed, she'd utterly cast aside her own wishes. If she'd kept her mouth shut, Mackinnon would likely have broken with her father.

Aye, things would have gotten ugly then, and blood might have been spilled. But now, instead, she'd made the relationship between the two clans watertight.

Hades, she'd even promised one of their sons would be fostered at Meggernie Castle.

"I think I might have gone too far," she admitted huskily.

Her father harrumphed and took a large gulp of wine. "Nonsense. Ye were magnificent. Mackinnon slunk out of here like a beaten dog!"

Makenna's pulse stuttered, and she inwardly cringed on her husband-to-be's behalf. She'd shamed him, and part of her was sorry for it. All the same, his capitulation had surprised her. He'd been so angry initially, but when she'd burned the document that his father had signed, something akin to respect had flared in his silvery eyes.

Suddenly, she'd been in control of the meeting. It had been a heady sensation, and she'd pushed her advantage. She couldn't believe she'd had the nerve to take a seat at her father's desk and write a new agreement. She'd never before done something so bold.

In the end, she'd written two copies of the same document, and both clan-chiefs had signed it in their own blood.

And now it was done.

For a moment, she'd spied an escape from this union—but then, she had been the one to slam the door shut in her face. Frankly, she felt like weeping, not toasting to their success.

Oblivious to her inner turmoil, the clan-chief strode to the table, where his copy of the agreement still lay. "This is better than I could have hoped for," he said, picking up the parchment and scanning it once more. "Not only will I have military aid, but trade. Meggernie will prosper." His gaze glinted then. "The extra men will be useful when I deal with those devil-spawn Campbells."

Makenna didn't reply. She literally couldn't. Her throat now felt as if a plum lodged there, threatening to choke her. She too wanted to take on their foes—but soon she'd be far from Meggernie.

Meanwhile, her father rolled up the agreement and secured it with a leather tie before carrying it across to an alcove in the wall. There, he pulled out a key from a pouch on his belt, inserted it into a lock, and opened the iron lid before placing the valuable document inside. He then firmly closed his safe box and deposited the key back in its pouch.

Turning back to Makenna, he flashed her a victorious grin. "Come, lass ... let's join everyone for the noon meal. We have happy news to share."

7: SILENCE AND SOLITUDE

MACKINNON DIDN'T SHOW his face in the great hall.

Makenna couldn't blame him. She too wished to hide—anything to avoid her father's crowing. Around her, Makenna's sisters and mother listened wide-eyed as the clan-chief regaled them with the tale of how she turned a desperate situation around. The pride in his voice was evident, yet she just felt queasy.

Likewise, Rae and Alec were riveted, and when her father finished his story, Rankin gave a low whistle. He then flashed Makenna a wry smile. "With skills like that, ye are wasted as a wife."

"Alec!" Liza elbowed her husband in the ribs.

"I mean it," Alec replied, rubbing the side of his chest, his smile turning contrite. "Makenna's talents would be of great use to our king. He could send her to negotiate with the English."

"Aye, she'd have the bastards cowering in no time," Makenna's father agreed.

"Ye did well," Rae rumbled, eyeing her. "Yer love for yer clan clearly knows no bounds."

Makenna's belly started to burn. How she wished the lot of them would stop blethering. No one here seemed to understand what that meeting had cost her. She wanted to remain here. To protect her clan. But no one cared about that.

"Our wee sister is indeed the fiercest of us," Alma said, with a proud smile. "But none of this nonsense about her working for the king. Instead, she will make a fine clan-chief's wife."

Makenna swallowed. Lord, the biliousness that had followed her downstairs was worse now. She feared she wouldn't be able to take a bite of the fine grouse pie the serving lads were carrying to the table. Hopefully, the meal would distract her companions and give them something else to talk about.

"And where is Mackinnon?" Alma's husband, Rory, spoke up then, a glint in his eye.

"Likely cowering somewhere, licking his wounds … and nursing his bruised balls," Connor MacFarlane, Sonia's husband, replied, and the two men shared a meaningful look. "Can't say I blame him. No man likes to be outwitted by a woman." Sonia shot her husband a withering look at this, yet Connor ignored her. Instead, he shifted his attention to Makenna—and the glint in his eye made her want to punch him.

She'd never warmed to Sonia's husband, nor Alma's, for that matter. And despite that she disliked Mackinnon, she didn't like the way the two men were speaking about him. He didn't deserve such humiliation.

Suddenly, she'd had enough of this, enough of the teasing and smug expressions. If she had to weather any more of it, she'd explode.

Stomach churning, she pushed herself up from the table. "Please excuse me," she muttered.

Makenna's mother frowned. "Is all well, lass?"

She forced a nod, even as her heart started to pound. "I just need some air." With that, she turned and fled the great hall. Someone called her name as she departed, but she ignored them. Let them congratulate each other *without* her presence. They didn't need her anyway.

Jaw bunched, she pushed her way out through the throngs of MacGregor, Mackinnon, and Maclean warriors who were still making their way inside for the meal. But once out in the entrance hall, she kept going.

The walls were closing in on her. She had to get out. She had to find a place where she could hide for a while and put herself back together.

"Makenna." Captain Lloyd Walker greeted her as she rushed out into the bailey. He was approaching the tower house, his stride brisk, for he was running late. Walker was even busier than usual at present. When she'd gone up to the walls at dawn, Makenna had noted he'd put more men than usual on the Watch. Meggernie continued to remain on the lookout for trouble. "Ye are going in the wrong direction, lass."

"No, I'm not."

He slowed his long stride. "Is something wrong?"

She shook her head, drawing to a reluctant halt to face him. "No ... *Everything* is."

Concern shadowed Walker's blue eyes. "Do ye wish to talk about it?"

Makenna's chest started to ache. Walker had taught her to fight, had never doubted or demeaned her. But his kindness now made her feel wretched. "Later," she gasped. "Can we spar together this afternoon?"

He inclined his head. "I thought yer father didn't want ye to train with me any longer ... not with yer intended in residence."

Aye, he didn't—but that didn't mean she'd obey him.

"One last time, Lloyd." She wished she didn't sound so desperate, but she couldn't help herself. Her breathing came fast and shallow now, panic bubbling up. "Please."

Walker huffed a sigh, his leathery face creasing into a rueful smile. "Go on then ... meet me by the armory once the shadows lengthen."

"I will." She gestured to the tower house then. "Ye'd better hurry up ... they're serving the pie now, and with so many hungry warriors in there, ye risk missing out."

Then, not bothering to wait for the captain's reply, she sidestepped him and set out across the bailey. It was an effort not to break into a run. Urgency beat inside her like a Bealtunn drum now. The wide courtyard was empty at this hour, save for the row of guards on the walls. Often, Makenna would have joined them, but not any longer. Nor did she retreat to the roof, as she sometimes did when she needed to be alone for a while. The orchard wouldn't do either. No, she had to get out of the castle.

She needed silence and solitude, to be far away from the prattle of others.

As such, she hurried toward the gates, passing under the portcullis moments later. Her boots thudded on the lowered drawbridge that spanned the River Lyon.

The water sparkled in the sunlight and skylarks trilled, while lapwings waded amongst the rushes.

Usually, she'd have slowed her step and taken in the beauty of it all, but today, she barely saw any of it. Hands clenched at her sides, she marched across the drawbridge and crossed the well-trodden road beyond, before stepping onto the meadow that stretched south of the castle. She strode across the grass then, toward the woodland to the south. She'd find refuge amongst the sheltering trees.

The rich scent of greenery embraced her as she left the meadow behind, the soft ground springing underfoot as she wove through the dark sycamores and under spreading oak and beech. Presently, she came to where a small burn bubbled over grey rocks, and there, she lowered herself onto a moss-covered rock.

Surrounded by the gentle babbling of the burn and the whisper of the breeze amongst the trees, she covered her face with her hands. She wanted to blot the world out, but she couldn't, even in this quiet place.

No man likes to be outwitted by a woman.

Connor's words taunted her then. Satan's cods, she'd just made life even harder for herself. She'd already given her husband-to-be plenty of reasons to dislike her, but after this morning, he'd despise her. And soon they'd be married, and she'd have to lie with him.

Reaching up, she massaged her aching temples. Nausea still burned the back of her throat. She felt thoroughly wretched.

Idiot. Idiot. Idiot.

Breathing deeply, she tried to master herself. She needed to calm down—or she wouldn't get through the next few days.

Eventually, her pulse slowed, and the queasiness subsided. The peacefulness of the woods wrapped itself around her, distancing her from everything that waited for her back at the castle. Here, none of it mattered.

Maybe I should stay out here a little longer. Her sisters were expecting her in the lady's solar after the noon meal, yet she wasn't in the mood to talk to any of them—not even Liza and Kylie. Aye, she'd linger here until her training session with Lloyd.

"Ye can't hide from them all forever though," she murmured aloud. "Ye can't flee from the fate ye've woven for yerself."

The snap of a twig underfoot had her reaching for the dirk at her side then. She whipped around to see a tall, red-haired man standing behind her.

Bran Mackinnon looked as if he'd been in the process of backing away—as if he'd just stepped out of the encircling beeches and discovered her sitting near the burn.

Makenna's heart jolted. *Cods!* Had he overheard her muttering to herself like a madwoman? Had he seen her leave the castle and followed her into the woods?

However, one glance at his face and it was clear he wanted to see her as little as she did him. When he'd left her father's solar earlier, he'd been stunned, yet now his silver-grey eyes were sharp. He cut a fine figure though, standing in the glade with the breeze ruffling his wavy flame-red hair. The quilted gambeson he wore over a dove-colored lèine was the same silver-grey hue as his eyes. His clothing molded his lean frame.

Aye, he was comely. It was a pity he had all the charm of a buck goat.

Rising to her feet, Makenna sheathed her dirk. Her pulse, which had only just settled, started to thud in her ears once more. The bastard had just shattered her peace.

Ironically though, there was an odd camaraderie in meeting him like this. He too would be licking his wounds. Makenna's chest tightened then; it wasn't usually her way to demean others so. She was sorry for it.

"Good afternoon," she said huskily.

"Afternoon," he replied.

An awkward pause followed.

"It's peaceful in the woods, isn't it?" she murmured lamely.

"It *was*," he replied, his tone clipped. They eyed each other in silence for a few moments before he spoke once more. "That was quite a performance earlier."

She swallowed. "Aye."

His gaze narrowed. "Is that all ye have to say?"

"I've said more than enough … don't ye think?"

He folded his arms across his chest. "Was it worth it to ye then?"

"Worth it?"

"Aye … ye could have rid yerself of me."

She pulled a face. "I'm well aware of that. But my clan is too important to me. I could see ye were trying to get out of yer bond … and I couldn't let ye."

Silence followed this admission before Mackinnon's frown deepened. "So, instead, ye made the agreement between us ironclad." To her consternation, he moved toward her then, in a long, stalking stride that made her want to draw her dirk once more. "There's no escaping me now."

"No." Her pulse quickened. "I try not to think about that."

He snorted. "Well, ye will have a lifetime to repent … I know *I* will."

Lord, how resentful he sounded. He'd stopped before her now, and Makenna had to raise her chin to meet his gaze. Up close, his glare burned into her.

She started to gnaw at her lower lip then, something she only ever did when agitated. However, when his gaze lowered to her mouth, she abruptly stopped. Heat washed over her. "What are ye doing out here anyway, Mackinnon?" she asked, drawing herself up and lashing out to disguise her discomfort. "Lurking?"

His auburn brows drew together. "*Lurking?*" He reached up and raked a hand through his hair. A gesture that left it mussed and spiky. "I'm out here trying to escape my fate … if only for a short while."

Makenna's shoulders slumped, the fight draining out of her. "I didn't plan for things to go so far," she admitted, cutting her gaze from his now. "I only wished to prevent ye and Da drawing yer dirks and going for each other … but then I got carried away."

"Ye did," he agreed roughly.

Makenna's cooling temper flared hot once more. He had the gall to blame her for this mess. "It wasn't all me," she snapped. "I wouldn't have needed to intercede if ye hadn't tried to slither free of the agreement."

His jaw muscles flexed, high spots of color appearing on his cheekbones. "Yer father tried to deceive me. I'm sick of all the lies. I'm tired of being *used*."

She made a disgusted sound in the back of her throat.

"Do ye have any idea how bitter ye sound? *Ye* made the decision to come here." He actually flinched at that, but she plowed on, the bit between her teeth now. "Watch out … or one day that scowl will fix itself upon yer face. Ye won't be so pretty then!"

He made a hissing noise through his teeth.

"And ye need to get a hold on that vile temper too," she added, chin kicking up. "I pity yer household. I'd wager all yer servants cower under yer miserable glare."

"Ye shall find out soon enough," he said hoarsely. "Although they'll need to brace themselves for ye … a woman with a mouth that won't stop."

She stifled a gasp at his rudeness. "Not everyone is threatened by a lass with something to say for herself," she hit back. "A *real* man wouldn't be."

"There ye go again," he replied with a sneer. "I'm surprised no one's tried to sew yer flapping lips closed."

Her hand strayed to the hilt of her dirk. "Just try."

His gaze glinted. "Is that a challenge?"

"Aye."

His eyes widened for a heartbeat, and then, to her surprise, he barked out a laugh. "I'm not fighting ye again."

Makenna inclined her head, even as the urge to wipe that condescending look off his face pounded through her. "Afraid, are ye?"

He stilled then, his gaze narrowing. "No."

"Liar."

What are ye doing? A shrill voice intruded then. *Are ye trying to make him yer enemy?*

She'd never dared goad a man so. It was foolhardy, yet she'd passed the point of no return now. Something had ruptured within her. She couldn't keep her anger, disappointment, and frustration leashed any longer.

Mackinnon made a sound in the back of his throat that sounded very much like a growl.

Unintimidated, she continued to stare him down. "Go on then. Teach me some manners."

Something feral flared in his eyes at this, and in response, a strange, fluttery sensation awoke in her belly. It was both exciting and unsettling, although she quickly pushed it aside.

Mackinnon stepped back then. Her gaze tracked him as he took off his dirk-belt and tossed it aside. "Very well … I shall."

8: SMOKE AND STEEL

UNBUCKLING HER OWN dirk-belt, Makenna set the weapon down upon the moss-covered stone where she'd been seated. As she did so, she was aware of the pounding of her pulse in her ears.

They were going to do this.

Makenna didn't doubt her abilities; however, fighting the man she was to marry soon wasn't the cleverest idea she'd ever had. Nonetheless, the hunger to put him in his place sang in her blood now, and there was no ignoring it.

She'd learned from the best. Captain Walker and the other experienced members of the Meggernie Guard first, and then Alec Rankin. Finally, Tormod MacDougall—a warrior at Dounarwyse, and the most skilled of them all—had trained with her the previous summer. These days, she preferred not to think about MacDougall. He'd been dangerous, yet, eager to learn from him, she'd trained with the warrior often.

Until the day he tried to rape her.

Shoving aside the memories, which still chilled her blood, Makenna moved away from the bank of the burn to a space in between the waterway and the edge of the encircling beeches. Here, the ground was spongy with moss, with no brambles, rotting branches, or rocks to harm themselves on. It was the ideal spot for a fight.

Mackinnon was rolling up his sleeves now, revealing toned forearms dusted with red hair. The man was lithe—a similar build to Tormod MacDougall. Such men were quick on their feet. Even though she was strong for a woman, her muscles honed by hours of training with the Guard, Makenna knew she'd never best even the smallest of men in strength.

No, it was her speed, skill, and cunning she'd rely on now.

And luckily, both Rankin and MacDougall had taught her several tricks.

Judging from the way her betrothed's gaze glittered, she'd need them.

"Ready?" She let her arms hang loosely at her sides and moved her legs apart, bending them slightly at the knee.

Mackinnon nodded, and they began to circle each other, each taking their opponent's measure.

He favors his left hand.

Aye, she recalled that from knocking elbows with him at supper the eve before. That made him trickier to fight, for she was used to fighting those who, like her, were stronger with their right.

His gaze held a calculating light now, his movements smooth and supple.

A frisson of danger skated down Makenna's spine, honing her already sharp senses further.

They both knew the only reason she'd bested him so easily the day before was because he'd tripped on a tree root. Before that moment, she'd been impressed by his skill. She'd never admit that though.

She waited for him to attack, impatience curling within her when he didn't. He wanted her to make the first move. Despite the predatory way he was watching her, she sensed his hesitation.

Makenna smiled inwardly. That was the greatest of her advantages. He'd never fought a woman hand-to-hand before, she wagered. He was afraid of hurting her.

She rushed at him then, aiming a strike just below his ribs.

He quickly side-stepped, his own fist grazing her flank. They danced apart.

Makenna flashed him a grin, even as her pulse quickened further. He was fast. Almost as quick as Tormod had been. She attacked again, this time letting him think she was going for the same spot, only to strike out with her left fist.

Her knuckles connected with his jaw, and his head snapped back.

They sprang apart once more, and Mackinnon flexed his bruised jaw, his attention never leaving her face. That smoky gaze was smoldering now, and the odd sensation that had ignited in Makenna's belly earlier returned. It made her breathless and a little weak in the knees.

Focus!

She wasn't sure why she'd responded this way, but she couldn't let it continue.

Makenna went for him again. But this time, he caught her wrist, hauling her close.

Of course, at close quarters, he thought she could do less damage. He then blocked her other fist as it drove up at his face.

He's good. Aye, she'd admit it—but she couldn't let him win.

Snarling a curse, she tried to kick his shins, but he avoided her blows deftly.

Anger surged up then. Earlier, she'd used his hesitation to her advantage, yet it frustrated her now. The bastard wasn't fighting her properly, as he would a man. Instead, he was trying to subdue her. He was trying to best her without landing a punch.

She wouldn't let him get away with it.

Twisting one wrist free, she grabbed him by the neck and yanked his head down—her forehead colliding with his mouth.

Mackinnon released her and reeled back. He then wiped his forearm across his lips, and it came away bloody. "Hellcat," he growled.

"Shit-eater," she taunted. "Ye want more of that?"

He did attack her then, moving with such speed that he took her by surprise.

The next thing Makenna knew, they were on the ground, rolling over and over, as he tried to pin her under him, and she tried to twist out of his grasp.

He was using his strength against her now, although she tried every trick she knew to get free. She tried to headbutt him again, but he was wise to that. She tried to knee him in the cods, but he flattened her to the ground, his lower body pressing her into the bed of soft moss beneath them. She tried to bite him, yet he wisely kept his hands away from her face.

And all the while, his moves were to defend himself or subdue her—not to attack as she had.

They continued to struggle, her curses ringing through the glade, until, finally, Mackinnon managed to pin her arms above her head. With one hand, he grasped her wrists, holding them against the moss, while with the other, he pressed down on her shoulder. With the full weight of his lower body against hers, she was trapped.

Fury hammered through her as she glared up at him. "That wasn't a fight," she snarled up at him. "Ye refused to engage."

Mackinnon's lip curled. "Did ye really think I was going to rough up Bruce MacGregor's daughter ... two days out from our wedding?" He shook his head then. "Ye must believe me to be witless."

No, she didn't. Instead, she had a grudging respect for the bastard. She wasn't going to admit such though, and so she spat a curse at him, writhing in his grip. Unfortunately, her movement merely ground their hips together—intimately.

"Stop it, Makenna," he growled, his voice sharp with warning.

His command only made her struggle harder. He grunted then, alarm flashing in his eyes. And then she felt it: a rigid hardness pressing against her belly.

Mortified, Makenna ceased her wriggling. *What the devil is that?*

Meanwhile, her betrothed glared down at her.

They were both panting and sweating from their fight.

Curse her, she was now far too aware of him. A faint sheen glistened on Mackinnon's brow, and blood trickled down his chin from where her forehead had collided with his mouth. This close, she could make out the flecks of smoke and steel in his irises.

He had long auburn eyelashes, tipped with black. A faint stubble of red beard covered his jaw, and a livid mark, from where she'd struck him, was coming up there. He'd soon have a bruise.

Her gaze fastened on his mouth then. His lower lip was split and starting to swell, yet she'd never noticed just how sensual the curve of his upper lip was. The scent of his skin, both spicy and woodsy, filled her nostrils, and dizziness suddenly assailed her.

She was in trouble.

"Ye are crushing me," she finally wheezed, sagging against the ground. The fight went out of her now.

Mackinnon's gaze darkened with what looked like worry, self-recrimination even. He then breathed a curse. A moment later, he lifted his lower body from hers.

"Got ye." Makenna brought her knee up and drove it into his groin.

Grunting, he let go of her wrists as if burned. Seizing her chance, she shoved him off her and rolled to her feet. Then, staring down at the man as, cradling his injured cods with one hand, he rolled onto his side, she caught his eye.

"Ye showed me mercy, Mackinnon ... that was yer first mistake."

He glared up at her, a nerve flickering in his cheek as he tried to focus through the pain she'd just inflicted. "And my second one?" he rasped.

Makenna moved back from him and retrieved her dirk-belt, buckling it around her waist. To her consternation though, her hands were a little unsteady.

That fight hadn't gone as she'd expected. Trying to ignore her reaction, she cut him an imperious look. "Letting yer guard down."

Bran limped into the bailey.

The throbbing in his bollocks was fading, although each stride chafed them.

Ire pulsed under his breastbone. Indeed, he'd fumed with every painful step back to the castle. However, some of that anger was directed at himself. What had he been thinking, accepting her challenge? The woman was a warrior and hadn't taken kindly to him pulling his punches. By doing so, he'd insulted her. He'd thought subduing Makenna would be the end of it, but when she'd wriggled like a pike on a hook under him—and to his horror, he'd found his rod stiffening for her—he'd been distracted.

And she'd seized her chance.

Even now, the shame of his arousal made his cheeks burn. He couldn't believe his body had betrayed him like that. Aye, he'd marked the lass's attractiveness from the first the day before, yet he didn't think he'd respond to her so strongly.

"What happened to ye?" A male voice, laced with faint amusement, drew his attention then.

Turning, Bran's gaze alighted upon Alec Rankin. He was leaning against a nearby wall, arms folded across his chest.

Bran's mouth twisted. "Nothing."

"I just saw Lady Makenna stalk past," Rankin drawled, eyeing Bran speculatively. "Her face was red, and she had a murderous glint in her eye." He paused. "Were ye responsible?"

Bran snorted. He wasn't going to dignify that with a response.

Rankin shook his head and pushed himself off the wall. "Ye didn't attempt to dishonor the lass, did ye?"

The anger pulsing under Bran's ribs flared hot once more. Was this *pirate* about to defend Makenna's virtue? "Go stick yer head in a dung hill, Rankin," he snarled. "I don't answer to ye."

Bran tensed as his father's killer approached. He hadn't seen Kendric Mackinnon fall on that fateful day. The final fight had taken place out on the water. The crew of *The Blood Reiver* had boarded the clan-chief's birlinn, and there, the two men had dueled. He reminded himself then that death in battle wasn't murder, and that there was no better way for a warrior to die. Even so, the sight of the pirate still curdled his gut.

Rankin halted around three yards distant. His gaze then narrowed. "If I find out ye've—"

Bran's angry curse rang out across the bailey. "The woman goaded me into fighting her ... and then when I did, she used my chivalry against me."

A beat of surprised silence followed, and then to Bran's shock, Rankin barked a laugh, delight sparking in his blue eyes. "Clever lass."

Bran clenched his jaw, his fists balling at his sides. If the bastard didn't stop yapping, he'd make him.

The pirate smirked then. "I might have taught her a few of the moves she used on ye."

"So, I have *ye* to thank then?"

Rankin shrugged. "She wanted me to teach her how to fight dirty … and I did. Makenna is a canny warrior, yet she knows that size and strength go against her." He paused then, folding his arms across his chest once more. "So, the wedding's off, I take it?"

Bran's lip curled. How he wished it was. However, he'd signed his name in blood that morning. He'd made a promise that he was now bound to honor.

9: FIGHTING FAIR

SWEATING, MAKENNA BLOCKED yet another strike, the thud of her bound blade colliding with Walker's carrying through the bailey. Meanwhile, despite that he was over twenty-five years her elder, the Captain of the Meggernie Guard appeared barely out of breath.

A moment later, she aimed a kick at his booted ankle, trying to catch him off balance.

Walker stumbled back before snorting. "What have I told ye about playing tricks like that?"

Makenna grimaced. "Sometimes, it's necessary."

The captain cast her a quelling look. "A warrior should fight fair."

"Honor will only get ye so far," she replied, remembering her fight with Mackinnon in the woods earlier in the day. Walker wouldn't have been impressed by her behavior, and now that her temper had cooled, she wasn't either.

Aye, in that case, it would have been wise to hold back. She hadn't just bruised her husband-to-be's cods, but his pride as well. Her behavior had been hot-headed and foolish, although she wouldn't openly admit to it. "Such moves could save my life."

"Well said, lass," an amused male voice intruded. "It's good to know ye listened to me."

Shifting back from Walker, lest he use her moment of distraction against her, Makenna cast a look into the shadows of the bailey, where Alec stood with his stepson, Craeg. Unbeknown to her, they'd both been watching her spar with the captain.

Embarrassment flushed through her. Indeed, Alec had said those very words to her around a year earlier when they'd fought for the first time. Initially, she'd thought his advice cynical, although these days, her perspective had altered. Life wasn't fair. Honor was all well and good, but their enemies had no morals.

Walker murmured an oath. "So, it was *ye* who taught the clan-chief's daughter to fight like a mercenary?"

Alec laughed, not remotely contrite. "Maybe."

Makenna realized then that a few warriors had left their posts to watch Walker and her fight. Like her, they knew it was possibly the last time they'd witness what had been until now a regular occurrence.

Surveying their familiar faces, and the respect and affection in their eyes, Makenna's breathing grew shallow. How she'd miss them all.

Walker shrugged out his shoulders, releasing the tension that had gathered there during their fight, before a smile tugged at his lips.

"Makenna is a natural," he replied, and the pride in his voice made an ache rise under her breastbone. His praise was hard won, and it meant much to her.

She didn't have any living uncles. Her father's younger brother had died in a skirmish when she was a bairn, and her mother had come from a large brood of daughters. But she'd grown up with Lloyd and saw him as kin.

"Care to spar with someone new, Walker?" Alec asked then, a gleam in his sea-blue eyes. "Maybe a former sea dog can teach ye some of his tricks?"

Lloyd barked a laugh, rolling his neck and flexing his fingers on the hilt of his bound blade. "Very well, Rankin ... grab yerself a practice sword, and let's get to it."

Makenna left the two men to face off. Meanwhile, Craeg lingered by the wall, his face alive with excitement at the prospect of seeing his stepfather fight.

Unwrapping the cloth from 'Arsebiter's' blade, she resheathed her longsword and crossed the bailey. She should—finally—join her sisters in the lady's solar, for there were finishing touches that needed to be made on her wedding gown.

Her gut clenched at the thought, for the reminder made her think about Mackinnon.

Halfway across the bailey though, her gaze alighted on the low profile of the infirmary—a small building tucked in behind the bakehouse.

Her step faltered, guilt constricting her chest. Tadhg Mackinnon had taken a nasty wound to the abdomen the day before—all because she'd acted in haste. She should really look in on him.

And so, she changed course, crossing the cobbles as the thud of blades colliding rang behind her. Men's voices followed as the watching guards urged Walker and Rankin on.

The interior of the infirmary was dimly lit and smelled of pungent healing herbs. Garia, the healer, was standing in one corner, mashing up something with a pestle and mortar. She glanced up when Makenna entered, her weathered face crinkling into a broad smile. "What brings ye here, lass?"

Makenna smiled back, although a trifle awkwardly. "Is Tadhg awake?"

"Aye." Garia jerked her chin over her shoulder. "Ye have time for a chat … before I change the poultice on his flank. Go on."

Makenna nodded before walking down the narrow aisle between empty cots to where a big man with wavy auburn hair sat propped up in a nest of pillows. It was a relief to see that he was the only one in here. Other warriors—on both sides—had received injuries in that skirmish, but none of them were serious enough to confine them to bed.

The hush inside the infirmary, so different from the activity of the busy castle outside, made her slow her step. Garia's space had to be treated with respect, like a kirk.

And as she made her way down the aisle, she observed the Mackinnon warrior closely. Guilt jabbed her once more when she saw how pale he was. Lines bracketed his mouth. He glanced her way then before scowling.

Makenna cleared her throat, embarrassment stealing over her. "Good afternoon, Tadhg."

The warrior didn't respond. If anything, his glower darkened.

She attempted an encouraging smile. "How are ye feeling?"

"I've been better."

"Are ye in pain?"

He grunted. A heavy silence fell in the infirmary then. Tadhg didn't seem bothered by it though. The look on his face made it clear he wished she'd leave. However, she couldn't. Not yet.

"I'm sorry for attacking ye yesterday." Her pulse started to race. Apologies didn't come easy to her; it was something her kin had all complained about over the years. But Tadhg could have died because of her, and for that reason alone, she swallowed her pride now. "It was rash."

He pursed his lips.

"I mistook ye for the enemy," she pressed on. "The Campbells of Breadalbane razed one of our villages." Her breathing grew shallow as she recalled the devastation that greeted her patrol two days earlier. "They grow increasingly aggressive ... I fear that one day, they'll try to take Meggernie for themselves." She paused there, resisting the urge to squirm. Tadhg was a man of few words. His stony silence made her babble like a fool. "My clan is everything to me," she concluded hoarsely. "I know it's a poor excuse ... but I wanted ye to know."

"Ready, lad?" Garia approached then, her healing basket full of bandages and unguents over one arm.

Tadhg nodded. His expression softened slightly as his gaze shifted to the healer.

"I shall leave ye to tend yer patient then." Makenna stepped back. She'd tried her best, but it had been like talking to a stone wall. She wouldn't linger where she wasn't welcome.

She was turning away when Tadhg's gruff voice forestalled her. "Has the Mackinnon forgiven ye yet?"

Makenna swung back to face him. She then frowned, giving him his answer. Just the mention of her husband-to-be made her temper flare. She didn't want Bran Mackinnon's forgiveness. "He's not an easy man to like," she replied stiffly. "I don't know how ye all put up with him."

Tadhg snorted. "Och, Mackinnon's not that bad … ye just need to learn how to handle him."

Garia coughed, as if smothering a laugh, at this, while Makenna's cheeks started to burn. "Any other advice?" she asked, unable to stop censure from creeping into her voice.

His gaze glinted. "Ye could start by talking to the man rather than swinging a blade at him."

10: BATS IN THE EAVES

"YE DID, WHAT?"

Kylie stared at Makenna, her lips parting in shock.

"Kneed him in the cods." Makenna dug her needle into the hem of the green damask surcote she'd wear for her wedding. "Although not hard enough, I fear."

Kylie murmured an oath. Meanwhile, Liza made a choking sound.

"Do ye wish for a husband who's … incapable of performing his … duties?" Liza asked, incredulous.

"That would be a boon, aye," Makenna replied. Heat rose to her cheeks then as she recalled the feel of Mackinnon's arousal, hot and hard against her belly—and the dizzying wave of excitement that had rolled over her in response. Curse her, she'd tried to forget that incident. After visiting Tadhg in the infirmary, she'd gone straight upstairs to join her sisters—although she was now wishing she'd hidden in her bower instead.

Tensing her jaw, she made two more neat stitches upon her wedding surcote. She usually liked needlework. It was a vastly different task from taking her turn at the Watch on the walls, riding out on patrol, or sparring with the other warriors, but she enjoyed the detail, and the sense of accomplishment afterward. Sewing relaxed her. Not now though.

"Mackinnon had it coming," she muttered.

Kylie sighed before reaching up to pinch the skin between her eyebrows. She then met Liza's eye. The two women sat opposite each other before the gently smoldering hearth. "I think our sister wishes to make her marriage a battlefield."

"It would seem so," Liza replied as she continued to wind wool upon a spindle. "But she'll learn better soon enough."

"She could do far worse than Bran Mackinnon."

"Aye," Liza agreed. "She could have ended up being wed to a man like Leod."

Kylie's brow furrowed. "Or Errol."

"Stop comparing my situation to yers," Makenna snapped, vexed that the two of them were carrying on as if she weren't even there.

Liza fixed her with a stern look. "Ye should try to put things right … *before* the ceremony."

Makenna's chin kicked up, heat flushing over her.

Liza's dark eyes narrowed. "A man's wounded pride isn't something to be taken lightly. Ye may feel justified, but since it was *ye* that ensured this marriage must take place, I suggest ye swallow yer pride and apologize." She paused then. "It'll make yer wedding night easier, at least."

"Liza's right," Kylie chimed in. "I know it's not what ye wanted … but ye will have to lie with him soon."

"For the love of God," Makenna choked out, mortification flooding through her. "Don't remind me."

Her sisters annoyed her further then by exchanging knowing looks.

Of course, they were both experienced in the ways of the world, while *she* was a virgin still. Neither knew it, but Makenna hadn't even been kissed. There had been men in the Guard she'd fancied over the years, men she wouldn't have minded a kiss from. However, they'd all been too intimidated to try their luck. And now, here she was, three and twenty. A lass who'd never been kissed, but who had killed. Her lack of experience frustrated her. She liked to feel capable in all areas.

"Mackinnon is a little proud and fiery to be sure," Liza said then, "but he's a fine-looking man." Her mouth quirked, her dark eyes glinting wickedly as she winked at Kylie. "And he's got large well-shaped hands … a favorable sign, indeed."

Kylie snorted a laugh, while Makenna yelped as she accidentally stabbed herself in the finger with the needle. Sucking her stinging digit, she glared at Liza. "What the devil have his hands got to do with it?"

Liza's smile widened. "Och, lass … ye have been well-cosseted, haven't ye? The look of a man's hands tells ye much about his character … and the size of his—"

Makenna gasped an oath, cutting her off.

Both her sisters were smirking now. It was too much, and she closed her eyes to block them out. Her cheeks were burning. She wondered if she should tell them that she already had an idea about the size of her husband-to-be's manhood, after today's incident. She checked herself though. Revealing such a thing would only encourage them.

"Christ's teeth, what nonsense," she muttered.

However, neither of her sisters was listening to her.

Liza flashed Kylie an impish grin. "Have ye seen the size of Alec's hands?"

"Can't say I have," Kylie replied with a giggle. "However, Rae's got hands like a blacksmith's. When I saw him unclothed for the first time, I got a pleasant surprise, let me tell ye. He had—"

"That's it!" Makenna threw down her wedding gown in disgust and leaped to her feet. "Ye won't drag me into such lewd talk!"

Kylie flashed her a look of mock hurt. "Lewd?" Her sister was so different these days. Before falling in love with Rae, bitterness had cast a shadow over Kylie. She'd been prim and easily offended. But now, she laughed easily and took life more lightly.

It's as if our roles have been reversed.

Nonetheless, Makenna wasn't going to linger here and listen to any more of this. She had the sneaking suspicion her sisters were just getting started. But this wasn't a show put on for their benefit. It was her life. *Her* future. Jaw clenched, she headed toward the solar door, her boots sinking into the soft sheepskins that covered the wooden floor.

But Kylie wasn't letting her escape without a parting volley. "Go on … seek yer betrothed out," she called after her. "And *mend* things."

It galled her to admit it, but her sisters did have a point. If she didn't try to repair her relationship with her husband-to-be, their wedding day—and night—would truly be an ordeal.

And in the man's defense, he'd thought he was protecting her by not engaging during their fight.

Unfortunately, Bran Mackinnon wasn't easy to find.

Makenna searched for him in the bailey, and in the orchard and gardens, before checking inside the guard barracks, the chapel, and the great hall. She'd even gone out into the woods again, although he was nowhere to be found.

Eventually, irritation buzzing inside her like a hive of bees, she climbed the steep spiral staircase that led up to the highest level of the tower house. It was the only place left to look. Stepping out onto the narrow walkway that led around the edge of the roof, she halted a moment. A breeze feathered across her face up here, the soft coo of pigeons drifting across the ramparts.

Rounding the corner of the square tower, she halted, her gaze alighting upon the lanky figure that leaned upon one of the battlements. Mackinnon was in profile and hadn't yet seen her. As such, she halted, her gaze raking over him.

Damn him, he was far too attractive, with his flame-colored hair and patrician features. Her betrothed appeared to be a hundred leagues away at present, his attention trained west. He was looking in the direction of home, and no doubt wishing he were there right now.

Makenna cleared her throat.

His gaze cut right, spearing her—tension rippling through his body. His eyebrows then drew together above narrowed eyes.

Fighting her discomfort, Makenna forced a tight smile. "I see ye have found my favorite spot at Meggernie."

He pushed himself off the ramparts, his expression shuttering. "I shall leave ye to it then."

He made to move off, but Makenna forestalled him. "Wait." Hades, her voice sounded as if someone were throttling her. "I wish … to … apologize."

Twice in one day. This was unheard of.

His jaw bunched, and heat sparked in her belly. Her heart started to pound against her ribs then, and she silently cursed Kylie. What a daft idea this had been.

"I don't need an apology," he replied coldly.

She started to sweat. "Nonetheless, I shouldn't have insulted ye, baited ye … or kneed ye in the cods."

In response, he cut his attention away, a flush staining his high cheekbones. "Aye, well … some of yer insults cut a little close to the bone," he muttered. "Life *has* turned me bitter before my time."

Makenna stilled at his candidness. Nonetheless, frustratingly, he didn't elaborate.

"I can be reckless when riled," she admitted before grimacing. "And I don't like being bested, I'm afraid."

"No one does."

Makenna's gaze shifted to where he now lay a hand on a battlement. The other hand rested on the pommel of his dirk. Liza had described his hands as 'large and well-shaped'—and they were, with broad palms and long tapering fingers. The nails were clean and trimmed. She noted a thin silver scar that marked the back of the hand resting on the battlement and wondered where he'd gotten it.

She continued to study him, her attention straying upward to his mouth. His lower lip was swollen from where she'd head-butted him.

With a sigh, she took a few steps closer before leaning up against the sun-warmed stone at the base of the doocot.

Silence fell between them, broken only by the soft warbling of pigeons. It wasn't a companionable hush though. She could have cut the tension between them with a blade.

"I've never seen a doocot on the roof of a tower house before," Mackinnon said, eventually shattering the awkwardness. "Those birds make a right noise."

Makenna cast him a veiled glance to find him leaning his back upon the ramparts, arms folded across his chest. His attention wasn't trained on the view west any longer, but upon the conical-shaped stone structure that perched behind her.

"They do … but I like the sound," she replied. "It soothes me." She paused then, forcing a smile. "I hope ye like pigeon?"

"Aye … well enough."

"Good. Cook and his assistants are baking pigeon pie for our wedding feast."

Her pulse quickened then. The ceremony was inching closer. By the time they sat down to pie, Father Malcolm would have bound them as husband and wife.

Lord help her, she wasn't ready for this.

She started gnawing at her lower lip before finally asking, "I didn't hurt ye … badly … did I?"

Mackinnon's features tightened. "Could we leave that incident behind us now?" he growled.

She nodded, relieved.

They lapsed into another silence, and, eventually, she pushed herself up off the doocot's wall. She then cut Mackinnon a veiled look. It was difficult to tell if he'd forgiven her or not. "Come." She took a step back and beckoned. "While we're up here, I might as well show ye something."

He scowled, and she sighed. "Fear not, it's nothing unpleasant … follow me."

She led him along the walkway that skirted the large square roof. She then descended into the stairwell, taking him down a few feet to where a narrow slitted window let in the afternoon sun.

Turning, she found Mackinnon right behind her.

He was closer than she'd expected, now looming over her, and his proximity made her heart kick hard against her ribs. His scent filled her lungs, and his heat radiated toward her like a furnace. It reminded her of what it had felt like in that glade, with his lean, hard body pressed against hers. Hastily shutting down her reaction, she moved down another step. "Look through the window," she said, her voice oddly husky, "and up."

Mackinnon indulged her, leaning toward the window and tilting his chin up. A moment later, his lips quirked. "Bats ... lots of them."

"Aye ... there must be at least two hundred roosting here during the summer."

"They're tiny," he murmured, a trace of awe in his voice.

"Aye, they're pipistrelles ... some are small enough for two of them to fit in my palm."

Mackinnon moved back from the window then, allowing her to squeeze in and look.

Many of the lasses at Meggernie shuddered at the very mention of the colony of bats that had made the eaves of the tower house their roosting spot, but she loved them. Her gaze alighted then upon the clutch of small bodies, each covered in a tawny pelt, their dark, leathery wings tucked in as they slept.

"In an hour or two, they'll emerge," she said softly, "and fly through the early gloaming ... looking for moths and midges to feed upon."

Her betrothed didn't answer, and she glanced his way.

He was watching her. His expression was veiled, yet there was something in his eyes—something that made her heart skip a beat.

Pulse pounding, she hurriedly looked away.

11: A WEDDING GIFT

NIGHT FELL OVER Meggernie in a soft black curtain. Rolling down the sacking over her bower window, Makenna tried not to think about what the morning would bring.

The day before her wedding had sped by in a blur, as if she were on the back of a galloping horse, and it now had the bit between its teeth. She'd risen early in the morning and taken a walk, alone, on the walls. The crisp air in her lungs and the feel of her dirk brushing against her thigh had reassured her.

But the solitude didn't last. A short while later, she'd joined her kin and guests for bannocks and porridge in the great hall. Mackinnon had also been present, a silent, brooding presence at her side as she forced down mouthfuls of porridge. Usually, porridge was her favorite breakfast, especially drizzled with honey and cream, but she'd had little appetite.

After the first meal of the day was done with, she'd retreated to the lady's solar to make the finishing touches on her wedding surcote.

All four of her sisters came and went as she worked, fussing over her, and bickering over the details of how she'd wear her hair the following day. It was the first occasion all five of them had spent time together in seven years. That fact should have made a lump form in Makenna's throat. However, as she'd listened to Sonia and Liza argue about what flowers she should wear in her hair, irritation had wreathed up.

She couldn't bring herself to care about such things—not when she was days from leaving Meggernie.

"Violets are everywhere in the meadow outside the castle," Liza had enthused. "They'll be perfect."

"Too commonplace," Sonia sniffed. "Ma's carpet roses have a lovely scent ... and they're more befitting a clan-chief's bride."

"But they have thorns."

"Aye ... but so does our wee sister."

They'd all snorted with laughter at this—although Makenna merely glowered.

Both Liza's and Kylie's gazes had shadowed then. Her ill-temper worried them. Indeed, it was a shame that she'd been so grumpy today. Who knew when they'd all be together like this again? All the same, she couldn't help the resentment that had knotted in her gut.

Apart from mealtimes, she'd seen little of Bran during the day. She'd hoped their conversation on the roof of the tower house might have made things a little easier, but it hadn't. They didn't seem to know what to say to each other now. It was all so awkward.

And now, here she was, readying herself for bed.

Her maid, Fiona, had just finished brushing Makenna's hair, and was about to settle herself into her cot in the corner of the bedchamber, when a knock sounded on the door.

Fiona crossed the chamber and opened the heavy oaken door to find Kylie standing on the other side. Makenna's elder sister had a small leather-bound book in one hand.

"Come to tell me to cheer up?" Makenna couldn't help the acerbic edge to her voice. She was almost out of patience with her family today.

Kylie inclined her head. "Would it help?"

"No."

Her sister glanced over at Fiona, who was watching their interaction with interest. "Can ye leave us for a short while, lass?" she asked. "I wish to have a few words in private with my sister."

Fiona nodded before flashing Makenna a glance. "Would ye like some hot caudle from the kitchens, Lady Makenna?"

Considering the offer, Makenna nodded. She'd barely eaten all day, although she did love caudle—a thick, rich drink made from oats and sweetened with honey. It would be comforting. "Aye ... thank ye."

Fiona departed, her soft footfalls receding in the narrow passageway that led between the family chambers that made up the top two floors of the tower house.

Makenna eyed Kylie then, bracing herself for yet more well-meant but vexing sisterly advice. However, none was forthcoming.

Intrigued, Makenna's gaze drifted to the book tucked under her sister's arm. "What's that?" she asked finally.

Kylie favored her with a secretive smile. "A wedding gift."

The northeastern shore of Loch Tay
Perthshire

The same night …

The woman he craved was just a day's ride away now. All he had to do was claim her.

Tormod MacDougall watched the moon's reflection glisten in the still waters of the loch and listened to the croaking of puddocks in the rushes. Behind him, the rumble of men's voices around the fire rose and fell, while the scent of woodsmoke laced the crisp air.

Shifting on the boulder at the water's edge, he fought impatience.

It had been nine months since he'd last set eyes on Makenna MacGregor—but during that time, his need for her had grown. It had gotten to the point where every quiet moment he had, like now, thoughts of her plagued him.

The challenge glinting in her moss-green eyes.

The flash of her blade as she fought.

The haughty tilt of her chin as she answered him.

That strong, lush body that begged to be ravished.

He'd never met a woman like her—beautiful and feminine yet with a backbone of steel and fighting skills to rival most men. Even him.

She'd fought him off when he'd tried to rape her, hadn't she?

Tormod's lips thinned as he recalled how she'd pulled a blade on him. She wouldn't be so feisty the next time he had her alone.

No, next time, he'd tie her to a bed and make sure there were no sharp objects within reach before he took her. He shifted uncomfortably upon the boulder then, a chill feathering down his spine.

Taking her might prove a problem.

Ever since two months earlier, when Makenna's sister Kylie had stabbed him in the cods, his prick wouldn't stiffen. The wound the bitch had dealt him that day—when he and the Ghost Raiders had attempted to take Dounarwyse Castle—was healing, but even when he took himself in hand, his member refused to respond. Lucky for him, the dagger hadn't pierced any vitals, and his bollocks and rod were still intact. Even so, he'd nearly bled out as he slid down the storm drain and out of the fortress. By the time he'd reached *The Night Plunderer* offshore, he'd been weak and in agony.

Only rage had kept him going.

Aye, one day he'd get even with Kylie. And what better way to start than ruining her beloved sister?

He summoned fresh images of Makenna then—naked yet still defiant. He'd let her hiss and spit at him as he spread her wide and plowed her sweet furrow. As he enjoyed the fantasy, he rubbed his knuckles at the groin of his braies.

Nothing.

Gritting his teeth, he tried to ignore the dread that clenched his gut. *It'll heal ... I just need time.*

"All's quiet?"

A gravelly voice behind him jerked Tormod from his thoughts.

Straightening up, he glanced right at where a large man had stepped up to his side. "Aye ... only the toads are awake at this hour."

"Don't let the stillness fool ye, lad ... the MacGregors often scout these parts ... for we are near the eastern borders of their lands now."

In the moonlight, 'Black' Duncan Campbell's long face and prominent nose appeared carven out of marble, his deep-set eyes dark pits. His long brown hair was pulled back and tied at the nape and his beard neatly trimmed.

Tormod observed him for a moment before shifting his gaze back out across the waters of Loch Tay. They were still a full day's ride out from Meggernie, but close enough to their destination that the Campbells had grown wary. This mission was bold, dangerous, but Tormod had insisted on being included. It was his chance to show his loyalty to Duncan Campbell, while at the same time ensuring that Makenna was captured.

He'd turned up at Finlarig Castle barely a month earlier, announcing that he too was an enemy of the MacGregors, and that he wished to swear fealty to the Campbells and help bring them down. He'd been honest with Duncan—it was best to, for the man was sharper than a boning blade—revealing what had happened at Dounarwyse, and how Bruce MacGregor's daughter had knifed him in the cods. He hadn't mentioned Makenna though.

Some of the Campbell men had guffawed at this tale, and Tormod marked which ones—for he'd pay them back one day—although Duncan hadn't.

Instead, he'd allowed Tormod to kneel before him and swear upon his blade. And then, over the days that followed, Tormod had proved just what an able warrior he was, just how ruthlessly he wielded a dirk or broadsword.

Campbell didn't give much away, but Tormod had sensed he was impressed with him. And now, here they were, on a raid together.

"Ye trust the man who brought word from Meggernie then?" Tormod asked after a pause.

Campbell nodded. "I sent him north to live among the MacGregors a few years ago … waiting for this moment." He paused, his mouth twisting into a thin smile. Tormod observed him, impressed. In Campbell, he'd met his equal when it came to cold-blooded ruthlessness. He wasn't a man one crossed. "And my hounds now hunger for MacGregor blood."

Tormod glanced over his shoulder then, at where the pack of massive liver-colored dogs with long ears and heavy jowls slept near the men: bloodhounds that had been trained to hunt MacGregors. Duncan Campbell's son, Robbie, who sat drinking by the fire with two other warriors, had bred the dogs. The chieftain's son boasted that he'd weaned the pups on the milk of MacGregor women, although Tormod could not help but believe that tale was an exaggeration. Nonetheless, the Campbells were convinced these hounds would help them hunt their enemies.

"And ye believe we'll be able to catch the clan-chief?" Tormod asked after a pause, focusing on the chieftain once more.

"Aye. Bruce MacGregor loves nothing better than a stag hunt … and my spy tells me that it's a family tradition to take any new son-by-marriage out … the day after any wedding celebrations." Campbell's hawkish features tightened. "I can't prevent this wedding that will unite the MacGregors and the Mackinnons … but I can ensure the couple's union is a short one."

Tormod's pulse quickened. *Makenna will ride with them.*

Aye, the lass wouldn't want to be left behind—and when they captured her father, he'd take her as well.

12: THE KISS

"OH, LASS, YE look a picture." Carmen bustled forward, gently nudging Sonia and Kylie out of the way so she could get a proper look at her youngest daughter. Her dark eyes glistened as she reached out and brushed some lint off Makenna's shoulder.

All the MacGregor women were inside the lady's wardrobe—a room adjoining the clan-chief's chamber, where Carmen dressed each morning—and were fussing around Makenna like a clutch of excited fowl.

Makenna favored her mother with a tight smile before she glanced over at the long looking-glass that stood to her right. "It is a bonnie surcote," she admitted grudgingly.

"Aye, and it fits ye like a glove," Liza added.

"Yer husband-to-be won't be able to keep his eyes off ye." Alma flashed her a grin from behind their mother.

Makenna scowled. She didn't want Mackinnon to stare at her. She just wished to get through today without disgracing herself. But then, traitorously, she recalled the way he'd looked at her two days earlier in the stairwell.

She'd thought the man despised her, but it wasn't hate that she'd seen in those smoky eyes.

"My youngest," Carmen murmured huskily. "I can't believe that soon ye will all be gone from Meggernie." Her throat worked then as emotion threatened to overwhelm her. "How fast time passes. It seems like just yesterday I was carrying ye at my breast, lass."

Makenna stiffened. Despite her resentment toward her mother and sisters—as they fussed around her—she suddenly felt sorry for Carmen. Family was everything to her. After her other daughters had flown the nest, there had just been the two of them at Meggernie. How many long afternoons had they passed together, seated in the lady's solar, sewing and gossiping?

This marriage would be a wrench for them both.

Their mother's hand strayed to the iron crucifix she always wore about her neck, her fingers fastening around it. It was a gesture Carmen made when she was making a silent prayer.

Makenna's chest tightened. She'd miss her. "Stop it, Ma," she said huskily. "Or I shall start bawling."

Carmen snorted, her full lips curving into a smile as she knuckled away a tear that escaped. "We don't want that, do we? Turning up to the chapel with a blotchy red face won't do. We don't want ye looking like a freshly dug neep."

Sonia and Alma laughed at this joke, although Liza and Kylie both grimaced.

Meanwhile, Makenna ground her teeth, her sadness fleeing. "Christ's blood," she growled. "Don't any of ye understand how hard this is for me?"

"Of course, we do," her mother soothed, putting a hand on her forearm.

Makenna shook it off. "No, ye don't." She cast a vicious look around the solar, at where her sisters looked on, their faces stiffening in surprise. "I may have locked myself into this marriage ... but that doesn't mean I *want* it. Protecting Meggernie ... and my people ... is my *life*." She broke off then, anger pounding in her chest. "Go ahead and enjoy yerselves today ... throw some rose petals, feast, drink, and dance ... but don't expect *me* to smile about it."

Sunlight bathed the sandstone bricks of the chapel, turning them a dull gold. It was a bonnie spot, on the edge of the apple orchard, and an excited crowd of well-wishers had gathered, baskets of rose petals in hand.

However, Bran didn't share their excitement.

Standing on the steps of the chapel, next to the portly priest, he tried not to grind his teeth as he waited. *Let's get this over with.*

A piper started playing then, the mournful wail of the Highland pipe echoing off stone. Whispers and murmurs erupted around him, and Bran turned, following their eager gazes between the rows of apple trees to where Makenna MacGregor approached. Clad in flowing green with small white roses threaded through her unbound hair, she was comely indeed.

Nonetheless, dizziness assailed Bran. God's bloody rood, if only there were a way out of this.

Makenna's expression was pinched. The lass walked slowly, her arm linked around her father's, and the smug look on the clan-chief's face made Bran's temper quicken. Of course, the man was pleased with himself. He'd now secured his much-coveted alliance between their clans.

Makenna's mother and sisters trailed behind her. All the women were attractive and dressed in their finest surcotes—but despite her furrowed brow, his bride outshone each one.

Aye, as much as he hated to admit it to himself—and by God, he did—Makenna was mesmerizing. The woman was a shrew and had no business wielding a blade or challenging men to fights, but there was no denying she had the body of a temptress, milky skin, a large sensual mouth, and green eyes a man could drown in.

Catching himself, Bran clenched his jaw hard.

The crowd parted to let the bride and clan-chief through. Rae Maclean and Alec Rankin were among the party. Both wore wide smiles, and heat washed over Bran. Captain Walker was there too, as well as a few members of the Guard. Even Tadhg had made it out of the infirmary, leaning heavily on a stick as he took his place amongst the Mackinnon warriors who'd also gathered here. Everyone looked in high spirits, except the bride and groom.

"Go well, Makenna!" Walker called out. "I hope Mackinnon knows how lucky he is!"

The warriors flanking their captain shouted their agreement, and Makenna's cheeks turned pink. All the same, she favored Walker with a smile—her eyes softening with affection.

No one called out well-wishes to Bran though. No kin stood amongst the crowd, wishing him well. His parents were dead, his sister was as good as, and the only blood relative he had was a grasping cousin on Mull; a man he didn't trust in the slightest.

Aye, he was truly alone.

He was dwelling on the fact that his family's bloodline was close to ending, and trying to ignore the hollowness in his gut, when Makenna stepped up to his side. Meanwhile, the MacGregor shifted back, taking his place to the right, alongside his teary-eyed wife.

Bran forced himself to look at his bride, and she met his gaze with her usual directness. Nonetheless, he marked the pallidity of her face and the nerve that ticked under one eye. The lass looked as if she wanted to bolt.

That made two of them.

Father Malcolm cleared his throat then and moved so he stood between Bran and Makenna. "Shall we begin?"

The ceremony passed in a blur. There was the binding of their hands, with a length of MacGregor clan plaid, and then the priest droned on. After that, he got them to recite their vows. However, all the while, Bran felt as if he was merely going through the motions, as if this wasn't really happening to him.

He'd known this day would come, and that his choice of bride was his father's, not his, but the reality of it hit hard.

Finally, the ordeal ended with Father Malcolm declaring them husband and wife. And then someone in the crowd shouted. "Kiss her, man!"

Alec Rankin—the dog's arse.

Bran's first instinct was to bestow Makenna with a hasty peck on the cheek.

But then something shifted within him.

Until now, she'd had the advantage in every interaction, while he'd been constantly on the back foot. This was his chance to turn the tables—and to get a little revenge. If the crowd wanted a show, he'd give them one.

Makenna stood there, jaw set as she braced herself.

Pulse quickening, he stepped in close to his wife. He then reached up with both hands, gently weaving his fingers through her thick hair, careful not to dislodge or prick himself on any of the roses. The heady scent of the white buds wrapped itself around him then. She smelled enticing.

Keeping his focus though, he drew her head back so that her face tilted up to his.

The look in her eyes was quizzical and vaguely alarmed. She was wondering what he was up to. Good. Let her worry.

He lowered his head then, his mouth slanting over hers in a lusty kiss. The crowd roared as he cupped the back of her head, holding her in place, and plundered her mouth.

Lord, she was sweet, like blossom honey. Vengeance tasted better than he'd expected, and he drank her in. He kissed her boldly, his tongue stroking hers. And all the while, the wedding guests clapped and whistled.

And when he finally drew back, he was surprised to find his blood pounding in his ears, excitement tight in his belly. For a few instants, he'd forgotten where he was.

Makenna stared up at him, pink flaring across her cheekbones. Her eyes had darkened. She looked furious—and beautiful.

Her rage drew him in, and something deep inside him answered her.

Suddenly, all he wanted was to haul her back into his arms and kiss her senseless.

Reining in the urge, he slid his hands from her thick hair and stepped back, putting much-needed distance between them.

Seated in the great hall, a steaming pigeon pie before her, Makenna tried to concentrate. It was difficult though, for she found herself fantasizing about jamming her elbow into her husband's ribs.

The bastard had put on that mortifying spectacle outside deliberately.

The challenge in his eyes as he'd pulled back from her had made her blood boil. Especially since her lips still tingled from his kiss. Her mouth tasted of him. Worse still though, hunger had clutched at her lower belly.

Curse him. He'd shocked her … but she'd enjoyed that kiss.

The musician who'd piped her into the chapel earlier had followed them inside the tower house. He now stood by one of the gently smoldering hearths, cheeks puffing as he played a rousing tune for the feasters.

The mood inside the hall was merry. Men, women, and bairns lined the long trestle tables, and the aroma of pastry and rich meat filled the warm, smoky air.

Those seated at the clan-chief's table were all smiles too, especially since her father had opened his oldest barrel of Castilian grape wine for this occasion. Serving lads circled the table, filling up everyone's goblets.

But two people at this table didn't share the gaiety.

Despite his 'performance' earlier, Mackinnon sat tense and silent at her side. Heedless of his son-by-marriage's mood, her father now regaled him with tales of his most successful hunting expeditions. Now that the marriage had taken place, he was in high spirits—and well into his cups. She heard him promise Bran then that they'd ride out the following day, to the mountains in southern Breadalbane, where they'd hunt stags in the narrow valleys and dark woods. He didn't seem to care that Mackinnon said little, although the younger man had the wits to make polite noises at the right times.

Makenna spoke to no one. Liza sat next to her and attempted to draw her into conversation. However, she responded in short sentences, distracted and on edge.

More servant lads appeared then, with wheels of aged cheeses, cured meats, and baskets filled with an array of breads studded with seeds and nuts. However, both she and Mackinnon picked at their meals.

"Bring me my quaich!" her father boomed, gesturing to the lad nearest.

The boy scurried off, returning with a large wooden cup with curved edges and two horn handles. It was her father's 'friendship cup', one he always asked for when he wished to build a bond with his guests.

Makenna's stomach tightened.

Having seen her father offering his quaich before, she knew what was in store.

The MacGregor poured the quaich nearly to the brim with ale. He then lifted it to his lips and took a sip before handing it to Mackinnon. "Yer turn," he instructed.

Jaw clenched, the young clan-chief copied MacGregor's act, taking a small sip of ale while holding the cup by both its handles. The two-handed design of the large cup engendered trust, on the part of both giver and receiver—for a warrior couldn't draw his dirk while handling it.

"Pass it to Liza now." Makenna's father went on. "The lady laird of Moy must take a drink to seal us all in friendship ... as must the chieftain of Dounarwyse."

Leaning down the table, Mackinnon stiffly did as bid. Makenna's sister sat, regal and serene, at Alec's side, her eyes glowing as she took a sip. Her father's gesture meant a lot to her. Drinking from his quaich made it clear he approved of her ruling Moy.

Lastly, Rae lifted the friendship cup and drank. However, his expression was veiled when he handed it back to MacGregor.

Makenna shifted uncomfortably on the bench seat. She wasn't surprised Rae wasn't overly impressed. Her father meant well, yet he was trying to force things. The Macleans wouldn't have forgotten the Battle of Dounarwyse, and that the MacGregors had sided with the Mackinnons against them. Sharing a quaich with his former enemies was all well and good. Nonetheless, if her father truly wanted Rae's loyalty, he'd have to earn it.

But if MacGregor marked Maclean's shift in mood, he showed no sign.

"Let us drink to a long-lasting friendship between our four houses," he announced, eyes gleaming. With that, he raised the quaich to his lips and drained the rest of it in one long draft.

13: INEVITABLE

THE FEASTING DRAGGED on. Around Makenna, the revelers grew more raucous. And when trays of honey cakes were brought to the table, and one was placed on a platter between the newlyweds, it was made clear the couple were expected to feed each other one.

Until this point, Makenna had done an admirable job of ignoring her husband. Likewise, he'd been too busy fielding questions from the clan-chief to focus on his bride. Her father had cannily shifted the conversation to matters of trade and Mackinnon answered him in terse, short sentences.

But now a cake sat before them, there was no getting away from interacting with the man she'd just wed.

Reaching out, Mackinnon broke off a piece. It dripped with a heavy honey syrup and smelled delicious. All the same, at present, Makenna had no appetite for it.

She sat rigidly as her husband lifted the cake to her lips.

A challenge sparked in those silver-grey eyes then. Everyone was watching, and he dared her to refuse him. What would he do if she did? Kiss her again?

Pulse quickening, she parted her lips and took the morsel of cake he offered.

The flavor of butter and honey exploded in her mouth as she chewed and swallowed. And then, trying to pretend all gazes weren't on them now, she picked up the other half of the cake and fed it to her husband.

After the feasting, they pushed the tables back, and a lively cèilidh began. And of course, the newlywed couple were dragged into the center of it.

By this stage, both Makenna and Mackinnon had drunk their fair share of rich grape wine. It had soothed the knots in her belly a little, although the awkwardness and tension between them remained.

Her husband danced well enough, yet he hadn't smiled during the feast, and as he swung Makenna around him on the floor, his lean jaw was set in grim determination.

Like her, he was suffering through this. Not for the first time, an odd feeling of camaraderie rose up within her. Everyone else was making merry, yet they were apart from it all.

Makenna's sisters were having a wonderful time. There was nothing they liked better than a cèilidh. Liza squealed as Alec swung her in one direction and then the other. Kylie and Rae danced a few feet from Makenna and Mackinnon. They were both grinning, their cheeks flushed.

Meanwhile, Ailean, Lyle, and Craeg capered around the dance floor like imps.

Her parents had even joined the dancers, and her father moved with surprising grace.

Makenna's throat tightened as she watched the dancing. She felt bad about her outburst before the ceremony. Her mother and sister had all looked so hurt, and the worry in Kylie's and Liza's eyes had cut her to the quick. They'd likely corner her at some point and try to get to the bottom of things.

But there wasn't any point in discussing it. The deed was done. She was Bran Mackinnon's wife now. An ache rose under her breastbone. Her breathing grew shallow and fast, and then dizziness assailed her.

"Let us rest for a bit." She jolted as Mackinnon's voice intruded. Cutting him a glance, she found him watching her, his gaze slightly narrowed. It surprised her that he'd marked her change in mood.

She nodded, grabbing the opportunity with both hands. "Please."

They slipped from the dance floor, returning to the empty clan-chief's table, which had been pushed back near the hearth.

Sinking down upon the bench seat, Makenna grabbed a ewer and filled her goblet. "Wine?" she asked Mackinnon, remembering her manners.

"Aye," he replied, still slightly breathless from the dancing.

She filled his goblet too, and they sat together, unspeaking, as the music halted for a moment and the revelers applauded the piper. The lull didn't last long though before the piper began a lively jig. Whooping filled the hall, and the dancers were off again.

"They don't need us, do they?" Mackinnon muttered finally. "I'm sure we could walk out of here and no one would notice."

"Don't be fooled," she replied, wishing her voice didn't sound so strained. "We'll be dragged back out onto the floor soon enough."

He made a strangled noise at this, and she cut him a sidelong glance. Her husband wore a hunted look. His gaze met hers then. "Better?" he asked.

Makenna stiffened. His unexpected concern flustered her. "Not really," she admitted huskily.

"Are ye upset about leaving yer family?"

An awkward pause followed before she nodded. Of course, she'd miss them. However, that wasn't why she was wrestling with panic.

Eventually, Mackinnon cleared his throat. "Yer family is a close-knit one … I envy ye that."

Once again, his reaction surprised her, and she glanced at him again. "Really?" Her mouth curved into a wry smile then. "We're loud, bossy, and always sticking our noses in each other's business."

He snorted. "Aye … but there's a warmth between ye." A strange emotion rippled over his face then. "I have no idea what that's like."

Makenna's face burned as she marched out of the hall.

Of course, no one was letting them leave quietly. The men shouted out coarse, lewd comments, and the women giggled.

Most of the crowd was well into their cups by now. Indeed, the MacGregor was swaying in his chair. Carmen had to ensure he remained upright as he lurched to his feet and bid the couple a slurred farewell.

The revelry had stretched on, continuing long after dark—eventually though, the time came for Bran and Makenna to take their leave of the great hall and climb to their bedchamber.

Leaving the jeering behind, Makenna clambered up the steep stairwell as if pursued by wolves. She was in no hurry to be alone with her husband, but at least when they reached her bedchamber, they'd be away from the heckling. And as she climbed, she heard the scuff of her husband's boots on the damp stone behind her.

Neither of them spoke while they made their way up to the landing on the fourth level of the tower house. Makenna then led the way down the narrow passageway, lit by guttering cressets, to her bower. It had been readied for them, with an oaken log burning in the hearth, and flickering candles upon the mantelpiece and the window ledge.

And some thoughtful person had scattered rose petals over the bed.

Makenna clenched her jaw at the sight. Curse it. This was really happening. She wasn't the least bit ready for her wedding night, and when she turned to face her husband, one look at Mackinnon's face told her that the sentiment was mutual. He wore a look of grim determination, as if he were about to have a boil lanced.

"Well." Hades, her voice sounded like a frightened sheep's bleat. Clearing her throat, she tried again. "This is it, I suppose."

"Aye," he grunted. "It was inevitable."

Makenna stilled. *Inevitable.* Aye, she supposed it was.

She eyed him then, still trying to find the measure of the man who was now her husband. Mackinnon cut a fine figure today. She'd noted how striking he'd looked as she walked toward the chapel on her father's arm. He wore a snowy-white lèine tucked into fawn-colored braies. The bright Mackinnon clan sash draped across his chest, although it was no match for his flame-red hair. Earlier it had been combed neatly, but now, as their wedding day drew to a close, it was mussed, flopping boyishly over one eye.

Things could be worse, she supposed. Her husband could be as ugly as a toad.

Comely or not though, she had no wish to disrobe in front of him and do any of the things that couples did behind closed doors. Her heart kicked then, and faintness swept over her.

"I could do with another cup of wine," she announced, moving across to the table where a ewer and wooden cups sat waiting. "Would ye like one too?"

"Aye … thank ye."

They'd both imbibed a great deal over the course of the feasting and dancing, although Makenna still felt alarmingly sober. She wouldn't get through this unless she took the edge off.

Relieved to have something to do, she poured them generous cups and handed him his. She then retreated to one of the two high-backed chairs before the fire.

It wasn't a cold night out, yet the glowing hearth was comforting, and she was drawn to its reassuring warmth.

Meanwhile, Mackinnon didn't move from the center of the bower. Instead, he stood there, holding his wine, watching her with a veiled expression now.

"Ye might as well take a seat too," she said, a trifle ungraciously. "Ye make me nervous ... looming over me like that."

He snorted. "I doubt anyone could ever make *ye* nervous."

Makenna pulled a face. "Ye'd be surprised."

He obliged her then, moving to the chair opposite and stretching out his long legs and crossing them at the ankle. He took a draft of wine, his gaze settling upon her. "If it makes ye feel any better, I too am on edge."

Aye, the knowledge did help, although it was surprising. She hadn't expected him to be so candid with her. Not for the first time this evening, his frankness had caught her off-guard.

Raising the cup to her lips, she took a fortifying gulp. "I suppose I can understand why." She grimaced. "I did knee ye in the cods recently."

He winced. "Can we *not* bring that up tonight?"

Their gazes met and held for a few moments before Makenna took another sip of wine. This was so awkward. She had no idea what to say to this man. This stranger who was now her husband.

The silence settled, heavy yet brittle, until eventually, Mackinnon broke it. "There's something ye should know," he said roughly.

Makenna inclined her head. "Aye?"

"I've never bedded anyone before."

14: WE ALL WEAR MASKS

MAKENNA BLINKED. "YE haven't?"

He nodded, a muscle feathering in his jaw.

Warmth flushed over her. "Well … neither have I."

He pulled another face. "That's expected, Makenna … ye are a woman."

She studied him, noting the faint flush that rose upon his high cheekbones. And in that moment, compassion stirred in her breast. It took courage to admit he was a virgin, and she found herself admiring him for it.

"It's not an affliction, Bran," she replied gently, surprising herself by using his first name. "Although, by the way ye kiss, I'd never have known."

He harrumphed, his blush deepening. "Aye, I've never had a lass," he muttered. "But I'm not a bloody priest."

Makenna couldn't help it; she giggled. "And so, how is it … that a braw man of three and twenty has never tumbled anyone?"

He cut his glance away and took another, large, gulp of wine. "I never intended it to be that way." He paused then, clearly rallying himself. "When I was sixteen, my father took me to Tobermory one eve and dumped me in a brothel … telling me that it was time to 'wet my prick'."

Makenna didn't wince at the coarse language. She'd heard far worse amongst the Guard. "But ye didn't?"

"I had my coin purse on me, and I paid the lass well for her silence."

She inclined her head, intrigued by his response. "Ye weren't tempted then?"

His brows drew together. "Of course, I was … I was sixteen and randy."

"So why didn't ye tumble her?"

He swallowed before lifting the cup to his lips and draining it. A long pause followed as if he was steeling himself to continue. "Because my father ordered me to … and I'd be damned if I'd let the bastard control *every* aspect of my life."

Makenna took these words in, weighing them. There was no mistaking the resentment in his voice. "Ye didn't like him much then?" she asked, softening her tone once more.

He snorted. "No … but I *minded* him for the most part." Leaning forward then, he stretched out a hand, and the thin silver scar she'd marked a couple of days earlier gleamed in the firelight. "This was from when I told him he should put his lust for revenge against the Macleans aside."

She studied the scar, surprise arrowing through her. "He *stabbed* ye?"

"Aye, he slammed his eating knife through my hand … pinning it to the table … and asked me if I had any other opinions."

Silence fell, the air turning weighty between them, before Makenna pursed her lips. "I take it, ye didn't?"

Her husband withdrew then, leaning back in his chair. His expression veiled now. "No."

She took another sip of wine, considering what she'd just learned. He hadn't been exaggerating earlier about the lack of warmth in his family. His father had been a bully. Growing up under such tyranny would have been awful.

Moments slid by, and she considered whether to tell him that she'd befriended his sister during her time at Dounarwyse the year before, to reveal that Tara deeply regretted their estrangement. Something checked her. Tonight was difficult enough without her bringing Tara up. Instinct told her that he wouldn't appreciate it.

"Thank ye for telling me that," she said after a long pause. "I feel as if I understand ye a little better now."

He pulled a face at that. "We have barely scratched the surface with each other, Makenna."

Her fingers tightened around her cup. He was right. A couple of confidences didn't make them friends. Hades, it was awkward now. She wasn't sure what to say. After a few moments, she cleared her throat. "It's been difficult for ye … since ye stepped into yer father's boots … hasn't it?"

His eyes narrowed, and for a moment, she thought he'd tell her to mind her own business. But then he huffed a sigh. "At times."

Silence fell, and she refrained from filling it. She wouldn't pepper the man with questions. If he wanted to tell her more, he would.

His gaze dropped to his cup, and he swirled the wine within, a rueful look flickering over his features. "Sometimes, I think my people would have preferred I'd defied Loch Maclean."

"But he'd have killed ye for it."

"Aye ... but then they could say I'd died defending the Mackinnon honor."

Makenna couldn't help it; she snorted.

Bran's attention snapped up. "Ye should understand such a sentiment ... yer clan's honor matters greatly to ye."

Their stare drew out, and she shifted in her seat, uneasiness fluttering in her belly. "Ye think that's all I care about?"

He quirked an eyebrow. "I know ye'd die to defend Meggernie."

Her breathing grew shallow. She would—although soon she'd be taken from this place, from her people.

"I *admire* yer loyalty to yer clan," he said then, surprising her. "Ye'd never kneel before an enemy."

Not like I did. The words were unvoiced, yet they shivered in the air between them.

Her skin prickled at this observation. Somehow, he'd managed to compliment her and cast a slur upon himself. It struck her then that it wasn't so much his clansmen's disappointment in him that galled him—but his own decisions. Her chest tightened. The man was far too hard on himself. Of course, she'd thrown those things in his face during that meeting with her father.

She wished she hadn't now.

"Maybe not," she said softly. "But I'd be wiser to bend sometimes ... it would make for an easier life."

His sensual mouth tugged up at the corners. "An easy life would bore ye."

Surprise jolted through her once more before she gave an unladylike snort. "Aye … probably."

Another pause followed. Talking about herself made her uncomfortable. She needed to bring the focus back on him. "Yer father's been dead a while … why haven't ye taken a lass to yer bed in that time?"

Mackinnon growled an oath, reached up, and dragged a hand down his face. "Christ's bones … can we leave this be?"

She flashed him an arch look. "Ye brought it up, remember?"

"Aye … the wine must have turned me witless," he replied with a grimace.

She laughed, appreciating the wry edge to his humor. "It's good ye are being honest with me," she replied. "It will make things *easier* between us."

Their gazes locked then and held, silence swelling between them.

"I felt ye should know," Mackinnon answered finally. "That way, if I fumble … ye'll understand why."

Nerves fluttered in her belly, and she glanced away. "Since I'm not experienced … I probably wouldn't notice anyway." She swallowed then, embarrassment sweeping over her in a hot, prickly wave. "We shall learn together."

"Aye."

"There's no need to rush things … we have all night." She broke off then, flushing. "And I can teach ye what I like as we go."

Her mouth snapped closed then. Dear Lord, what had she just said?

His gaze hooded in a way that made her heart flutter. "Ye will?"

She nodded mutely, even as her face burned like a hot coal. She couldn't believe she'd blurted out such a thing. What must he think of his MacGregor bride?

Her pulse thumped in her ears while he stared at her for a few moments. And then, to her relief, his lips lifted at the edges into one of his rare smiles. "Ye never fail to surprise me."

"I do?" Frankly, she'd shocked herself. She was starting to sweat now, suddenly far too aware of him. They were seated a few feet apart, but it felt too close.

He nodded. "Yer boldness is something to behold."

She pulled a face, not sure whether his comment was meant as praise or a rebuke, before taking another gulp of wine. "Things aren't always what they seem," she blurted out, heat flushing over her once more. "Ye don't have to scratch far beneath the surface to discover much of my confidence is bluster."

Her heart slammed against her ribs then. What was wrong with her tonight? Deliberately avoiding his eye, she put her cup down next to the hearth. *No more wine for ye!*

Resisting the urge to fidget, she eventually forced herself to look at him. A groove had etched between his eyebrows, although he now watched her in a way that both exhilarated and frightened her.

Makenna's breathing hitched. Somehow, he made her feel … seen.

"We all wear masks," he admitted with a wry smile. "It's how we survive."

Their stare drew out—the air between them heavy with tension now. Once again, a sense of kinship flooded over Makenna. Despite the fiery start to their relationship, there was something about this man that made her want to trust him.

She exhaled sharply. "So … what happens now?"

His gaze met hers, challenge flickering in his eyes. "Now … we go to bed."

15: I SHALL BE GENTLE

DON'T PANIC. BREATHE.

Makenna MacGregor was a brave woman. No shrinking violet. She'd faced men in combat—and had killed. But the thought of disrobing before her husband, lying upon the bed with him, and rutting with him, made her heart race like a bolting hind.

The unknown loomed before her, but she forced herself to stand up and face it. Face him.

Likewise, Mackinnon rose from his chair and stepped toward Makenna. He towered over her, and his nearness made her pulse flutter.

Dragging in another deep breath, she closed her eyes.

"I shall be gentle."

Her eyes snapped open, and she raised her chin to meet her husband's smoky gaze.

She nodded, relief suffusing her. He was paying attention—and had marked her anxiety.

Wiping her damp palms upon the skirt of her surcote, she wet her suddenly parched lips with the tip of her tongue. That was a mistake, for his gaze slid down to her mouth.

Suddenly, she remembered the sensual kiss he'd given her after the wedding ceremony. At the time, she'd wanted to lash out at him for taking liberties. Even so, the feel of his mouth on hers had been a brand and had sent her senses reeling.

"Ye might as well kiss me again then … Bran," she murmured, her voice wobbling slightly. It was time for her to stop thinking of him as 'Mackinnon' now though. He was her husband, and they were about to be intimate. She couldn't keep treating him like a stranger.

"Very well," he replied. And with that, he stepped closer and lifted a hand. His fingers brushed her jaw before he took hold of her chin. An instant later, he leaned in, brushing her lips with his.

It wasn't like the kiss after the wedding ceremony. No, this was softer, almost as if he was making sure he was welcome. This time, there was no audience. Nothing to prove. He wasn't trying to even the score. Now there was just the two of them locked in an intimate moment.

And she answered by brushing her mouth against his in return. The scent of him—oak, leather, and male—filled her nostrils then, and when his mouth found hers once more, she closed her eyes.

His tongue traced the seam between her closed lips, and with a sigh, she opened for him.

He kissed her deliberately, thoroughly, with a tenderness she hadn't expected—and after a moment or two, she responded by stroking her tongue against his.

Bran made a sound low in his throat. His hand slid along her jaw to her neck, before he cradled her nape as he deepened the kiss.

And Makenna couldn't help it. She melted into him.

Her hand rose then, her palm resting on his chest. She could feel the heat of his body through the thin material of his lèine. Unbidden, her fingers curled, digging in as their tongues tangled, as they tasted each other deeply.

And she liked how he tasted. She liked the rasp of his chin against her softer skin, the swell of his lower lip, and the sensual curve of the upper one. And when he caught her lower lip between his teeth and gave it a gentle nip, Makenna's belly clenched, neediness sweeping over her.

Neediness?

Oh, aye, just one kiss had her dissolving in his arms like spring snow. She couldn't believe the mouth that she'd bloodied two days earlier made her ache so. But it did. Fortunately, to her relief, his split lip was healing well; although she was still careful with it as their embrace continued.

When they eventually drew apart from the long, languorous kiss, they were both out of breath.

"Turn around," Bran ordered huskily. "I shall unlace yer surcote."

Wordlessly, meekly, she obeyed. There was nothing submissive about Makenna usually, but tonight, she didn't feel herself. Not at all. Standing in the midst of her bedchamber, she closed her eyes once more, waiting as he undid the back of her surcote. Usually, Fiona would help her undress. It felt scandalous that a man should do so.

But it is his right.

Her pulse fluttered as the realization fully sank in. She was Lady Mackinnon now. A clan-chief's wife.

He removed her surcote, and Makenna was about to turn to face him once more when he stepped in close—so close she could feel the heat of his body burning into her—and swept the curtain of hair aside. His lips skimmed her shoulder, above the neckline of the edge of her kirtle, and up to her neck.

His hands then slid around to her front, where they began to unlace her kirtle.

Makenna couldn't concentrate on how he was undressing her though. Instead, she shivered as his lips traveled up the side of her neck. His tongue then explored the shell of her ear, and her legs started to tremble.

She hadn't expected to feel such a sensation. The neediness in her belly had spread, and the tender flesh between her thighs had started to ache. Her pulse galloped now. She felt strangely breathless and leaned into him as he continued to disrobe her.

Finally, she wore nothing but a filmy ankle-length lèine.

Bran took hold of her shoulder then and gently turned her to face him again. Eyes flickering open, she obeyed. And when their gazes met once more, she marked the flush upon his cheekbones and the way his eyes had darkened.

He looked *hungry*.

They hadn't even done anything truly intimate yet, but she could feel an odd quickening inside her. A wildness that scared her a little.

His gaze raked down her, taking in the lines of her body, which were clear through her thin linen tunic. The lèine left little to the imagination.

Like all the women in her family, she had full breasts. Her nipples—small and hard—were clearly visible, thrusting perkily toward him.

Bran brushed the back of his hand across one of them, and pleasure darted straight through her core.

Biting down on her lower lip, she watched as he stroked his thumbs over both nipples, teasing them both into even harder peaks.

She swallowed a groan. Her belly churned now. The throbbing between her thighs intensified, and she stifled the urge to squirm. These new sensations made her feel oddly restless.

"Ye can touch me too ... if ye wish?" he said, his voice strained now.

Aye, of course she could. She knew that. Pulse skittering, she reached out and tentatively untucked his lèine from his braies. Her fingers slid underneath, her breath catching as she explored the warm, smooth skin of his flat belly. Her hands slid upward, over the hard ridges of muscle to the sculpted planes of his chest.

And all the while, Bran watched her, his gaze hooded now.

Her fingertips found his nipples then, and she brushed her thumbs over them, as he'd done with her, thrilling as they grew hard under her touch. His sharp intake of breath told her that he was as sensitive as she was. He made a sound in the back of his throat before stepping back from her and pulling off his lèine and clan sash. Firelight flickered across the lean, strong lines of his finely muscled torso and arms.

Makenna studied him, her breathing coming shallow and fast.

She'd always thought she was attracted to men who were big and brawny—but Bran's body was simply beautiful. Lean with a leashed strength that made her wonder what it would be like to be under him.

She'd soon find out. Her pulse went wild then.

Holding his eye boldly now, she reached down and took hold of the hem of her lèine, pulling it upward and wriggling out of the garment before her courage failed her.

There, she stood—naked—before him.

Bran didn't avert his gaze either. Instead, he looked his fill, his gaze traveling over her swollen breasts, over the curve of her belly, dip of her waist, and flare of her hips, to her thighs. Makenna had a strong body, muscled from hours spent training with the rest of the Guard, but she had a woman's softness too. And when she marked the way her husband's pupils grew large, she knew he liked what he saw.

He then heeled off his boots, unlaced his braies, and pushed them down.

Makenna couldn't help it. She *had* to look.

His rod was as beautiful as the rest of him, long and shaped like a thick arrow shaft. It was also as stiff as one.

Her mouth went dry, her blood roaring in her ears. He was going to put *that* inside her.

Bran stepped into her once more, his hands all over her as his mouth found hers this time. His kiss was demanding, and she answered him with a voraciousness of her own. How exciting it was for them to be standing here together naked, so aroused by each other.

And he *did* arouse her. Her skin was flushed and exquisitely sensitive, her breathing rapid.

The wild churning in her belly was impossible to ignore. All the same, she was nervous about what they were about to do. She imagined it would hurt the first time.

However, his kiss chased her fears away, and when he moved closer still and brought their bodies flush, it was difficult to hold any thoughts in her head. Shyly, she stroked her hands up his chest once more, before linking her arms around his neck. She then wriggled herself against him, desperate to get closer.

Bran groaned against her mouth. His hands swept down the arch of her back and cupped her backside. Then, one hand caught hold of her thigh, and he hauled her up against him so that their most intimate places were pressing together.

And there, he ground himself against her.

Clinging to him, even as their kisses grew hungrier and deeper now, Makenna found herself mimicking his action. She ached for friction.

The feel of him, bone-hard and hot, rubbing against the slippery, throbbing flesh between her thighs was quickly turning her witless.

"Are ye ready, Makenna?" he asked then, his voice husky.

"Aye," she gasped back.

A moment later, he picked her up, allowing her to wrap both legs around his hips, as they continued to kiss. He then carried her over to the bed and laid her down upon the coverlet. As he did so, she felt the tremor of tension in his body.

The scent of rose enveloped them, but Makenna barely noticed. She was too busy staring up at her husband.

His gaze *devoured* her. In the past, she'd disliked it when men gave her a carnal look. Now though, it made her blood catch fire.

Bran favored her with a nervous smile, her breathing catching at the vulnerability he'd just revealed. This wasn't just lust between them, but discovery. However, when he lowered himself to his knees before the bed, took hold of her ankles, and drew her close, she started to tremble.

"I just want to see ye," he murmured. And then, before she could reply, he pushed her legs wide apart and stared between her spread thighs. A moment later, a ragged sound escaped him, and he breathed an oath.

Watching his face, and the flush that had now risen upon his high cheekbones, Makenna thought she might burst into flames. This was too intimate. She wasn't ready for it. Raising a hand, she placed it over her face to hide her embarrassment.

"Makenna." His voice was low and rough. "All is well?"

"Aye," she lied, even as her voice came out in a mortified squeak.

"Look at me."

Swallowing, she pulled her hand away from her eyes and forced herself to look at where he knelt between her spread thighs.

His gaze was surprisingly steady. In contrast though, her face burned like the sun.

"I want ye to watch this," he went on, that nervous, shy smile returning. "To make sure I'm doing it right."

She started to sweat at these words, even as her belly clenched.

She didn't trust herself to answer him either—not without humiliating herself—and so she gave a jerky nod. She then raised herself up onto her elbows, her gaze lowering to where his hands parted her most intimate place.

"How do ye wish to be touched?" he asked, the catch to his voice betraying his excitement, his nerves.

Heat flushed over her once more. She couldn't believe that he was asking such a question—yet she knew just how to answer. "Stroke with yer fingertip ... above my ... entrance," she whispered. "Circle."

He nodded. A moment later, his finger slid against her, and she gasped at just how sensitive she was down there. And when he began to touch her as asked, stroking and circling, a delicious wave of pleasure rippled through her loins.

She couldn't help it; she whimpered.

Bran's gaze rose to find hers once more, even as he continued to touch her. "Is that good?" His voice was strangled, sweat gleaming on his brow.

"Aye," she ground out. It was hard to respond though, not when wild excitement pooled and coiled in her lower belly. "Very."

He then lowered his gaze, fixing his attention upon her sex once more. "What next?" He sounded out of breath, as if he'd been running.

"Slide a finger *inside* me."

Heavens, she was sweating now too, caught halfway between mortification and excitement.

And when he obeyed, Makenna choked out a curse, a shiver rippling through her. He worked her gently with that finger before adding a second without needing to be asked.

"Can I taste ye?"

Makenna gasped at his question, heat flooding through her loins. "Oh ... aye."

Murmuring another oath, he sank his fingers deep inside her before leaning in and covering the flesh above them with his mouth. His tongue started to gently flick, and she cried out.

She couldn't help it. This felt too good. And then, her embarrassment dissolved, her restraint falling away. Finally, she let herself give in. Lifting her hips off the mattress, she pushed against his mouth and fingers, urging him to continue. "Higher," she panted. "And bend yer fingers a little."

And he did as bid—gaining confidence now as he slid his fingers in and out and curled them up each time they sank in her. Meanwhile, his mouth devoured the pearl of flesh he'd found.

Makenna watched him, excitement clenching in her gut. Sweat slicked both their bodies. She couldn't believe Bran wanted to do such things to her. But he did, and as the moments slid by, she was gradually losing control. Her body trembled now, her loins throbbing. "Oh, God," she gasped. "Bran!"

"Aye?" he growled against her.

"I can hardly bear it!"

"Do ye want me to stop?"

"No!" Her cry echoed through the bedchamber.

He laughed, his breath feathering against her quim. "Well ... in that case." He redoubled his efforts then, sucking the aching bud nestled between her thighs as he thrust his fingers into her now. Like her, he'd left nervousness and embarrassment behind and let himself revel in this.

That did it. Pleasure broke, taking her over the edge in a giddy rush.

She shuddered, letting out a squeal that would have embarrassed her in other circumstances. However, right now, she was too busy writhing against him as he continued to eagerly work her, drawing out the rippling, pulsing waves of ecstasy until she collapsed onto the bed, panting.

16: A BLADE-TONGUED HELLCAT

BRAN PUSHED HIMSELF to his feet, surprised to find his limbs shaking. His prick ached, and his bollocks throbbed cruelly, but he didn't care.

Pleasuring Makenna so intimately had been the most exciting experience of his life, as had watching her unravel. She'd enjoyed everything he'd done to her—had directed him where needed—and had been desperate for his touch by the end.

Over the years, he'd heard other men talk about bedding women, but most of the time, it was just boasting and lewd gestures. He'd never learned anything useful. But Makenna had shown him what she wanted, and how she liked to be touched. Her confidence impressed him. He'd never experienced anything so intoxicating.

Still breathing hard, his wife lay there, spread out on the bed, her face flushed, her soft pale skin gleaming with sweat.

And the sight of her made his already racing heart start to kick like a wild pony against his ribs.

He wanted to fall upon her, to sink his rod to the hilt in that delicious wetness and ride her like a savage. But he wouldn't. She was a virgin, and he wouldn't use her so roughly. Instead, he climbed on the bed and stretched out next to her.

After a while, she rolled to face him. Her eyes were wide and full of wonder. "I liked that," she admitted, and her husky voice went straight to his groin. His shaft was rigid and throbbing against his belly, leaking from the tip.

"So did I," he replied, wishing his voice didn't sound quite so strained.

"I can pleasure ye too," she replied, rising onto her knees. Her gaze was upon his prick now. "If ye like?"

"Aye," he ground out. God's blood, he couldn't believe this was happening. "Please."

Her full lips quirked. "So polite, Bran Mackinnon." Her small hand reached out and wrapped around the root of his straining member. "Let's see if I can make ye *forget* yer manners."

Heat ignited at the base of his spine at these words, and his rod jerked in her grip. Her voice was deliciously throaty, and she couldn't help but challenge him. Even now. "I don't know how long I'll last," he managed, each word ripping from his chest. "I—"

She lowered her head to his groin then, her mouth swallowing the crown of his shaft, and he lost the ability to speak.

Her hot mouth and eager hands, one stroking his bollocks now while the other worked his rod, utterly undid him.

He had no idea how she knew how to pleasure him so well, and he didn't care either. Her eagerness inflamed him.

How quickly things had changed. Just three days earlier, he couldn't stand the woman, and now, all he could think about was losing himself inside her.

He tangled his hands in her thick hair then, slowing her a little and pushing her head down to take more of him. His lower belly clenched as she groaned low in her throat. As he'd warned, he was too excited to last long though—and a short while later, he arched up off the bed, his head falling back. "Christ's blood! Makenna!" Pleasure shot up his spine as he spilled deep inside her mouth.

She drank him down, her throat bobbing. And when she finally sat back on her heels, face flushed, eyes gleaming, Bran had never seen anything so beautiful. Of course, he'd noted her strong, lush body before tonight. Clothed, she was striking. Naked, she was a goddess.

Their gazes met then and held for a long moment. Neither of them spoke. How could he articulate what he'd just experienced? He was still reeling from it.

"Come here," he rasped eventually, catching her hand and drawing her down next to him.

She came, her body warm and soft against his, nestling her face in the hollow of his shoulder. And as they lay there, listening to the crackle of the fire, Bran trailed his fingertips down the curve of her spine.

Makenna closed her eyes, giving herself up to the gentle rhythm of Bran's fingers up and down her back. She liked how that felt, how his body molded against hers.

They hadn't spoken of what they'd just done to each other, almost as if they were both wary of breaking the enchantment that had woven around them. Uniting them.

She'd never imagined doing something like that to a man, but she'd enjoyed it—especially when Bran forgot himself, arching up to meet her mouth and calling out her name. She'd felt powerful. Sensual. And as they lay there, her core throbbed gently, greedy for more of him.

Earlier, she'd been nervous and embarrassed about lying with him for the first time. But now, the anxiety had fled. She didn't care if it hurt; she wanted him inside her.

It wasn't long before his shaft grew hard once more, straining eagerly against his belly. But Bran ignored it at first. Instead, he rolled to her, his mouth finding Makenna's. They kissed for a long while—deep, sensual kisses that made her gasp and sigh—and then he moved down to her aching breasts, sucking each one until she trembled underneath him.

Only then did he move farther down her body.

Spreading her legs wide, he pushed them up so that her pelvis tilted toward him, exposing her to his hungry gaze. "I don't want to hurt ye," he said, the roughness of his voice making lust slam into her with dizzying intensity.

"Ye won't," she panted. "Just don't hurry."

His lips tilted into a smile that made her heart stutter. He then stroked the tip of his rod over her sex, making her shiver. Nestling it at her entrance, he worked his way inside her with delicious slowness.

Halfway in, Makenna started to sweat.

Despite that she was ready for him, she was so tight. It was uncomfortable, almost painful.

Bran was patient though. He experimented—slowly circling his hips, withdrawing, and then pressing deeper. The discomfort eased as he did so. Heat kindled deep in her womb as he finally sank home, bringing their bodies flush.

His sharply indrawn breath excited her, as did the look of wonder on his face. Although she didn't have time to linger upon it, for he rolled his hips once more. It didn't seem as though he needed any more instruction from her. The man had most definitely found his stride.

Pleasure rippled through her, followed by a hot rush of wetness. Makenna gasped, bucking against him. Bran growled something under his breath and pulled out of her, almost to the tip, before sinking deep once more. Meanwhile, his hands gripped her thighs, keeping her spread open for him.

He rode her like that, in slow, deep thrusts, and before long, sweat gleamed on both their bodies.

Makenna trembled now, tension coiling tight deep inside her womb. She'd thought the pleasure he'd given her earlier couldn't be bettered, but this … this was … she didn't have the words.

She was aware then of a woman's shrill cries filling the bedchamber and vaguely recognized them as her own. She couldn't bring herself to care. The ecstasy that thundered through her was too great to be borne silently. She couldn't keep quiet. It was so good—and it just went on and on.

Bran's groans joined her squeals then, and he went rigid, his head throwing back as he plunged one last time inside her.

She watched, fascinated, as his eyelids flickered and pure pleasure rippled across his face.

Makenna fell asleep immediately after their coupling. A boneless, exhausted slumber that dragged her into its delicious embrace. She awoke to find the first rays of dawn peeking around the edge of the sacking. The fire had died, although a blanket covered her and Bran—he must have awoken during the night and retrieved it.

They lay together, limbs tangled.

Bran was snoring softly, and Makenna carefully pushed herself up onto an elbow so she could see his face.

Asleep, he looked younger. His skin was even paler than hers, with more freckles scattering the bridge of his nose and cheeks. His beautiful lips were slightly parted.

Makenna gazed upon him with fascination.

The man might have been a virgin before last night, but he certainly hadn't come across as awkward. And he'd taken instruction eagerly, without questioning her.

They hadn't conversed since their long and sweaty tumble, and warmth rolled over Makenna. What if things were awkward now? What if the magic of the night before had fled now that the sun was rising? What if, when they conversed again, they vexed each other as they once had?

She didn't have time to dwell on her worries though, for at that moment, he stirred, his eyes slowly opening. Their gazes met and held.

"Did ye sleep well?" he murmured.

"Aye," she whispered. "Very well."

His mouth quirked, and he lifted a hand, brushing a lock of hair off her face. "Ye look bonnie in the morning light," he murmured. "Yer hair wild … yer eyes soft."

Makenna's heart did a little skip. She raised her hand, pushing her hair back. Indeed, it was a tangle—a reminder of their passion. She cleared her throat then, suddenly embarrassed. "Well … at least our wedding night is over with."

His gaze shadowed at her words, and she immediately kicked herself. Why had she said that?

"I didn't bruise ye … did I?" he asked after a pause. A groove etched itself between his eyebrows, one she itched to reach out and smooth away. Clenching her hand, she prevented herself. "I meant to go slower but forgot myself in the end."

"Ye didn't hurt me," she assured him, even as her cheeks warmed. Indeed, after the initial discomfort, there hadn't been any pain. Just gut-twisting, soul-pounding pleasure.

His gaze met hers then, his expression solemn now. "It's not right … the way all of this was done." He paused then. "If I were a farmer and ye a local lass, we'd have had the chance to get to know each other … for me to *woo* ye before we tumbled."

She snorted. "Instead, I tried to kill ye … and then we fought."

He huffed a laugh. "I suppose love play takes many forms."

Makenna stilled. *Love play.* They both knew that wasn't what had happened on the days leading up to their wedding. Could one lusty night wash all the resentment away?

Their gazes met again, and then Bran lifted his hand once more. This time, he brushed the back of his knuckles across her cheek. "I'll not pretend things between us will be easy," he said softly. "But I'm willing to try … if ye are?"

There it was—another challenge issued. Already, he'd learned that Makenna could never resist a gauntlet thrown down before her.

A pause followed before she lowered her gaze. "Once ye discover more about me … ye might wish ye hadn't."

It was his turn to snort. "Before our wedding, I thought ye were a blade-tongued hellcat … but last night, I learned there's more to ye."

Her chin kicked up. *A blade-tongued hellcat?* "And I thought ye were a haughty lairdling with a pike stuck up yer arse."

His eyes snapped wide at her response. And then, to her surprise, he threw back his head and roared with laughter. He then propped himself up on an elbow and grinned at her. "Ye know ... I think we might be well-matched."

"Aye?" His mirth both affronted and flustered her. She'd just insulted him, but he didn't appear to mind.

"Aye." His grin faded now, his smoky eyes growing limpid. He then drew back the blanket covering them, his gaze dragging down the exposed length of her body. Her skin tingled under the weight of his stare, her breathing suddenly shallow. He cupped her face with his hand, his attention shifting to her mouth. "Now ... let's put that sharp tongue of yers to better use."

17: THE MORNING HUNT

BRAN ROSE FROM the bed and gave a long, languid stretch. A sense of well-being, unlike any he'd ever experienced, washed over him then, and a smile tugged at his mouth. This morning felt like a new start—for them both.

Maybe marriage to Makenna wouldn't be so onerous, after all.

He glanced over his shoulder at where his bride still lay abed, and the sight of her delicious curves made his breathing grow shallow. Makenna was dozing, sprawled on her front, her long auburn hair tangled after their last tumble. His gaze raked down the curve of her back and the twin rounded globes of her buttocks. She was just lovely.

They'd feasted on each other, but he couldn't wait for the day to pass so that he could be alone with her again. There was so much more to discover.

Stretching once more, Bran then padded across to where the privy sat behind a screen. Once he'd used it, he roused the fire and put another log on. Ruddy light flooded through the bower as he crossed back to the bed.

The light peeking in around the sacking on the window was brighter now. Soon, a servant would bring up their morning bannocks; he should really get dressed. Even so, the urge to join Makenna once more was stronger.

He was about to do just that when he noticed the book sitting on a shelf next to the bed.

Curiosity wreathed up. He wondered if it was a book of poetry. His mother had one that Tara loved reading.

Reaching out, he picked it up. However, when he turned it over and read the title embossed upon the red leather cover, he frowned. *The Art of Coupling*. That didn't sound like a poetry book to him.

He opened it and scanned the first page. He then turned to the next. And the next.

Eventually, he cleared his throat. "Makenna?"

"Mm?" She was still half-asleep.

"What's this?"

Murmuring something under her breath, she rolled onto her side to face him. Her full breasts gleamed in the firelight, their small pink nipples tempting him.

Trying to focus on what he'd just discovered rather than his wife's glorious tits, Bran waved the book. "This."

Her gaze snapped wide. "Oh, cods."

He raised an eyebrow. "Indeed."

She swallowed. "How much have ye read?"

"Enough."

Muttering an oath, she sat up, her wild hair spilling over her shoulders. "I meant to hide it ... I should have."

Her response was oddly endearing, as was the blush that now stained her cheeks. He liked seeing Makenna flustered.

Deliberately keeping his expression veiled, he looked down at the page he'd just finished reading—which described in graphic detail how to pleasure a woman's quim. Realization dawned then. The night before, he'd been delighted by how well his virgin bride had known her body, how confidently she'd instructed him.

Now, he understood why.

"Where did ye get it?"

She gnawed at her bottom lip. "One of my sisters gave the book to me ... as a wedding present." The blush on her cheeks glowed now. "Kylie wanted my wedding night to be ... easier."

Bran fell silent as he considered this revelation. So, Rae Maclean's wife had given Makenna this 'love manual'. He frowned, even as his gut tensed. He preferred not to think about the chieftain of Dounarwyse, whom he still considered an enemy, rutting his wife.

"Are ye vexed?" she asked finally.

Her question made him still. Makenna's eyes were shadowed. She was worried she'd offended him. She hadn't, although she *had* taken him by surprise. Life with this woman certainly wouldn't be boring.

"No," he replied, his lips tugging into a teasing smile. "Although I can see I will need to study this later ... in readiness for tonight."

Licking honey off her fingers, Makenna caught her husband giving her a hungry look that had nothing to do with the delicious griddle scones and blossom honey Fiona had brought up for them. Their gazes locked, and her breathing grew shallow as her belly fluttered. Her desire for him didn't yet show any sign of abating. Instead, it was growing.

When Bran had discovered The Art of Coupling, she'd been mortified. What must he think of her?

But his response surprised her. Tossing the book aside, he'd climbed back into bed and hauled her into his arms. He'd taken her hard as the dawn light filtered into her bower, plunging deep while she wrapped her legs around his hips, dug her heels into his arse, and raked her fingernails down his back. Her eager response had driven him wild, and his hoarse cry had joined hers when he'd shattered.

She'd thought he'd be sated, but one look in his eyes now told her he wanted her again.

Her quim started to ache in response. Despite that she was a little sore down there now, she needed him too, with a force that made dizziness sweep over her.

She was grateful that they were able to break their fasts alone. Fortunately, they weren't expected to join everyone else in the great hall this morning. Just as well, for Makenna wasn't ready to face her sisters—Liza and Kylie, especially—and their knowing smiles. The tower house's walls were thick, but she and Bran had made a lot of noise during their coupling. Her especially.

"If yer father and his hounds weren't waiting for me downstairs, we wouldn't be leaving this chamber," he growled.

Makenna's breathing quickened. There was time for him to take her again. They didn't have to disrobe. He could push her up against the wall, lift her skirts, and—

A brisk knock cut off her heated thoughts then, and her gaze jerked to the door.

"Hurry yerselves up." Her mother's lilting voice carried through the thick oak separating them. "Yer father wants to get an early start."

Makenna grimaced, all lusty thoughts fleeing. "Aye, Ma," she called back. "We shall be down shortly."

She glanced back at her husband then, to find Bran wearing a half-smile, even as heat still smoldered in his eyes. Their gazes held for a long, delicious moment, and she found herself wishing it were the evening already.

"*Arsebiter* ... that's quite a name for a sword."

"Aye, a fitting one too," Makenna replied, glancing over at Bran. He rode next to her through the woods. Ancient beech, oak, and ash formed a canopy overhead, with dappled light filtering through the greenery. She then gestured to the heavy claidheamh-mòr strapped behind his saddle. "And what did ye name yer broadsword?"

"I didn't ... it was my father's." He pulled a face. "*Bonestrike*."

Makenna studied him for a few moments before answering, "Ye should have another sword forged. One that suits ye ... one that ye can name yerself."

He raised an eyebrow. "Why is that?"

"The bond between a warrior and their blade is a vital one … a partnership. *Bonestrike* was yer father's, but ye are a different man and require a different sword."

He gave a slow nod at this, his brow furrowing. "Ye have a point … I might do that."

The trill of a skylark interrupted them then, an enchanting melody that made Makenna's lips curve. How she loved the woodland around Meggernie. It was a peaceful morning, with hardly a breeze stirring the sweet, soft air.

Despite a long night of revelry, the rest of their company was in good spirits. Her father rode at the front, flanked by Alec on one side and Rae on the other. The three men were ribbing each other good-naturedly, the low rumble of their voices carrying through the morning's stillness. Rae's tension after her father had produced his quaich seemed to have eased.

A knot of warriors, quivers of arrows and longbows slung across their backs, followed. They'd brought half a dozen leggy deerhounds with them too, and the dogs loped alongside the horses.

Likewise, both Makenna and Bran carried longbows. This stag hunt would take them deep into the valleys at the feet of the southeastern arm of the mountains. And as they rode out of the trees and up a heather-strewn hill, Makenna caught sight of the sprawling mountain range before her and the mighty bulk of Ben Lawers. Those mountains divided her father's lands from the long expanse of Loch Tay to the south. Unfortunately, though, the territory south of the mountains belonged to the Campbells of Breadalbane and 'Black' Duncan Campbell.

Every time her gaze rested on Ben Lawers, she couldn't help but ruminate about the enemy.

She still chafed about the fact that her father wouldn't share his plans with her. After she departed for Mull, he'd deal with the Campbells, and not before. She felt shut out, pushed aside.

"It's a fine country this," Bran noted then. He admired the mountain range. "I can see why ye love it here."

"I do," Makenna agreed softly, even as something knotted deep within her chest. "I can't believe I'll soon be leaving."

"Ye shall grow to love Dùn Ara too." She glanced his way to find him watching her now. "My castle perches high upon a rocky outcrop above a sheltered harbor with woodland to our back and the glittering sea to the north." Pride laced his voice, even as his lips curved into a hesitant smile. "My father added onto the original dùn. Its curtain wall is now five feet thick."

"It sounds mighty," she replied, unable to resist teasing him.

"It is."

Makenna cut her attention away then. Suddenly, she was loath to speak of her new home, for it reminded her that she was abandoning her clan. She and Bran had passed a surprising night together—and discovered a passion that had left them both reeling—but that didn't change the truth of things.

This was an arranged marriage, not for their personal benefit, but for that of their clans. Their union would hopefully make both the MacGregors of Meggernie and the Mackinnons of Dùn Ara stronger and forge a lasting relationship. Her happiness, or his, didn't matter. They were both strong-willed too, and it was likely their marriage would be a stormy one.

A shadow settled over her, chasing away her earlier sense of well-being, and dimming the beautiful morning.

She glanced Bran's way again, to find him looking ahead once more as he rode.

His profile was proud, and the sunlight made his wavy hair look as if it were on fire. He was dressed in a lèine, chamois braies, and a leather vest this morning, although he'd also donned his clan sash. The brightness of it stood out. Seeing it reminded her of Bran's arrival at Meggernie. He'd been so angry, so bitter—such a contrast to the night before.

Tension coiled under Makenna's ribcage as her gaze slid over his chest. He'd worn that sash deliberately—to remind everyone here he was, and would always be, a Mackinnon. Aye, he'd drunk from her father's quaich, but that didn't mean they were friends. After their revealing conversation before coupling, she felt as if she understood him a little better.

"I met yer sister at Dounarwyse."

His body jerked, his gaze swinging Makenna's way. His eyes then narrowed. As she'd expected, this wasn't a subject he wished to discuss. In truth, she wasn't sure why she'd brought it up, only that she'd liked Tara and hadn't forgotten the pain in her eyes. All the same, the stiffening of his spine challenged her. She couldn't let it go now.

"Tara is a good woman ... with a kind, generous soul," she continued. "She wishes to be reconciled with ye. Why won't ye bury the ax?"

His gaze hardened. "What lies between my sister and me is *our* business, not yers."

His tone was sharp, and Makenna lifted her chin as she eyeballed him back. "So, ye'll not forgive her then?"

A muscle feathered in his jaw before he looked away. "No."

And with that short exchange, the easy rapport between them shattered.

It surprised Makenna that it had taken so little to stir up their earlier animosity. However, the trust they'd built overnight was clearly as fragile as thistledown.

She focused once more on her gelding's furry ears, her belly clenching. *Why did ye do that?*

She'd known he wouldn't want to speak of Tara. Not yet—not while things were so new between them. But she'd done so anyway and driven a wedge between them. For an instant, she'd enjoyed challenging him, yet the sensation had been fleeting.

And in the aftermath, shame washed over her.

Bran urged his cob into a canter, following the men through a steep-sided valley. The hounds were on the scent, racing after a large roe stag that bounded ahead of them.

Noon was approaching, and it was the second hunt of the day. Earlier, two roe deer hinds had fled across their path. The dogs had gone after them, using their speed and keen eyesight to track the hinds through the trees.

The riders followed, catching up with the deerhounds just as they ran both deer down. The carcasses were now slung over the backs of the garrons they'd brought with them.

This coursing came as a welcome distraction for Bran. The stag was young and would take a while to tire; this would be a grueling hunt. Just as well, for he needed to settle his temper.

The morning had started so well. The beginning of their ride south had been enjoyable too, for things had been easy between him and Makenna.

For a short while, he'd dared believe his ill luck had come to an end—that for once, things might work out for him.

But he'd marked Makenna's shift in mood when she'd spoken of her love for Meggernie. She hadn't seemed that impressed by his description of Dùn Ara either.

Yet when she'd brought up Tara, she crossed the line.

He wouldn't have her telling him how to conduct himself with his sister. Makenna had grown up in a secure and happy home. She had no idea what it was like to be betrayed by kin so deeply.

All the same, a hollow sensation had settled in Bran's chest in the aftermath. Last night had been like stepping into someone else's life. For the first time in a long while, he hadn't felt alone. Instead, he'd lost himself with a beautiful woman—and had foolishly believed it was a turning point for him. Maybe this marriage wouldn't be the awful burden he'd feared.

But the reality was that he'd wedded a strong-willed woman. This wasn't the first time Makenna had challenged him—and it wouldn't be the last either.

Up ahead, the MacGregor whooped. "We're gaining on him!"

The warriors following shouted, bloodlust igniting in their veins. The going was rough here, for the valley floor was knotted with tree roots, yet their surefooted coursers leaped burns and wove in and out of trees with ease.

In the distance, Bran caught a flash of tawny brown. The stag was tiring. Soon, it would stop, turn, and face its pursuers. At that point, they'd bring it down.

As he rode, Bran was aware of Makenna following just behind him.

Now and again, he'd catch a flash of green, for she wore a pine-colored leather vest over a kirtle of the same color and woolen leggings underneath. Crouched over her horse's withers, she rode confidently, her gaze trained on the hunt.

She was magnificent, although part of him didn't want her here. His father had always insisted that a woman's place was by the hearth, taking care of bairns and managing a household. Not riding like a man on a hunt. It wasn't seemly, but *his* reaction went deeper than that. He was protective of her. Worried that she might take a fall.

Vexed that he'd be concerned about such things—for Makenna was far more capable and tougher than most men—Bran focused once more on the stag.

They'd just ridden into a narrow glade alongside a meandering burn. And here, the exhausted beast made its stand. Sides heaving, it stopped, turned, and lowered its antlers, ready to fight.

The hunters drew up their horses, while MacGregor whistled to his hounds, commanding them to circle the stag rather than attack.

Pulling up his own horse, Bran's gaze settled on their quarry. The stag was beautiful, with a sleek brown coat, dark eyes, and massive antlers. His chest constricted then, the excitement of the hunt fading. He never relished this part of it. The stag was valiant yet outnumbered. It wasn't a fair fight—but then, there was little that was fair about life. He'd learned that early.

"Go on, Mackinnon," MacGregor boomed, drawing his attention. The clan-chief's face was red with exertion, his eyes bright, his grin wide. "Bring it down."

The tightness in Bran's chest increased. Of course, his father-by-marriage was doing him an honor. He could have asked any of the men present to kill the stag or have claimed the right himself. But he wanted his new son-by-marriage to do it.

Bran couldn't disappoint him.

Setting his jaw, he nodded and unslung the longbow from his back. A moment later, he plucked an arrow from the quiver. Shifting in the saddle, he turned his torso, raised his bow, drew back the bowstring, and sighted his target. He was positioned to the right of the stag and had a clear view of its head and neck. It would be a clean kill. The beast wouldn't suffer.

And so, he loosed the arrow.

18: YE CANNOT CLIP MY WINGS

MAKENNA KEPT STEALING glances at her husband as they turned and made for home.

The rest of their party were in high spirits.

Alec and Rae were firm friends, it seemed. The two of them conversed at length as they rode side-by-side up ahead. Her father led the way, riding alongside Captain Walker now. Although she couldn't hear them clearly, she knew they'd be talking about the hunt—about the things that had gone well, and what they could have done better—as they always did after a day of coursing.

But Bran had been silent ever since bringing the stag down.

His aim had been impressive. A single arrow into the soft spot above the eye. The shaft had driven into the stag's brain and killed it instantly.

Cheers had filled the glade afterward, although Makenna had marked that her husband didn't share in the revelry. The man barely raised a smile. Was he still vexed with her for asking him about his sister?

The stag now hung across the back of the sturdiest of the garrons they'd brought with them. Meggernie would have plenty of venison to feast upon in the coming days.

"Ye wield a longbow well," she said finally, breaking the weighty silence between them.

His attention swung her way, although his expression and gaze were both veiled. "Aye," he replied without a trace of arrogance. "It's always been my weapon of choice."

"Did yer father teach ye?"

"No, a man named Fergus … who once captained the Dùn Ara Guard. He fell at Dounarwyse." His gaze shadowed at this admission.

"He was a friend then?"

Bran shifted his gaze away, focusing ahead. "Aye … he had the patience for teaching that my father always lacked."

Makenna gave a soft snort. "My father is the same … after our first swordplay lesson, he threw up his hands and refused to teach me again." She paused then, her gaze flicking to where the Captain of the Meggernie Guard had just snorted at something her father had said. "Fortunately, Walker has infinite patience. I've certainly tried his over the years."

She'd deliberately made a self-deprecating comment, in the hope of lightening the mood between them, of seeing that beautiful mouth quirk into a smile. However, Bran's expression didn't change. In truth, she was now truly sorry about baiting him earlier in the day.

She'd wanted to challenge him, but it hadn't tasted as sweet as she'd expected. And now, she found herself wishing things were easy between them again.

"Is the hunting good on Mull?" she asked finally, when it became clear he wasn't going to respond to her comment. "I didn't go out coursing at Moy or Dounarwyse while I was there last year."

"Aye … there are plenty of deer and even a few boar in the woodlands."

"And are the woods like these?" She wanted to keep him talking, to thaw the ice between them.

"Similar … oak and ash mainly. Many ancient oaks grow along the coast, although the wind blows them into twisted shapes."

Her mouth curved. "I remember seeing those … near Moy Castle." She paused then, awkward. She wasn't used to feeling on the back foot. "I look forward to us exploring the isle on horseback and hunting together."

He didn't answer immediately, and when she looked his way once more, she marked the groove that had etched between his eyebrows. "Things will be different when we return to Mull. Ye won't be serving in the Dùn Ara Guard … and I don't want ye training with them either. Nor will ye carry weapons like a man." He paused then, his gaze shadowing. "I don't wish for ye to come to any harm."

Makenna snorted, even as her heart kicked against her ribs. "I'm not made of eggshell. I've already bested *ye* twice."

Irritation flared in his eyes. "No … but a husband must protect his wife," he answered firmly. "It will be for yer own good."

"This is who I am," she said, fighting to keep her tone even. He might think such a declaration was protective, that he was doing her a favor. Instead, it was smothering, and she wouldn't stand for it. "I will bear ye bairns, sew and weave, and manage yer castle as chatelaine … but ye cannot clip my wings, Bran. I won't let ye."

His face flushed then, and their gazes locked in silent combat. Eventually, her husband growled his answer, "Ye are my wife, Makenna … ye will do as ye are told."

Fire ignited in her belly. "Then ye will have to lock me up," she ground out. "Ye won't rob me of my dirk and sword … or forbid me from riding and hunting … without a fight."

An answering heat flared in his smoky eyes. "Yer father has indulged ye … as has Captain Walker … but I'll not let ye make me the laughingstock of Mull."

"I thought ye wanted to *protect* me?" she countered, her gaze narrowing. "But it sounds that ye are more concerned about how other people see ye."

Her voice was rising now, causing the men riding ahead of her to glance over their shoulders in surprise. Makenna ignored them.

Meanwhile, her husband's expression turned stony.

They stared at each other, anger crackling like a summer storm between them. Neither of them was willing to give ground.

Disappointment tightened Makenna's chest. The night before, she'd been delighted to discover her husband was far more sensitive and deep-thinking than she'd anticipated. But this morning, he'd revealed yet another side to him—one she liked far less.

If he got his way, she foresaw a miserable life awaiting her on the Isle of Mull.

"Ye named yer father a tyrant," she said finally, even as her pulse thumped in her ears. "Yet it appears to me that ye wish to emulate him."

Bran flinched as if she had just struck him across the face. "I'm only trying to be a proper husband." He bit out the words. "And take care of my wife."

"No, that's just a ruse! Ye wish to dominate me, I see it now."

"Ye see *nothing*. Don't act as if ye know me. Ye don't."

The baying of hounds cut through the woods then, severing their argument.

Makenna stiffened, her gaze sweeping the tangle of hawthorn at the path's edge. The noise wasn't coming from their dogs, for the six deerhounds they'd brought with them trotted alongside the horses, exhausted after a day's coursing.

"To arms!" Her father roared then from ahead, his voice slicing through the warm afternoon air. He yanked his dirk free of its scabbard. All those following him did likewise, including Alec and Rae.

Cursing, Makenna did the same.

She glanced to her right then, to see that Bran had unslung his longbow and already notched an arrow.

Huge muscular dogs burst from the trees, followed by a stream of men on horseback.

The twang of Bran's bowstring followed as he loosed his first arrow. It struck one of the riders leading the group of attackers in the chest, knocking him off his horse. An instant later, Bran had notched another shaft. He let that one fly too, and it hit a second warrior in the throat.

And then the warriors were upon them.

Things moved swiftly. So fast that Makenna had no time to take a good look at their attackers. Most of them were big men clad in leather and woolen cloaks. And the expression on their faces was savage.

Their dogs were beasts. Their jaws were huge and slavering, their dark gazes feral. Bloodhounds, yet bigger than any she'd ever seen.

The hounds reached them first. Some savaged the deerhounds while others leaped at the horses. Curses and grunts followed as the warriors fought them off. The riders came after their dogs moments later, dirks slashing.

Makenna twisted to the side, narrowly avoiding a blade. Heart pounding, she slid down from her horse and drew Arsebiter, ducking as another dirk slashed at her.

An agonized grunt followed, and the warrior who'd just tried to stab her toppled off his horse, grasping a feather-fletched arrow buried deep in his neck.

Bran had just brought him down. Like Makenna, he'd dismounted. All of them had. It was easier to fight on foot.

Their assailants swarmed around them now. Campbells.

The bastards.

Makenna leaped forward, engaging one of their attackers, who'd just leaped from his mount and lunged for her. The ring of clashing steel echoed through the woods, and suddenly she was fighting for her life. There was no time to look at her father, or even glance Bran's way. One moment of distraction and it would be over.

Meanwhile, those massive hounds were wreaking havoc. They'd bested their deerhounds and were now swarming around the fighting warriors, jaws snapping.

Makenna looked frantically around her. They were surrounded. Outnumbered.

Two of their warriors fell close by—Tyree and Brec, men she'd grown up with—the wet sound of their final breaths cutting through the woodland air. With a roar, she launched herself at their killers, her blade flashing bright in the afternoon light. But it wasn't enough. There were men all around her, hemming her in. Their gazes gleamed, and they grinned toothily. The whoresons had them—and they knew it.

Panting, Makenna found herself fighting back-to-back with Bran. He'd cast aside his longbow to use a dirk at close quarters.

And then, amongst the press of large leather-clad bodies, she caught a glimpse of a man with white-blond hair. He'd just stuck his dirk through the throat of a warrior and kicked him to the ground. The pale-haired warrior fought with a skill she knew intimately, for she'd trained at swordplay with him many a time. Trained, and lost every fight against him.

A chill washed over her, dousing the fire of battle in her veins. She'd only ever met one man she truly feared, but believed she'd never set eyes on him again.

No ... it can't be.

19: TWO BIRDS WITH ONE STONE

THEY WON'T GET away with this. The Meggernie Guard will come after them.

Makenna tried to keep up her spirits with rallying thoughts. But underneath her mantle of courage, it was difficult not to worry. It was difficult not to despair—or to let fear unravel her.

Tormod MacDougall is alive.

Her belly twisted as she recalled the moment he'd shifted his attention her way during the fight. His gaze was as pitiless as before, although his face seemed crueler. And the slow smile he'd given Makenna had made her heart stutter.

They hadn't spoken, although she'd seen him watching her as she'd had her ankles and wrists bound. And the look in his pale-blue eyes had made her tremble.

Makenna wasn't a lass who was easily frightened. Nonetheless, she'd never forget what Tormod had tried to take from her the year before, and his threat as Rae Maclean's men dragged him from the broch after the laird had flogged him still haunted her.

It isn't over between us, lass ... ye shall see me again.

Wrists and ankles bound and slung over the withers of a horse, she stared down at the grass they now cantered over. Hanging upside down like this had made the blood rush to her head. A wedge of filthy cloth gagged her, and the side of her head throbbed from where one of her captors had hit her when she'd tried to stop him from tying her up. Closing her eyes, she tried not to think of Tormod. She couldn't allow herself to do so. Instead, she silently cursed the Campbells.

Cursed every dog-humping one of them.

They'd been forced to surrender eventually. It was either that or die. Six of their party—and all her father's beloved deerhounds—had fallen in the skirmish, their bodies left sprawled amongst the trees. The rest of them were taken captive: Makenna and Bran, her father, Captain Walker, Alec, and Rae, as well as the two remaining MacGregor warriors, Aodh and Mungo.

Bloodied but not beaten, her father had raged at them at first. Yet his outburst had caused a man with a long face, hooked nose, and pitiless eyes to push his way through the circle of warriors and dogs. He'd then stridden over to him and struck the MacGregor hard across the face, bringing him to his knees.

It was then they'd discovered that this wasn't just a Campbell raiding party, but 'Black' Duncan Campbell's warband.

The chieftain himself had accompanied his warriors. They'd come north hunting the MacGregor clan-chief—and they'd found him.

Staring down at the clumps of coarse grass, thistles, and heather, Makenna wondered how Bran was faring. He'd fought savagely in the end, only giving up when Tormod pinned him to the ground and placed a dirk-blade to his throat. Makenna had thought for a sickening moment that Tormod might kill him then. Her belly clenched at the memory.

Tormod hadn't slain him though. Instead, he'd held Bran still while others bound his feet and wrists. And now, Meggernie lay far behind them.

Aye, the Guard would come after them, eventually, but it would take time to track them, to catch up with this warband. In the meantime, Duncan Campbell had a big head start, and she had no idea what he was planning.

Frustration beat like a caged raven in her chest. She hated feeling so powerless. Seeing her father and Captain Walker taken captive had been an awful wrench too. They were now as helpless as bairns. The order of things had just splintered, and she couldn't see how to put things back together.

The afternoon stretched out into a golden evening. Their captors made the most of the long gloaming to get as far from Meggernie as possible. Finally though, they drew up in a narrow, wooded gully—a sheltered spot in a pass that cut through the eastern arm of the mountains—where no one would find them.

Makenna's temples pounded as she slumped onto the pebbly ground. Hanging upside down for hours had made her dizzy and nauseated.

Bran was then hauled over and thrown down next to her.

Blinking to see properly in the shadowy dusk, Makenna studied her husband's pale face. A bright bruise had come up on his cheekbone from his fight with Tormod. Nonetheless, his silvery gaze burned.

Tearing her attention from Bran, she looked over at her father and the others.

The MacGregor wore a glower that looked as if it might split his face—a mutinous look Makenna knew well. Her chest constricted painfully then. His anger wouldn't help him now. Next to him, Rae was bleeding from a shallow cut to his forehead. It seemed he'd given the Campbells some trouble moments earlier when they'd pulled him off the back of a horse. Meanwhile, Alec's handsome face was carved into hard lines, his blue eyes narrowed as he observed the men who milled around them now.

The Campbells ignored their captives for the moment; instead, they concentrated on lighting a fire and preparing supper. They ate dried meat and oatcakes, talking amongst themselves, but they didn't offer their captives any food. And it was only later that they removed the gags from their mouths and gave them some ale to drink, holding skins up to their lips.

Makenna drank thirstily, although the few gulps they gave her weren't enough. Glaring at the warrior who yanked the skin away before leering at her, she watched as he moved to Bran. Her husband looked as if he wanted to bite the warrior's hand off, yet, like her, his thirst was greater.

As the man moved over to the next captive, Bran shifted his attention to Makenna.

His gaze met hers then and held. His ire still simmered, yet there was a question in his eyes now, a shadow of concern. He wanted to know if she was hurt.

Makenna gave a barely imperceptible shake of her head. She wasn't going to snarl at him for being overprotective now, not when all their futures were uncertain.

"Ye won't get away with this, Campbell," her father rasped then. "Abducting a clan-chief is low … even for ye."

The Campbell warriors around him snorted with laughter and rolled their eyes at this. Duncan Campbell, who sat upon a rock by the fire a few yards away, merely shrugged. "Long have ye underestimated me, Bruce. Ye should have known this day would come."

"Aye … ye've had it coming, ye cattle-stealing whoreson," a younger man standing nearby sneered. By his looks, Makenna guessed this was the chieftain's son. He was dark-haired and rangy but without his father's intensity.

"Too right, Robbie," Campbell rumbled, his gaze never leaving Makenna's father.

"Shit-eating bastards." Undaunted, the MacGregor glared back. "Does the Campbell know about this?"

The chieftain's bearded jaw tightened a fraction. "Ian Campbell will thank me for dealing to ye."

Makenna stilled at these words—an admission that the Campbell clan-chief hadn't sanctioned this abduction.

Her father spat on the ground. "I shall have my reckoning against ye … mark my words."

Campbell merely exchanged a look with his son before smirking.

Makenna's chest tightened. She shared her father's rage. Nonetheless, the glint in the Campbell chieftain's eyes was a warning. There was something in his manner that reminded her of Tormod.

Her father was as strong as an ox, and a formidable warrior, but at his core, he was decent and capable of mercy. But Campbell and MacDougall were cut from a different cloth.

Fighting dread, she glanced over to where Tormod sat whittling a piece of wood by the fire.

The bastard was watching her.

She couldn't help it; she shuddered under the weight of his stare.

And seeing her reaction, he flashed her a wolfish smile.

Dusk slid into night. The Campbells gathered around the fireside, drinking and congratulating each other, while their beastly hounds lounged at their sides, eyes glowing in the firelight.

Leaning against a cold slab of rock, Makenna wriggled, trying to ease the chafing of the rope upon her wrists.

"They know how to tie knots, it seems," Bran murmured. He was seated next to her, so close their shoulders brushed. His nearness was reassuring. All the same, she wished she were sitting next to her father, and that she could speak to him. Unfortunately, he sat nearer the fire, under the eye of Campbell. The last thing the chieftain wanted was his prize escaping.

"I know," she grunted. "I can't budge them."

Silence fell then before Bran nudged her with his elbow. "That man with the pale hair has been staring at ye all evening. It's as if he knows ye."

Makenna's pulse quickened. "He does."

"Tormod MacDougall." Rae's voice intruded then. Makenna had forgotten he was seated next to Bran. "Kylie stabbed him in the cods around three months ago … but the rat-faced bastard didn't bleed out as we hoped."

"No," Makenna whispered, deliberately not glancing Tormod's way. He was looking at her again; she could feel the probing weight of his stare. "Last year ... at Dounarwyse ... he tried to rape me."

Bran made a soft hissing sound.

"I fought him off," she continued, "and Rae flogged him the following morning before banishing him from his lands." She halted there, her throat constricting. Although she hadn't admitted it to anyone, that attack had shaken her more than she cared to admit. It had been a chink in her armor—a reminder that she had vulnerabilities, after all. If she was honest with herself, she hadn't been herself ever since.

"But he found allies amongst the Ghost Raiders," Rae continued the tale after a lengthy pause. "Thanks to him, they discovered a way into my broch."

"Looks as if he's got new friends," Bran replied. His voice now held a rough edge.

Rae gave a soft snort. "Aye, unfortunately."

Silence fell between them then. Exhausted, Makenna leaned her head back against the damp rock and closed her eyes. Even so, her stomach was in knots, and she'd broken out in a cold sweat. "He wants *me*," she admitted finally, her voice barely above a whisper. "He told me we'd see each other again ... and he's made good on his threat."

"I remember his words," Rae answered gruffly, while Bran remained silent. "But he wants his revenge against me as well, lass. He'll be congratulating himself on bringing down two birds with one stone."

Bran's brow furrowed as he observed his wife. Makenna had been dumped a few yards away, and sat head hanging, shoulders slumped. When he'd caught a glimpse of her face earlier, he'd marked her strained features and shadowed gaze. It was unlike her to look so defeated, and something deep in his chest tightened.

He couldn't help it. He worried about her.

The Campbells had set off at dawn, traveling swiftly. They were now watering their horses and resting for a short while on the northern shore of Loch Tay. The sun warmed Bran's face and sparkled off the water of the loch. The day was the bonniest of the year so far, but he was hardly in the mood to appreciate it.

Instead, he couldn't take his eyes off Makenna.

Ye don't have to scratch far beneath the surface to discover that much of my confidence is bluster.

There was far more to his bride than met the eye. Beneath her arrogance, she was sensitive and caring. She could handle herself as well as him in a fight, yet she was vulnerable now. They all were.

Bran swallowed, trying to ignore his dry mouth and throat. The Campbells hadn't given them enough to drink, although he wasn't thinking about his own discomfort, but Makenna's. He hated knowing he couldn't shield her from harm.

She thinks I'm a tyrant. Aye, and he had only himself to blame for that. He'd come across as overbearing, and he was sorry for it.

The truth was he was forming an attachment to his feisty bride. Finding someone to care about after years of loneliness had made him act impulsively. He needed to ensure he didn't lose her. He didn't want to fail her, not like he had his sister. When Tara had returned to Dùn Ara after escaping her abductor, he'd stood by while their father had condemned and then humiliated her.

Was it any wonder she ran away?

Pushing aside painful memories, Bran tore his attention from his wife and glanced over at the man who'd tried to rape her. The night before, he'd noted that Tormod sat apart from the Campbells and didn't interact much with his fellow warriors. The chieftain favored him though. The pair had ridden side-by-side for most of the morning, at the head of the band.

Tormod didn't appear to notice Bran's scrutiny. Instead, he whittled a piece of wood with a small sharp knife while staring at Makenna. His gaze was hot and hungry.

Bran clenched his jaw. How he longed to drive a dagger through that dung-eater's eye.

And he made a silent promise to himself that he would.

Heart pounding, he stared down at his bound wrists. The rope had chafed the skin where he'd tried to loosen it. There was no getting free of these bonds.

The day before, Makenna had accused him of caring too much about the opinions of others. Perhaps he did. To many of his people, and the Macleans and the Macquaries—the other clans on Mull—he was the wet-behind-the-ears pup who'd crawled back to Dùn Ara after the Battle of Dounarwyse with his tail between his legs. Even years later, he burned with the humiliation of it.

Or he *had*—until the Campbells of Breadalbane took it upon themselves to kidnap the MacGregor hunting party a day after his wedding.

Suddenly, none of that mattered. He couldn't have cared less whether all of Mull hated him. He was too angry to care about anything but making the Campbells and Tormod MacDougall pay. The Mackinnon temper was something indeed. Cold and quiet, yet sharp as a boning knife. Mackinnons didn't rant and rage. No, they bided their time, and when they struck, they went for the throat.

But until that time, he'd let the Campbells think he wouldn't give them any further trouble.

The Campbells rode as if Lucifer himself were on their tail. A spine of mountains now reared up to the north.

Slung over the back of a horse, his body sore, his head aching, Bran did his best to keep track of their progress. Had someone picked up their trail yet? Was there a band pursuing them? Frustratingly, it was impossible to know, for the Campbells told their captives nothing.

They barely rested for the remainder of the day, and the shadows were growing long when they finally reached the southern edge of Loch Tay.

Fighting dizziness, Bran lifted his head to see high grey walls rising above a birch copse. Shortly after, they left the loch's shoreline behind and climbed the hill up a narrow path, single file now, before riding through a scattering of shielings.

Bran lifted his head again to see men, women, and bairns gathering before their thatch-roofed cottages.

They watched the chieftain and his warriors—and their captives—with nervous, cowed expressions. Campbell didn't bother to acknowledge them as he rode by.

Neck aching from the effort of keeping his head raised, Bran shifted his attention to the fortress that loomed to his right. His gaze narrowed as he inspected it. The tower house was high—at least four floors—although the dark-grey stone gave it a gloomy look. A high wall surrounded the keep. The gate was open to admit them, a dark maw with the spiky teeth of the raised portcullis.

Finlarig Castle awaited them.

20: TORMOD'S PRIZE

MAKENNA WATCHED IN horror while her husband was pushed roughly into a deep pit.

The other members of her party quickly followed, grunting and swearing as they landed on each other.

Finally, only Makenna and her father remained outside the hole. She'd never been in a hall such as this one. What laird had an oubliette for prisoners in one corner of his hall? It sat next to a much shallower stone-lined pit that had an ominous-looking curved, worn stone in its center.

It looked suspiciously like a chopping block.

Makenna's pulse went wild then, and she braced herself to be shoved over the edge as well. Two men held her by each arm, for they'd removed her bindings to bring her inside. However, the Campbell warriors merely closed the metal grate over the prisoners—the clang of iron ringing through the hall. They then pushed a heavy bolt home, locking it.

Heart thumping against her ribs, she watched Duncan Campbell move forward. He eyed both Makenna and her father before favoring them with a thin smile. "Welcome to Finlarig ... a fine castle, is it not?"

Neither Makenna nor her father answered.

"Of course, the pit is too humble for a clan-chief and his daughter," Campbell went on. "My men will take ye to private chambers on the upper floor ... where ye will be brought water for bathing and some supper."

"What do ye want, Campbell?" Bruce demanded. His eyes were a murderous green, and a vein throbbed in his temple.

The chieftain made a tutting sound. "Not so hasty ... there will be time for us to discuss matters later. For now ... just enjoy my hospitality."

"I don't want yer hospitality," her father shot back, his fury spilling over. He lunged for the chieftain then but was hauled back by the two men who held him.

Unperturbed, Campbell nodded to his warriors. "Take them upstairs."

Unsurprisingly, they put Makenna and her father in separate chambers.

Thrusting her through the doorway, the men slammed the heavy oaken door behind her. The grate of an iron key turning in the lock followed.

She flung herself at the window then, fingers grasping at the shutters. But they too were locked. Makenna cursed, whirling around and surveying the four walls enclosing her. There was no way out of this chamber.

A brick of peat burned in the hearth, and an oil lamp sat next to the canopied bed, casting the room in soft golden light. A bowl of water waited on a stand near the window, steam rising from its surface.

In other circumstances, she might have found this chamber comfortable. But now, she saw it for what it was. A prison.

The others have it far worse though.

Makenna choked out a curse. She'd thought Campbell may have announced his plans this evening, that he might have put them all out of their misery, but he deliberately hadn't.

He was playing with them.

Trembling, she sat down on the edge of the bed.

It was hard not to let fear take over now, not to let her imagination run wild. They were trapped in Black Duncan's web, and he clearly had plans for all of them. Tormod's presence among the Campbells added fuel to her rising panic.

Makenna's fingers clenched into fists, her nails biting against her palms. The pain steadied her and made her focus. "Hold fast, lass," she whispered. "The others need ye to be strong … to have yer wits about ye."

They did. She had to breathe deeply, calm her thoughts, and come up with a plan.

They weren't beaten yet.

Campbell wouldn't lock her up in here forever—and when she was brought before him again, she'd be ready.

"I have two favors to ask, Dunc."

The laird glanced up from where he was pouring himself a large cup of ale. "Oh, aye?"

"Aye." Tormod slid onto the bench seat next to Campbell, his gut tightening as he did so. He'd been biding his time before asking this, but he couldn't wait any longer.

"And the first?"

"Ye've got the clan-chief ... but his daughter ... I want her for my own."

They were alone at the table, for supper had ended and only a few men remained in the hall—a group of them playing knucklebones a few yards away. Robbie Campbell was among them. The chieftain's wife, Janet, had retired for the evening.

He had Campbell's ear now.

The chieftain didn't reply immediately, and the long pause irritated Tormod. He didn't like to be made to wait. Nonetheless, Campbell was the one with all the power here, and so he swallowed his annoyance.

"Makenna Mackinnon is a fiery one."

"She is that."

"Have ye met her before then?"

"Aye," Tormod replied lightly. "She visited Dounarwyse while I was there."

Campbell favored him with a long, hard look, one that made Tormod resist the urge to squirm. His deep-set eyes were like two dark pebbles. "Why haven't ye mentioned this before now?"

"It didn't seem important."

The chieftain inclined his head.

"It's a coincidence, is it not, that just a month before I abduct the MacGregor clan-chief and his newly wedded daughter, ye turn up at my door, offering me yer fealty?"

"It is," Tormod replied. He didn't like the way Campbell was looking at him now. "But let me assure ye that wasn't in my mind when I swore to serve ye."

A lie, but a smooth one.

"Ye have impressed me so far, Tormod," Campbell replied before lifting the cup to his lips and taking a sip. "But ye ask much ... ye haven't been at Finlarig long."

"My place is here, Dunc," Tormod answered, realizing as he spoke that he meant it. He had nowhere else to go. His uncle at Coeffin Castle had taken him in when he'd arrived, injured, on *The Night Plunderer*, but as soon as he was well enough, he'd told him to leave. And of course, the pirate ship had long set sail. Those men he'd rallied to fight with the Ghost Raiders had no loyalty to him any longer, and they'd sailed away on the pirate cog shortly after dropping him off.

Tormod could have a good life at Finlarig Castle. And with Makenna as his, he'd have no reason to leave. All he needed was Campbell to give him his due. After everything he'd been through, he deserved her. He'd been foiled at Dounarwyse, but he wouldn't let it happen again.

"She's wedded now, of course," Campbell pointed out then, his eyes glinting.

"Surely, ye won't let Mackinnon live?" Tormod shot back.

The chieftain's gaze narrowed. "I haven't decided what do to with him yet."

"He's merely a complication ye don't need. What if he was to have an 'accident'?"

Campbell smirked at this, although his gaze remained sharp. "Aye ... he might well have one ... especially if MacGregor proves uncooperative."

Tormod glanced across the hall then, at the pit. The prisoners had been silent all evening, and they were too far away to overhear the conversation at the chieftain's table. Nonetheless, Tormod's belly clenched whenever he thought of Bran Mackinnon. He'd wanted to be the one to bed Makenna for the first time, yet the red-haired whoreson had stolen his prize. He'd wanted to cut his throat after they'd attacked the MacGregors, but Duncan had instructed that the members of the wedding party were to be taken alive, if possible. Nonetheless, Mackinnon *would* die, whether by accident or otherwise. Tormod would see to it.

Silence fell between them then, and impatience simmered inside him once more. He should have known Campbell wouldn't give this to him easily. He'd have to work for it. He decided it was time to make his wishes clear.

"Makenna is mine," he admitted finally. "She just doesn't know it yet." Heat ignited in his veins at the thought of having her spitting and scratching in his bed, of all the things he'd do to her once his manhood recovered.

He paused then, wondering what was going through Campbell's thought cage now. Of course, the man was onto his third wife. Janet was sweet and meek, nothing like Makenna. Indeed, the chieftain gave a rueful shake of his head. "A lass like that is more trouble than she's worth."

"For some men, maybe," Tormod answered. "But not to me."

Another hush followed, broken only by the laughter of Robbie and the warriors, who'd just finished their game of knucklebones and were starting on a new one.

Campbell didn't speak. Instead, he continued to drink his ale, his gaze shifting to the iron grate over the pit. Suddenly, it seemed he was leagues distant.

Annoyed, Tormod eventually cleared his throat. "May I have her, Dunc?" God, it stung to ask for something that already belonged to him. However, he forced himself.

Campbell blinked, glancing his way. "Maybe ... let me think on it."

Tormod's gut clenched. He was nearly there, yet the chieftain was deliberately holding his prize just out of reach. *How dare he?*

Watching him closely now, Campbell inclined his head. "What was the second favor ye wished to ask?"

Drawing in a deep breath and attempting to smother the pulsing ember in his belly, Tormod pulled himself together. *Patience. Ye shall have her soon enough.* "Rae Maclean," he said, a rasp to his voice now. "I want him too."

Campbell flashed him a grin. "It's like *that*, is it?"

Tormod snorted. "Trust me, I have 'special' plans for the chieftain of Dounarwyse."

21: REGRETS

IT WAS DARK and fetid inside the pit—and cramped, with six men sitting in it.

Leaning up against the rough earthen wall, Bran listened to the muffled sound of voices in the hall beyond. There had been much noise earlier, boasting and numerous toasts to their 'victory'.

His temper had simmered with each one. Around him, his companions had fallen silent, each man lost in his own thoughts.

"How long do ye think they'll keep us in here?" One of the MacGregor warriors, Mungo, asked eventually. His voice was low, rough. The note of resignation in it worried Bran.

A snort followed. "Not long," Rae muttered. "This is a holding place … Campbell will have something else in store for us, I'm sure."

Rae's words were ominous, yet none of them contradicted him.

"Aye ... this pit is for show," Alec agreed. His tone was unusually subdued. "He put it in his hall for a reason."

Bran swallowed a curse. "Who does that?"

"Black Duncan." Captain Walker spoke up for the first time. "I'd heard the tales ... but thought them exaggerations. Long have folk whispered of how he beheads prisoners for visitors."

Alec harrumphed. "A bit of light entertainment, eh?"

Bran suppressed a shiver as he recalled the shallow stone-lined pit just a few feet from this one. "Looks like there was some truth to those tales."

"Aye," Walker replied, his voice grim. "It would seem so."

Aodh, the second of the two MacGregor warriors who'd been captured, growled an oath. "Well, that's it ... we're all done for."

A brittle silence fell then as each prisoner wrestled with the knowledge they'd soon be executed. And as the moments slid by, Bran could feel the hope leaching from his companions.

Clenching his jaw, he fought the same despair. No, he wouldn't resign himself to his fate. He'd fight until his last breath.

"So, lads," Lloyd said finally, rousing them from their brooding. "Any regrets?"

"Regrets?" Aodh asked, his voice thin with barely disguised fear.

"Aye ... we're likely to meet our maker tomorrow. Is there anything ye'd do differently?"

Silence followed this comment, stretching out until Aodh made a strangled sound in the back of his throat. "I wish I'd had the balls to ask Elsie Grant to wed me."

"Malcolm the blacksmith's wife?" Mungo asked incredulously.

"Aye ... I've been soft on her for years but was too proud to say so ... and *he* got in first."

"I wish I'd joined the Bruce's cause," Mungo added after a brief pause. "My brother went, and I always felt like a fazart for not following him." He halted then before asking, "What about ye, Captain?"

Lloyd gave a soft snort. However, there was no hesitation when he answered, "I wish I'd been a better husband."

"Aye?" Rae asked.

"Aye." There was an edge to the captain's voice now. "Freya was a good woman ... but I tried to change her. We fought like pit dogs as a result."

Bran's stomach clenched at this admission. Walker didn't realize it, but that comment was a little too close to the bone. "She's gone then?" he asked gruffly.

"Aye ... two summers past. Life hasn't been the same since." Lloyd's words were softly spoken, yet there was no mistaking the pain in them.

Silence filled the dark pit until, finally, Rae cleared his throat. "I had many regrets ... once," he murmured. "About my family, my first wife ... my choices. I used to carry them on my back ... but ever since meeting Kylie, I've let many go." He paused then. "And ye, Alec?"

"A pirate doesn't let himself have regrets," Alec replied after a few moments. A wry edge crept into his voice as he continued, "Quickest way to get him killed."

Bran pulled a face. Why wasn't he surprised by his attitude? "So, ye regret nothing, do ye, Rankin?"

He couldn't help but make the dig. After all, he shared a pit with his father's murderer and couldn't bring himself to forget it.

"Ending yer father's life, ye mean?" Rankin replied smoothly. Bran flushed hot. "Aye."

A pause followed, and when the pirate answered, his voice was serious. "There have been men I've killed over the years that didn't have it coming ... but yer father did."

Bran glared at Alec's dark form, seated directly opposite him in the pit.

"He sought to bring down the Macleans of Mull ... to seize their lands for his own," Rae added, his tone hardening. "To destroy and dominate ... to rule over all of the isle." He broke off then, letting his words settle for a few moments. "Is that what ye wished for too, Bran?"

The question was a slap across the face. A direct challenge. Bran's first instinct was to hit back, to tell Rae that, aye, he believed in his father's cause—that he'd wished to see the Macleans utterly crushed and driven from Mull.

But it would have been a lie.

"No," he admitted eventually, his voice rough. "I never wanted that."

"I thought as much," Rae answered. "Ye aren't like him."

Bran curled his hands into fists, leaning his head back against the rough wall of the pit. Part of him wanted to snarl at Rae, to tell him he had no business making assumptions about him. But there was another part that craved to hear those words—for, in truth, there had always been a part of him that wondered if, despite everything, he wasn't that different from Kendric Mackinnon, after all.

"And ye, Mackinnon?" Walker asked then. "We've all spoken of our regrets ... or lack of them. It's yer turn now."

Bran grimaced, grateful that no one in this dark pit could see his expression. Regrets. He was still young, but he had already amassed too many. His sister was his biggest one, but he couldn't talk of it here, with these men who were virtually strangers to him. It was too raw. Too personal.

Makenna knew though, which was why she'd dared raise the subject with him. And in return, he'd snarled at her—and now he might never have the chance to make things right.

He regretted that too.

"I wish I'd have had more time with my wife," he admitted finally, even as his chest tightened. "I'd have liked to know her properly."

Another silence fell then, the mood inside the pit even gloomier now.

No doubt, Rae and Alec were both thinking about their wives too. Bran had watched Rae interact with Kylie and noted also how happy Alec and Liza were together. They'd found their other half in each other, yet hadn't even had the chance to say goodbye.

"Enjoying yer accommodations are ye, lads?" A goading voice intruded then from above.

Bran craned his neck upward to see Robbie Campbell's leering face, ghoulish in torchlight, looming over the iron grate.

"Aye … the finest I've ever had," Alec quipped, unable to help himself. "Why don't ye come down and join us … there's plenty of room."

Robbie snorted a laugh. "I think not … ye lot reek like stags in rut."

"We're thirsty, Campbell," Walker said, not bothering to disguise his irritation. "Why don't ye stop yer empty blether and hand us down some ale skins."

"Thirsty, eh?" Robbie drew back from the pit, and a rustling sound followed.

Moments later, something streamed through the grate.

Warm liquid splashed on Bran's face, and he drew back in disgust. Meanwhile, around him, his companions cursed.

The whoreson was pissing on them.

Seated at the chieftain's table, Makenna looked around for a weapon.

She'd been handed a wooden cup filled with wine, but there were no eating knives within reach, not even a wooden spoon that she could use. A banquet lay before her: a spit-roasted suckling pig stuffed with chestnuts and apples, pottage, breads, wheels of cheese, and an array of custards.

She had no stomach for any of it. Not while she and her father were hostages. Not while her husband and friends waited in that foul pit a few yards away.

Her father sat a few feet farther down the table, in between two huge warriors. Makenna was also flanked by men clad in chainmail and leather. Both men were heavily armed, and one of them had a knife wedged into the back of his boot. She longed to lunge for it, but since the warrior in question watched her like a buzzard, she didn't dare.

After waiting a day—the longest wait of her life—they'd collected her from her bower and escorted her downstairs.

Like her father, she was freshly bathed and dressed in clean clothing. Servants had brought in a green kirtle that matched her eyes, with a wine-red surcote to wear on top. She'd initially refused to don the clothing. The servants had then disappeared before one returned with the news that her husband would have a finger cut off with every further refusal she made.

Teeth gritted, Makenna had done as bid. She couldn't let them maim Bran.

And now she sat at the chieftain's table, alongside Black Duncan, his wife, son, and two daughters. She was supposed to eat and drink, to pretend nothing was wrong. Likewise, her father sat rigidly upon the bench seat. She'd never seen him look so grim. His jaw was set, his mouth a thin, hard line.

Musicians appeared then, upon the stone gallery above the hall. Two harpists who struck up a courtly tune. The supper began. Serving lads circled the floor, refilling cups with ale and wine. The mood was convivial, as if they were celebrating Yuletide.

Makenna tried to eat, picking up morsels with her fingers, but every mouthful of pork stuck in her throat. What she wanted to do was rail at them, to smash things. But she restrained herself. Losing control wouldn't help anyone.

Bide yer time.

She drank sparingly, for she wished for her instincts to remain blade-sharp. She couldn't make her move now, but her mind had been scrabbling since the moment she entered the hall—and a plan of sorts was now forming.

A few yards away, seated at the end of one of the long trestle tables, Tormod ate from his trencher, his pale gaze never leaving her.

Makenna did her best to ignore him, even as her skin prickled and her pulse started to race. The man had the gaze of a serpent. Aye, he still terrified her, but she'd had time to rally, to raise her shields. He was the least of her problems right now though.

The feasting and drinking went on for a long while, and during that time, Campbell didn't even acknowledge his hostages. Instead, he spoke at length with his son while occasionally speaking to his young wife. Janet was slender and pretty with large—vacuous—blue eyes. The woman seemed oblivious to Makenna and her father's presence at Finlarig and didn't look Makenna's way once. Instead, Lady Campbell spent most of the meal conversing with the laird's two daughters, who were both barely five years her junior.

Makenna held fast, but underneath it all, dread grew like a stain. It made it difficult to focus.

Black Duncan was waiting.

And he was, for eventually, once servants carried the remnants of the feast away, the chieftain's female kin—and all the women present save Makenna herself—rose from their seats and left the hall. The warriors who remained behind pushed back the tables, leaving a clear space between the pit and the chieftain's table.

Makenna's heart started to drum against her ribs, and her palms grew damp.

Here, it begins.

22: BUT A SMALL FAVOR

CAMPBELL TURNED TO his son. "The parchment, Robbie … put it before Bruce MacGregor if ye please."

Smirking, Robbie withdrew a scroll from the breast of his gambeson and rose from his seat. He then moved around to the front of the table and, with a flourish, unrolled the parchment. However, before placing it in front of their captive, he glanced his father's way. "Shall I read it, for everyone's benefit?"

Makenna clenched her jaw. How she wanted to smash her fist into his sneering mouth.

"Very well." Duncan leaned an elbow on the table and reached for the jug of wine. "Indulge us."

Robbie cleared his throat and held the parchment up. "I, Bruce Nairn MacGregor of Meggernie, hereby give over rule of Meggernie Castle and all its lands to Duncan Fife MacGregor of Breadalbane. From this day forth, I abdicate all ownership of said lands and swear I shall depart from Perthshire forthwith, never to return."

The laird's son paused them, his smirk returning as his dark eyes glinted. "And following the tragic death of Bran Kendric Mackinnon of Dùn Ara, I give my blessing to a union between my youngest daughter, Makenna, and Robert Duncan Campbell of Breadalbane."

Silence followed his words.

Panic gripped Makenna by the throat. Suddenly, it was hard to breathe.

In just a few lines, they'd robbed her father of his lands, slain her husband, and given her to the enemy. Her ears started to ring like a kirk bell, and she closed her eyes for a moment, struggling to hold on to her composure.

Meanwhile, murmurs of approval whispered through the hall. The Campbell retainers clearly thought their laird clever. And when she opened her eyes once more, she noted that some of them were elbowing each other and grinning.

But Tormod didn't share their jubilant mood. He sat there, frozen in his seat, his face as white as milk.

Makenna had no time to dwell on his odd reaction, for her attention shifted back to Robbie. The young man's expression was smug now. Bile stung the back of her throat as she watched him place the parchment before her father.

They were both caught in Black Duncan's snare, victims of his lust for power. Of course, she was no stranger to the 'games' between clans. Her father had promised her to a man she'd never met. She'd resented that, but the agreement Campbell wanted the MacGregor to sign went far beyond anything her father would have done.

Her belly clenched then. *They're going to kill Bran.*

Silently, her father gazed down at it, reading every word written there. It was as if he hadn't believed his ears and had to read it for himself.

Eventually, his gaze lifted, shifting to Black Duncan. "I'll not sign this."

The chieftain quirked a dark eyebrow. "Oh, ye shall."

"No." The MacGregor picked up the agreement. He then ripped it to shreds, pieces of parchment fluttering like rose petals over the table. "The devil roast ye alive, Campbell." He bit the words out. "I. Won't. Sign. It."

A hush fell in the hall. The chieftain's men weren't smirking now. Instead, they watched the scene at the table intently, as if they were anticipating something.

Dizziness swept over Makenna. She applauded her father's response, but she couldn't help but believe that he'd just played into Black Duncan's hands. The man wanted a spectacle—and he'd just given him the opportunity to put one on for his warriors.

Tutting, Campbell glanced over at where a serving lad stood to his right. "Fetch fresh parchment, ink, pounce, and a quill from my solar."

The youth nodded and took off like a hare out of the hall.

"Ye are wasting yer time," Makenna's father snarled. "Take the wool out of yer ears. I said—"

Campbell silenced him with a wave. "Ye're all bluster, Bruce … but ye won't be for much longer." He shifted his gaze to where a group of his warriors stood a few yards away, clearly awaiting his command. "Haul Captain Walker out of the pit."

A short while later, the Captain of the Meggernie Guard stood, bloodied yet defiant, in the middle of the hall. He'd fought the warriors who'd retrieved him, but in the end, they'd bested him.

"A loyal man, Walker," Campbell drawled. He looked on, amused, as Walker was finally subdued. "But *how* loyal?" He leaned forward, his gaze spearing the tall, rawboned man. "Would ye die for yer clan-chief?"

"Ye filthy maggot," the MacGregor rasped. His face reddened then as he realized the game his enemy was now playing. "How dare ye—"

"Cede nothing, Bruce," Walker cut him off. His grey eyes were as hard as flint. "No matter what he does, don't give him what he wants."

"Brave words," Campbell replied smoothly. "But ye'll lose yer head nonetheless."

Makenna gasped. "No!"

All gazes cut to her, but she barely noticed. Instead, she lurched to her feet. "Cease this wickedness!"

The chieftain snorted. "I'm just getting started, lass." He nodded to the men flanking her, and they grabbed hold of Makenna's arms, yanking her back down onto the bench seat. Campbell then gestured to the men who restrained Walker. Wordlessly, they dragged him over to the shallow stone-lined pit.

They pushed him down so he knelt in the center of it, so that his throat pressed against the smooth, curved stone.

An executioner's block.

Fury splintered within her. "Barbarians!" she shouted. "I'll gut the lot of ye if ye touch him!"

The men on either side of her increased their grip on her arms. A warning. Meanwhile, mocking laughter rang in her ears. Robbie Campbell was now grinning like a wolf, while his father—of a more cunning disposition—wore an enigmatic half-smile. "She's got a sharp tongue this one, Robbie … are ye sure ye can handle her?"

"Oh, aye," his son assured him. He then looked over at Makenna and licked his lips.

A strangled noise erupted through the hall, and Makenna jerked her head toward it. Tormod was on his feet now, his hands clenched by his side. His face was twisted. "Ye promised her to me, Campbell," he ground out—each word biting. "Or do ye forget?"

Makenna's heart kicked like a wild pony. *What?*

The chieftain favored him with a veiled look. "I told ye I'd *think* on it, lad … and I have. MacGregor's daughter is too valuable to give to the likes of ye."

Tormod rasped a curse, yet Black Duncan merely smirked. "I'll give ye Rae Maclean though … I don't care what ye do to him."

"That's not—"

"Enough," Campbell cut him off sharply. "I have spoken." Shifting his attention from the warrior—whose face was now pinched with rage—the chieftain took the parchment, ink pot, bag of pounce, and quill from the out-of-breath servant who'd just rushed upstairs to do his bidding.

He then refocused on Makenna's father. "I will write out the agreement again, MacGregor. Will ye sign it?"

Makenna's father was sweating now, his green eyes tormented.

"Don't agree!" Walker called out from where the Campbell warriors held him down. One of them had taken a polearm from the wall. Its whetted ax blade gleamed in the torchlight. "Make my end worth something." There was no fear in his voice now, only outrage.

"No, Lloyd!" Makenna cried out, panicked. "We can't—"

"Quiet, Makenna!" her father cut her off sharply, even as his voice faltered. "Ye aren't helping, lass."

Her pulse started thudding wildly in her ears. "No," she whispered, the sound broken. She couldn't lose Lloyd. He'd trained her, encouraged her, and given her gentle support when she needed it. He was a good man—one of the best. They couldn't just stand by and watch him be executed.

And yet, if her father signed that contract, he'd lose everything. *They'd* lose everything.

Walker knew it and so did her father—as did she.

Makenna cut her gaze to the MacGregor. The grief in his eyes was raw, and yet he held his tongue. And after a long pause, he jerkily shook his head.

Black Duncan's mouth pursed, irritation sparking in those deep-set eyes. "Ye are going to be difficult, are ye?"

MacGregor remained stubbornly silent.

The chieftain huffed a sigh before glancing across at his warriors. "Kill Walker."

"No!" Makenna shouted, struggling against her captors' iron grip. "Leave him be. Leave him—"

But no one heeded her.

A scream began in Makenna's head as one of the warriors hefted the polearm high.

The noise grew shrill—a terrible song—cutting off as the weapon slashed down, the ax cleaving into the back of Walker's neck. It was a vicious blow—mercifully so—although it took another strike to take his head clean off.

The warriors holding him let go of his body, and it fell, twitching, into the pit.

Makenna's agonized cry echoed through the hall. She'd never made a sound like it before—a keening. And as she slumped against the table, held in place by her captors, something fractured deep inside her.

Vision blurred by tears, she forced herself to look her father's way. His eyes glittered.

Meanwhile, Black Duncan dipped a quill into his ink pot and bent over the unfurled sheet of parchment. The scratching sound of his writing filled the now-silent hall.

No one interrupted him.

Eventually, the chieftain finished writing. He then took a pinch of pounce and sprinkled the fine powder over the fresh ink, ensuring that it dried quickly and wouldn't smear. Afterward, he raised his chin, his gaze fixing on Makenna's father once more. "I'll not hand this over ... just yet ... for I have no wish to waste expensive parchment," he drawled. "I shall wait until ye give me the *right* answer. What will it be, MacGregor? 'Aye' or 'Nae'."

"Nae," the clan-chief choked out, the vein in his temple pulsing.

Black Duncan favored him with a thin smile. "Very well ... ye wish to play, I see." He glanced over at his waiting men. "Fetch Bran Mackinnon."

Warriors pulled Bran out of the pit. Unlike Walker, he didn't struggle.

"Much meeker now, aren't ye?" Robbie jeered from where he stood to his father's right. "Not so full of yerself now ye've been pissed on."

Laughter rumbled through the hall at these words.

The noise pierced the fog of Makenna's grief. Hot tears rolled down her cheeks now. She'd just witnessed Lloyd beheaded. Nothing else mattered. Her ears were ringing, and her pulse hammered in her ears. But even so, she was aware of the rough hands of the warriors flanking her, digging painfully into the flesh of her upper arms—it was a reminder that this ordeal wasn't over. Instead, it was just beginning.

Focus!

Walker wouldn't want her to give up. She had to make his sacrifice count for something. Blinking to clear her vision, she looked over at her husband.

Bran's expression was veiled as he surveyed Walker's body in the pit next to him, and the blood that pooled there. His red hair shone brightly in the torchlit hall. His handsome face was remarkably composed. Makenna's throat tightened. He was strong—far more so than she'd realized.

He glanced in her direction then, and their gazes fused.

His silver eyes weren't shuttered. No, they burned into her. Full of emotion. Full of things they'd never shared. Suddenly, she was sorry for locking horns with him, for being so proud. She wished she could go back in time, that she could relive their one night together.

I don't want to lose him too.

The realization slammed into her. She swallowed hard then, her vision blurring again.

"Ah, look at that," Black Duncan murmured. "Love's young dream, is it not?"

This snide comment brought more snorts of mirth from the warriors, but Makenna's attention remained upon her husband.

"I'm afraid, this young clan-chief is an inconvenience to me now," Campbell continued after another lengthy pause. "As I have written ... Makenna is meant for my son ... which means Mackinnon must 'tragically' die."

Makenna's father growled a curse, but Black Duncan merely shrugged. "I'll kill every man in that pit, if I have to, MacGregor ... and if that doesn't get ye to acquiesce, I'll break *ye* ... into tiny pieces." He paused then. "And I will make yer daughter watch."

A tremor went through Makenna. She'd spent years hating their neighbors to the south. The Campbells of Breadalbane had long harried their borders and terrorized their people. But this was something else. This evening, he'd crossed a line that could never be uncrossed.

The MacGregors of Meggernie would never forget this day. She'd make sure of it.

"Before ye cut off my head, I have a request," Bran spoke up then, his voice low and steady. "I wish to kiss my wife one last time."

Black Duncan pulled a face, irritation flickering across his hawkish features. "Ye aren't in the position to make such requests, Mackinnon."

Bran's gaze fixed upon him, unwavering. "It is but a small favor."

The Campbell chieftain snorted. "Ye are starting to vex me."

"I apologize," Bran answered. "But I don't want to die before saying goodbye *properly* to Makenna."

Smirks followed this comment.

"Go on, Campbell," one of the older warriors called out. "Let him stick his tongue down her throat one last time."

Robbie muttered an oath under his breath, while Tormod was ominously silent. Makenna didn't look either man's way.

"Aye," another man agreed, grinning. "He asked nicely enough."

Laughter erupted then, although Black Duncan was now frowning. "I'm going to enjoy seeing them strike off yer head," he ground out. "However, let it not be said that I'm *completely* without a heart." He gestured to the men holding Makenna. "Take the lass over."

The warriors did as bid, hauling Makenna to her feet, and pushing her around the edge of the table. She went willingly, not struggling under their rough handling. Her legs were wobbly, yet she'd managed to shove her sorrow down for the moment.

She concentrated on slowing and deepening her breathing, and the strength flowed back into her limbs. Her senses sharpened. That was better. She could think clearly again.

She wasn't sure what Bran was doing, but he'd unwittingly aided her.

The loose plan she'd been forming before coming downstairs this evening—the one that had dissolved when she'd seen Walker executed—relied on her being on her feet and away from the table. She needed room to move, and Bran had just given it to her.

She met her husband's eye once more, and something clenched deep in her chest. This was it. If she couldn't stop Campbell, she didn't want to walk out of here alive. She'd rather die on her feet than be forced to kneel for the enemy, to end up as a Campbell plaything.

And the glint in Bran's gaze told her he understood. Knowing he did made her resolve harden within her.

"Husband," she murmured, stepping close to him. After a day in the pit, he reeked like a barnyard dung heap, yet she didn't care.

"Wife," he whispered in return.

Campbell warriors still held them fast, yet the pair ignored them. Instead, Bran bent his head, slanting his mouth over hers. It was a bruising, passionate embrace, one that kept nothing back—and Makenna answered it, uncaring who looked on. The heat of his mouth, the way his tongue entwined with hers, the way his teeth grazed her lips, branded her, filled her with determination.

Their kiss went on, hot and wild, until Black Duncan made an annoyed sound in the back of his throat. "Enough of this nonsense … take her back to the table."

Makenna resisted the pull on her arms, while Bran's lips slid from hers and grazed across her cheek. "Lift the grate," he whispered.

A moment of confusion pulsed through Makenna before her heart kicked. Of course. When the warriors had hauled Bran out of the pit, they hadn't bothered to slide the bolt home afterward.

And now that she'd come forward to say goodbye to her husband, the pit was just a few strides away from her. She could make it.

23: SHOW HIM MERCY

AS THE WARRIORS pulled Makenna away from her husband, Bran moved.

They should have bound his wrists upon hauling him out of the pit, but they hadn't. They'd been arrogant, so sure that he wouldn't try to escape. As such, Bran took the man to his right by surprise as he drove an elbow into his gut.

An instant later, he'd swiped the man's dirk and driven it up under his jaw.

Makenna didn't hesitate.

She brought her slippered heel down hard on the foot of the man to her left and then twisted right, slamming her forehead into the mouth of the other warrior.

Fury turned her vicious. She didn't hold herself back. Instead, she used every skill she'd learned from Walker, every dirty trick Alec had taught her—and every subtle move *Tormod* had shown her.

Earlier, she'd noted the hilt of the blade peeking out from the boot of the warrior to her right. She'd known that was what she'd go for if she got the chance. And she did so now.

Grabbing it, she slashed the warrior to the left across the throat and then ducked a punch from the man she'd just head-butted, cutting him across the back of the knees.

A great roar went up in the hall—angry shouts and the hammering of booted feet as the chieftain's men reacted and lunged for her.

Makenna dove for the pit, reaching it moments ahead of the Campbell warriors. Yanking up the heavy iron lid—even as the muscles in her upper arms screamed at the weight—she let it fall to the floor with a heavy boom. She then turned back to face her attackers.

Just a few yards away, Bran was now fighting Tormod. The two of them slashed at each other with dirks.

Her belly dropped to her boots. *Christ's blood. Not him.* She'd sparred with Tormod often enough in the past to know just how good he was. Bran could handle himself in a fight, but he wasn't that warrior's equal. She hadn't met anyone who was.

But she couldn't focus on him right now, not when she was surrounded.

Meanwhile, her father had used the distraction to deal with the two men who held him. One of them lay face down on the table, blood pooling under his head, while the other grappled with his captor.

Campbell had leaped to his feet, drawn his dirk, and was bellowing orders. "Robbie!" he yelled. "To me!"

The chieftain's son, who'd rushed toward the pit with the others, swiveled, moving back toward the chieftain's table.

Together, father and son advanced on Makenna's father.

But she couldn't focus on him either.

Snarling curses, she struck at any warrior who came within reach. However, there were too many of them. She wouldn't be able to hold them off for much longer.

But she didn't need to, for now that the pit was open, the men inside had worked together to climb out of it.

A large broad-shouldered figure barreled past her, moving low.

Rae tackled one of the warriors around the thighs, bringing him down. Alec, Aodh, and Mungo were right behind the chieftain of Dounarwyse—and then, suddenly, the fight wasn't quite so one-sided.

Nonetheless, there were seven of them fighting against a dozen. The odds weren't in their favor.

Jerking back as a blade swiped at her face, Makenna kicked her assailant hard in the cods. She then drove her dirk into the soft flesh above his collarbone. She yanked her blade free as he grunted and fell to the floor.

Only then did she dare take her eye off the Campbell warriors still swarming around them, to see how the fight between Tormod and Bran was progressing.

And to her surprise, her husband was holding his own.

Bran had told her that a bow and arrow were his weapons of choice, yet he handled himself well with a dirk. Both he and Tormod were bleeding now though. Blood slicked Tomrod's forearm, and a shallow cut oozed on Bran's cheek.

Neither of them took their gaze off each other.

All the same, the savagery on Tormod's face chilled her blood, as did the coldness of his eyes.

That was what made him a better warrior than most—his utter lack of mercy.

Unless she did something, Tormod would eventually best her husband.

Meanwhile, Alec had fought his way through the press, collecting a blade as he went, and was now at her father's side. Black Duncan, Robbie, and three other warriors surrounded them, but the two men were doing an admirable job of holding them off. For the moment.

Another warrior rushed at Makenna then, drawing her focus once more, and after she'd bested him, her gaze returned to Tormod and Bran.

Tormod had backed her husband up. Bran now fought just a few feet from the wall. Any closer and he'd be trapped, and Tormod would strike.

She had to do something.

"Tormod," she yelled above the din. "*Tormod!*"

Aye, she knew the man was obsessed with her. It was a twisted attachment, one that had nothing to do with real love or affection. He wanted to dominate her, to have her as a possession. However, it was the only thing she had over him, and she'd wield it.

Hearing her voice, his chin jerked sideways. "Makenna!" he panted. "Ready to watch Mackinnon die?"

"Stop!" she gasped, feigning panic, as she moved toward them. "Please spare his life."

Bran made an outraged noise at this, but she ignored him.

"I'll go with ye now ... we can ride from here and never look back ... if ye promise to show him mercy."

Tormod's pale-blue eyes glinted, and she knew she had him.

And Bran did too. It was the moment of distraction he needed. She'd been waiting for him to take it—but, even so, the swiftness and brutality of his act surprised her.

One moment, the two men had been slashing at each other, the long thin blades of their dirks glinting in the light of the torches burning on the walls. The next, Bran swapped his blade to his right hand and lunged.

And he drove his dagger straight through Tormod's left eye.

The warrior had turned his face slightly, to see Makenna, unwittingly holding his head at just the right angle.

The two men fell, sprawling together on the rush-covered floor.

Even with a knife embedded in his eye socket, Tormod tried to fight. But his movements were clumsy, jerky.

Makenna looked on, impressed. She hadn't realized Bran could wield a blade so deftly with his right hand.

Pinning Tormod to the ground, Bran grabbed hold of his flailing wrist and stared down at the warrior's ashen face. Her husband didn't speak, yet the hardness in his eyes made his hatred clear. And as Makenna looked on, Tormod's body shuddered and then went still.

A shout echoed through the hall, and her attention was drawn to where more warriors had rushed inside.

They were still outnumbered, and yet something had changed.

The huddle of men fighting by the chieftain's table had dispersed, and Makenna quickly saw why.

Alec had managed to disarm the chieftain's son. He now held him captive, a blade at his throat.

Makenna's father stood at Alec's shoulder, and Rae, Aodh, and Mungo had joined them.

Murmuring an oath, Bran rose to his feet, his gaze cutting to Makenna.

Aye, the tide was close to turning in their favor—but they needed to get to the others.

They fled across the hall, dodging the warriors who now rushed at them, reaching their friends just as a circle formed around them.

Breathing hard, blood running down the side of his face now, Black Duncan glared at them. The chieftain was hunched over and was favoring his left side. Someone had managed to get under his guard. "It's over," he ground out. "We have ye surrounded."

"No ... it's far from over," Alec replied softly. He then pressed the blade harder against Robbie's throat, causing blood to well. "Unless ye want me to kill yer son."

The Campbell chieftain's face turned to stone. Meanwhile, Robbie made a strangled sound in the back of his throat—one that sounded very much like a plea.

Makenna's breathing grew shallow, and she adjusted her grip on the dirk.

A dull fatalism pressed down on her then. They had no way of knowing whether Campbell was willing to sacrifice his son's life or not. And if he was, then it really would be a fight to the death in this hall.

She wouldn't be taken prisoner again—and neither would her companions. Things might be about to get bloody.

Long moments drew out, and around them, the hall fell silent.

Campbell didn't give the order to attack.

Finally, Alec spoke once more. "Here's what will happen now, Campbell. Ye will stand aside while we leave. I'm taking yer lad with me, mind ... to ensure ye behave yerself."

A nerve flickered in Black Duncan's cheek.

The cunning, callous bastard had one weakness, it seemed. His son.

"How do I know ye won't kill Robbie?" he ground out.

"Ye will have to take my word," Alec answered, his blue eyes glinting. "And pray it means more than yers does."

A brittle silence fell then, drawing out until the Campbell chieftain gave a jerky nod. Then, moving aside, grimacing in pain as he did so, he gestured for his men to do the same.

And they did—one by one, each warrior shifted back, leaving the way to the door clear.

Alec nodded to his companions. "Go on … Robbie and I will follow."

Makenna obeyed. Flanked by her father and Bran, she edged toward the door, with Rae, Aodh, and Mungo behind her. Alec brought up the rear, walking backward, his knife never leaving Robbie's throat.

Moments later, they were in the entrance hall, and a short while after that in the barmkin that surrounded the tower house. They moved across the cobbled space toward the gates. Night had long fallen, and the sliver of the moon shone amongst a carpet of stars. Torches hanging on chains illuminated the barmkin, casting long shadows.

"Raise the portcullis, and open the gate!" Robbie cried. He didn't trust that Alec's blade wouldn't slip. However, the guards there hesitated. "Do it!" His voice grew high-pitched, panicked.

Reluctantly, the guards moved to obey. Nonetheless, the MacGregor party was made to wait while the portcullis was raised. The creaking of iron filled the humid night air, and then, finally, the gate rumbled open.

Makenna glanced behind her then, to see a tall, spare figure standing on the steps, flanked by his men. Black Duncan's hawkish face was harsh in the torchlight, his eyes dark pits of hatred. He still clutched his left side, his hand wet with blood.

"Let my son go!" he shouted, his rough voice carrying through the silence.

"Soon enough," Alec called back.

Together, they edged through the gate and along the path that led into the village beyond. Finlarig slumbered at this hour, the scent of woodsmoke heavy in the air. Light glowed from around the edges of closed doorways.

No one here would bother to stop them.

"When we reach the edge of the trees, we run," Makenna's father murmured as they strode along the road now, the castle rising in a dark silhouette above them.

"Aye," Alec grunted. "And what do ye wish me to do with our captive? If ye want vengeance for Walker, I shall give it."

Makenna's pulse quickened. He was letting her father be the one to choose.

Robbie made a panicked noise. "Ye promised," he rasped. "I—"

"Still yer tongue," MacGregor cut him off. "Yer whining unmans ye."

They'd reached the tree line—a dark press of beech waiting to receive them.

Makenna's fingers flexed around the hilt of her dagger. She longed to make someone pay for Lloyd's death. She'd be happy to take this rodent's life. It wouldn't bring her friend back, but it would even the score.

"As tempting as it is to slit yer throat, I shall let ye live. Although" —her father stepped closer and brought his own blade up— "I shall leave ye with a lasting memory of this day … a reminder of what happens when ye cross the MacGregors." And with that, he drew the tip of his blade down from the top of Robbie's eye and down his cheek, carving a deep, dark path.

Blood welled, and the chieftain's son whimpered a curse. Nonetheless, with Alec's knife still at his throat, he didn't dare move.

"Off ye go now," her father murmured. "Run back to yer Da."

Alec released Robbie, and the laird's son stumbled away, clutching his bloodied face. Such was his terror that he didn't curse them, didn't utter threats.

A heartbeat later, Makenna's father turned to his companions. "It's not over yet … they'll come for us soon enough."

"We can't outrun them," Rae pointed out, his tone grim.

"We don't need to," her father replied. "The alarm would have been raised in Meggernie when we didn't return. They'll be hunting for us." He paused then, his gaze glinting in the moonlight. "I have some of the best trackers in Perthshire in my Guard … they'll find us."

24: ÀRD-CHOILLE

THE HOUNDS STARTED baying a short while after they left Finlarig Castle.

They'd expected it. Even so, the sound made Makenna's pulse lurch. Black Duncan was hunting them now, and he'd be out for blood.

Meanwhile, the seven of them ran along the loch shore, setting a steady pace.

Some, like Bran, Alec, and Rae, ran easily, their long legs eating up the ground. But her father had started to wheeze now. He was bigger and older than the other men, and after a short while started to fall behind.

He'd spoken true earlier. The MacGregors of Meggernie were known for their expert tracking and hunting skills. Yet would their people dare camp this close to Finlarig? Would they find them in the dark?

Initially, Makenna tried to keep pace with Bran, although it wasn't long before her legs and lungs started to protest.

She dropped back next to her father. "Black Duncan is injured," she panted. "He was bleeding badly when we left."

"Aye, lass," he gasped. "I made sure to stick him good and proper!"

Under other circumstances, she might have grinned at this news. But knowing that they'd lost Lloyd, and that they were leaving his corpse behind at Finlarig, made it difficult to celebrate. They weren't out of danger yet, but now that they'd gotten out of the castle, grief hammered into her again. It was hard to think about anything else. It was hard to even breathe.

"I hope he bleeds to death," she ground out.

"With any luck, he will, lass," her father answered, his breathing labored.

The baying of the hounds intruded once more. Nearer now. The thunder of hoofbeats, approaching from the west, and the shouts of men, echoed across the still loch.

Makenna's already racing heart leaped at the noise.

"Cods!" her father cursed. "Where are the others?"

"There's a light up to the east," Rae shouted from ahead.

"A campfire, I'd say," Bran added, his voice rough from exertion.

Makenna's heart leaped. "It's them!" And just as well too, for sweat slicked her body, and her chest was burning. She wasn't used to running this far or fast.

"MacGregor!" Her father roared. Despite that he'd been winded just moments earlier, hope made him rally. His voice carried far into the night. He then followed with, "Àrd-Choille!"

High Wood! The MacGregor war cry.

Moments passed and then shouts echoed back at them from farther up the shore. "'S Rioghal mo dhream!"

Makenna's breathing caught, her skin prickling now at the sound of the MacGregor motto. It was the response they'd been waiting for—a way of telling friend from foe, for the enemy would have likely just shouted back 'Àrd-Choille'. Tears of relief welled in her eyes.

"Thank Christ," Mungo rasped from just ahead. "I can't run much farther."

"Keep moving!" Rae grunted. "Or one of those beastly hounds will take a bite out of yer arse."

That spurred all of them on and gave them the final burst of speed they needed to reach the MacGregor search party.

Relief crashed over Makenna at the sight of the warriors rushing toward them, dirks drawn.

"MacGregor!" One of the warriors called out, spying his clan-chief. It was Blair, Walker's second-in-command. Peering at the approaching men, she recognized her brothers-by-marriage: Connor MacFarlane and Rory Lamont.

"They're right behind us," her father shouted.

Reaching the MacGregors, they skidded to a halt.

Makenna swiveled on her heel to face their attackers. She was now gasping for breath. Next to her, Bran's chest rose and fell sharply as he also struggled to catch his breath. However, like her, his gaze was trained west, at where the enemy approached. Their torches glowed like fireflies in the dark, the outlines of horses and dogs frosted by moonlight clearly visible now.

As if sensing her stare, he glanced her way then, before a harsh smile tugged at his lips. "Ready to deal with the Campbells?"

Fire ignited in Makenna's belly as she nodded.

A crimson sunrise spilled over the sky at dawn, almost as if the blood that had flowed on the shore of Loch Tay had stained the heavens as well.

Victorious, the MacGregors left the bodies of their Campbell pursuers sprawled amongst the heather, took their horses, and set off east. A few of their men had been injured in the fight, but nothing serious. Once they returned to Meggernie, Garia would tend to them.

The bloodhounds didn't follow the MacGregors, for once they realized their masters were beaten, they'd fled back in the direction of Finlarig. The MacGregors didn't dare celebrate yet though, for there was a chance Black Duncan would send more warriors in pursuit. And as they rode side-by-side under the warm sun, listening to the flutelike whistle of thrushes, Bran found himself glancing often over his shoulder.

"Let them dare follow us," Makenna muttered. Looking her way, he saw that her hand then strayed to the dirk at her hip. His wife's expression was fierce this morning, her lovely face pale and splattered with blood. Lloyd's death had left its mark upon her.

Bran's chest constricted.

This woman was truly unique. He could travel the length and breadth of Scotland and never find her like. They'd come close to being separated forever back at Finlarig Castle, something that had hardened his resolve to fight back. He couldn't lose Makenna.

"It was a near thing back there," he admitted after a pause. "Tormod was close to besting me."

"The whoreson was a fiend with a blade," she replied. "That's why I interfered."

"Aye," he answered roughly. "I'm not foolish enough to be vexed about that." He winced then. "Although I'll admit, my pride was dented at the time."

"Ye killed him though. I gave ye that, at least." Makenna was watching him intently now.

"Ye did," he answered quietly. "I'd vowed to … for what he did to ye."

Their gazes fused then, the moment drawing out. A faint flush rose to her cheekbones, her eyes softening. "Thank ye, Bran," she murmured.

He swallowed. He wanted to tell her that he'd take on the devil himself to protect her. However, he was now painfully self-conscious. Things were still new between them, and he had no idea how she might respond to such a declaration.

Ahead, the rest of their party traveled in exhausted silence. None of them had rested during the night. There would be time to do so when they reached MacGregor lands once more. Once they were certain no one followed them.

Tearing his gaze from Makenna's, Bran cleared his throat. "I wish to apologize."

"For what?"

He glanced her way again, to find a groove etched between her eyebrows. "For being so heavy-handed … when we spoke of how things would be when we returned to Dùn Ara." He broke off there, his embarrassment growing. "I was an arse."

She snorted a laugh. "Och, with everything that's happened, I'd forgotten about that." She pulled a face. "Thank ye for reminding me."

"Aye, well ... I'm sorry." He raked a hand through his hair, wishing he was better with words. "And I want ye to know that I will never again tell ye to put down yer blade."

Her gaze widened. "Ye won't?"

"No, I give ye my word. I said those things out of fear, Makenna."

She stiffened. "Ye did?"

"Aye ... fear of failing ye ... of losing ye." He stopped there, his throat painfully tight.

Meanwhile, his wife continued to watch him, her green eyes softening.

Exhaling sharply, Bran pushed on. "But I know better now. Ye are a warrior. If I took that from ye, ye'd wither ... like a wildflower torn from a meadow." He paused, swallowing. "I want to see ye bloom at Dùn Ara ... for ye to have *purpose* there."

She raised an eyebrow. "So, ye won't grumble when I ask to spar with ye?"

"No ... just as long as ye train *only* with me." A wave of possessiveness swept over him. He meant it too. Makenna could handle herself, yet he didn't want any of his men leering at her or using training to take liberties.

To his surprise, an impish half-smile tugged at her lips. "Ye wish for me to give ye some pointers, do ye?"

He huffed. "Aye, well ... ye might as well teach me some of those 'dirty tricks' of yers."

At dusk, deep inside MacGregor lands once more, the party halted for the day and made camp. And as the last of the daylight faded from the sky, they sat companionably around a crackling fire while the carcasses of two hares spit-roasted over embers.

The aroma made Makenna's belly growl, for she'd lasted the day on nothing more than a few mouthfuls of bread and cheese. The day had been a fine one, with warm sun on their backs. They'd made camp in the heart of a pinewood, and the evening air was soft and fragrant with the scent of woodsmoke and resin.

Seated cross-legged before the fire, it was hard not to let her shoulders slump. Finally, they'd reached safety. Exhaustion dragged down at her, turning her eyelids heavy.

Holding up the skin of ale that Blair had just passed him, her father surveyed the faces of those seated around the fire. "At a time like this, I truly count my blessings," he said, his voice unusually solemn. "I have lost good men in the past days, and my heart is heavy … but when I look around this hearth, I see friends."

Makenna's throat constricted at this, her vision blurring. *Lloyd should be here with us.*

Sorrow twisted like a blade inside her chest then. Fighting to keep her composure, she looked over at Bran, and then her attention slid to Rae and Alec. Their gazes all gleamed. Meanwhile, Connor and Rory observed their father-by-marriage with a blend of wariness and surprise.

"Back in Meggernie, I had ye all drink from my quaich … I spoke of a 'friendship' between former enemies … but let's face it … we all know I was forcing things." He coughed then, a rare look of embarrassment stealing across his face.

"I thought that if we gathered together under my roof, I'd win yer loyalty ... yet it can't be bought, demanded, or stolen." He raised his fist to his heart then and thumped it hard. "I swear to ye now that the Macleans of Moy and Dounarwyse ... and the Mackinnons of Dùn Ara *all* have my allegiance. I need not sign my name on any contract, for it is carved upon my heart."

Swallowing, Makenna tried to ignore the ache that suddenly rose under her breastbone. Her father was a man who felt all emotions keenly, and his green eyes now shone.

"And ye have my allegiance, Bruce," Rae replied, mirroring the MacGregor clan-chief's gesture.

"And mine," Alec added. His mouth then quirked. "I'm speaking on behalf of my wife, of course ... but I'm sure the laird of Moy would agree."

A pause followed, and all gazes swiveled Bran's way.

Staring back at Makenna's father, her husband raised his hand, curled it into a fist, and slammed it against his ribs, to the left of his breastbone. "Ye have my loyalty as well," he answered. "Carved upon my heart."

Bran slept like a dead man, not stirring from the position he'd lain down in. Nonetheless, he awoke to find the sky still dark and the fire pit smoking. It was early. His companions, wrapped up in their cloaks, slumbered, their snores rumbling through the trees.

Rolling over, he tried to go back to sleep yet found he couldn't. Eventually, giving up, he rose to his feet and stepped over Makenna. She slept curled up like a kitten.

Something tightened deep in his chest as his gaze lingered upon her face. Looking at her now, it was hard to believe the woman was so fierce, but he'd seen just how brave she was.

Carefully, he picked his way through the sleeping figures and moved to the edge of the trees. He then approached where Blair kept watch.

"Ye're up before the lark this morning," the new Captain of the Meggernie Guard greeted him.

Bran pulled a face. "I always am … go on … get some rest before dawn breaks."

"Are ye sure?"

"Aye … I've rested enough."

Blair gave a jaw-cracking yawn and nodded. He then clapped Bran on the shoulder before he returned to the camp, leaving him alone amongst the dark pines.

Massaging a stiff muscle in his shoulder, Bran surveyed his surroundings. They were far from Campbell lands now, although it would be foolish to let their guard down. Black Duncan wasn't the sort to give up easily. It was just as well the bastard was badly injured, for he'd have other things to worry about right now.

Nonetheless, relief unknotted the last of the tension in Bran's chest. *Thank Christ that's over.* He didn't like to think about how close he'd come to having his head struck from his neck.

Lloyd Walker hadn't been so lucky.

The woods were quiet, for it was still too early for the first birds to begin their morning song, and as he stood there letting the last vestiges of sleep drift away, a calmness settled upon him.

Peace.

He'd rarely felt it.

There was something else too, for this morning, he sensed his own worth—deep down to the marrow of his bones. No one could dispute that his quick thinking had saved them all at Finlarig. Ever since taking his father's place, he'd chased true confidence, but it had eluded him. Until now.

"Ye aren't one to lie abed either, I see." Makenna's soft voice roused him from his thoughts, and he turned to see his wife approaching. She had slung her woolen cloak around her shoulders, and her hair was mussed from sleeping.

His chest started to ache. Lord, she was beautiful.

"No," he replied with a half-smile. "I've always liked to watch the dawn … it's the quietest time of day."

"Aye." She halted next to him, her face lifting to where a glow appeared through the trees to the left. The sun was rising. "At home, I get up before anyone else and go up on the walls … it gives me time to put my thoughts together."

"Ye'll be able to do that at Dùn Ara soon," he murmured. "The views from the walls are breathtaking first thing." She nodded at this, yet didn't reply. He cleared his throat then. "Times like these, ye realize how lucky we are to be alive."

"Aye," she whispered. "Staring death in the face does that to ye."

Silence fell between them then, stretching out as the first of the larks began to twitter amongst the treetops. However, Bran sensed Makenna's tension. She folded her arms across her chest and, after a while, started to tap her toes.

He inclined his head. "What is it?"

"Ye apologized to me yesterday," she said, keeping her gaze firmly on the approaching dawn. "And I should return the favor."

"Aye?"

She nodded, discomfort rippling across her face. She still didn't look his way. "I'm proud and rebellious by nature … asking for forgiveness doesn't come easy."

He snorted. "It doesn't for any of us. But ye don't need—"

"No … but I am sorry, Bran." She swung around to face him. "For snarling at ye as I have … for deliberately goading ye instead of trying to build trust between us."

Warmth kindled under his ribs. "Apology accepted," he replied softly. "Although, it takes two to quarrel."

They stared at each other for a long moment, the air between them growing heavy. "We are married now, and we should embrace it," she murmured. "I want us to start afresh. Can we?"

He nodded, even as his throat thickened. "I'd like that." Stepping near, he then lifted a hand and brushed away a lock of hair from her cheek. "Black Duncan came close to ending our short marriage," he said, his voice catching. "But we are free of him now … and I too want to begin again."

25: BE BOLD. BE BRAVE

CHAOS REIGNED INSIDE Meggernie's bailey.

Men, women, children—and dogs—swirled around the travel-weary band that clattered under the portcullis and into the wide cobbled yard beyond.

Rae's wife and sons clung to him, while his boisterous collie, who'd accompanied him from Dounarwyse, bounced around the huddle, barking.

Liza flew across the bailey and threw herself into Alec's waiting arms as he swung down from his horse, sobbing with relief as she hugged him. Craeg was close behind her and drawn into their circle as Alec assured them all was well.

Makenna's mother rushed to her husband, face distraught.

"All is well, mo chridhe," the MacGregor rumbled, pulling his wife into a hard embrace and then kissing her passionately. When he drew back, his gaze was shadowed. "Black Duncan Campbell attacked us on the return home from the hunt … and took us back to Finlarig Castle. But we got free."

His expression grew strained then, his eyes shadowing. "Lloyd is dead though."

Carmen's face crumpled at this news.

Watching her father comfort her mother, Makenna's throat started to ache. Lloyd had been with them for years; both her parents had been close to him. And after his wife died, they'd invited him to take supper with them most evenings in the clan-chief's solar. Her eyes started to sting then. Being back here without Captain Walker's steadying presence made her sorrow even sharper.

During the journey home, her grief had swelled and then receded in waves, like a rising and ebbing tide. All it took was a memory of Lloyd striding through the bailey, calling out to his men, and tears welled.

This castle wouldn't be the same without him.

Swallowing, Makenna dashed away a tear that trickled down her cheek. Lord, it was difficult to hold herself together.

Curse Black Duncan. Fury bloomed like a dark flower in her belly then, momentarily chasing away her grief. *We must make them pay.*

Meanwhile, her parents had forgotten she was even present. The bond between Bruce and Carmen MacGregor was so strong that sometimes they were oblivious to others. *She* grieved Lloyd too. Her mother would eventually withdraw from her husband's embrace and seek her youngest daughter out. But for the moment, she was invisible.

An arm went about her shoulders then, squeezing gently. Surprised, she glanced up to see that Bran had stepped close. It felt odd to have a man, who wasn't her father, hold her like this, and she momentarily stiffened.

However, one look at Bran's face told her he understood.

"Ye loved him, didn't ye?" he said softly.

"Aye," she whispered. "The world feels ... wrong ... without Lloyd in it."

His hold on her shoulders tightened. "He died bravely."

Makenna swallowed. Aye, he had. She needed to remember that.

Meanwhile, Alma and Sonia swept across the bailey and welcomed Connor and Rory back. Voices echoed off stone, the noise assaulting Makenna's ears. Suddenly, the full weight of everything that had happened in the past days slammed into her. They were safe now. There was no risk of the Campbells coming after them. All the tension she'd been holding dissolved then, and her legs started to tremble.

Bran's arm tightened slightly in response, and she leaned into him; his body was her rock. This was how it would be from now on. He would be her strength, and she his.

"Makenna!" Kylie disentangled herself from Rae and his sons and headed across to her. "Are ye hurt?"

"No," Makenna croaked, as her throat constricted once more.

A few yards away, Liza left Alec explaining what had happened to Craeg and moved toward her. Bran released his wife then, shifting back so that Makenna's sisters could both enfold her in a crushing hug.

"Thank the Lord, ye are home," Liza said huskily. "Safe."

Hiccoughing, as a sob clawed up, Makenna clung to her sisters. She wanted to appear stoic, but their concern made her crumble.

Makenna sank into the hot water with a groan. Never had a bath felt so good.

Beyond the screen, Bran made a noise in the back of his throat.

"What is it?" she called out.

"Nothing," he replied, although his voice was slightly strangled.

"Do I need to thump ye between the shoulder blades?" she asked.

"No, I'm fine."

Her brow furrowed. "Aye, well … leave some of the supper for me, mind."

He snorted. "I haven't yet touched it."

Makenna raised an eyebrow. Really? It had sounded like he'd just choked on a mouthful of something. Servants had brought up a meal of fresh bread, cheese, braised onions, and blood sausage. It now sat on a table behind the screen.

However, before eating, Makenna wished to bathe. And once she was done, Bran would take his turn.

Her belly fluttered then.

It was intimate, bathing in the same chamber as him—knowing that he was just a few feet away. Most married couples wouldn't bother to put a screen up, but when they'd retired, shyness had stolen over her.

They'd been naked together before, although their wedding night seemed to belong to another life. Another person. Indeed, she'd been on edge as servants had lugged up pails of steaming water to fill the bath and put up a screen for her.

Even the heat of the water, seeping into her weary, aching limbs, couldn't dissolve the tension that now tightened under her ribcage.

Trying to ignore it, she picked up a cake of rose soap and began to wash. The sweet scent enveloped her, a familiar perfume that she would always associate with Meggernie. Her mother ordered this fine soap from France; one of the many things her husband indulged her in.

It had been a fraught and emotional return home, and so everyone had retired to their quarters early. The following day at noon, they would bury the fallen warriors, whose bodies they'd recovered from the woods where they'd been left by the Campbells. However, there could be no burial for Lloyd Walker.

Sorrow tugged deep in her chest at the reminder. She closed her eyes, letting the pain rise and flow through her. Mother Mary, it hurt to think of him.

"Makenna?" Bran's voice reached her once more. "Ye've gone very quiet in there. Are ye all right?"

"Aye," she replied huskily.

Her gut twisted then. All *would* be well—after she got even with Black Duncan. Aye, both he and his son were injured, and they'd slain several Campbell warriors, but it wasn't enough. How she longed to burn Finlarig Castle to the ground.

Thoughts churning, she set about washing her hair, combing out the knots with her fingers. The warm water soothed her as she worked now, and she was tempted to linger in the bath for a while, to soak until her fingers and toes turned wrinkly. But Bran was waiting, and she didn't want him to have to wash in cold water.

She looked around for a drying sheet, her pulse stuttering when she realized she'd forgotten to bring one over to the tub.

"Bran," she said, ensuring her voice remained light. "Can ye fetch me a drying sheet? They're on the bed."

A pause followed before she heard his footfalls moving across the wooden floor.

A moment later, she glanced over her shoulder to see him emerge around the edge of the screen. She noted then, how he'd deliberately averted his gaze, his face turned away as he handed her the drying sheet. She also marked the faint blush that now stained his cheekbones.

God's troth ... were they back to awkwardness between them now?

"Thank ye," she murmured, taking the drying sheet from him.

Nodding, he disappeared back behind the screen.

Makenna watched him go, her brow furrowing. After the things they'd said to each other on the journey home, she'd have thought he wouldn't be embarrassed to be alone with her like this—yet he was.

Gnawing at her bottom lip, she rose to her feet in the tub. She then stepped out, her feet sinking into the soft sheepskin, and dried herself off before wrapping the drying sheet around her.

When she emerged from behind the screen, she found Bran seated by the hearth. Although it wasn't a cold evening, the servants had lit a fire. The castle was made of cold, damp stone, which meant that even in the summer months, the air grew chill at night. One booted ankle rested on his knee, he leaned back, cradling the cup of wine he'd been nursing for a while now.

"Yer turn," she said, flashing him a shy smile.

"Ye didn't take long," he replied, his gaze still averted.

"Aye, well ... I wanted ye to be able to enjoy the hot water too."

Bran did look her way then. A moment later, his eyes darkened, his lips parting as he dragged his gaze down the length of her body. Makenna swallowed, nervousness fluttering up. Although she was wrapped in the drying sheet, she still felt exposed. Still pink and damp from the bath, her hair falling in wet strands over her shoulders, she was sure she wasn't the most attractive sight, yet Bran stared at her as if a siren had just emerged from behind the screen.

Realizing what he was doing, her husband blinked, closed his mouth, and nodded. "Aye." His voice sounded odd, strained. "I certainly need one."

He then rose swiftly from his chair, fetched himself a fresh drying sheet, and disappeared behind the screen.

Makenna retreated across the room, retrieving her comb so that she could untangle the stubborn knots that had formed in her hair over the past days. She then sank down into the chair opposite where Bran had been sitting.

Moments later, she heard his sigh as he lowered himself into the tub. "That's better."

"There's soap," she called.

A snort followed. "Rose ... great ... I shall smell like a lass."

Makenna laughed, a little of the tension between them easing. "I won't mind."

He muttered an oath, yet splashing followed as he began to wash.

And as the sounds went on, Makenna couldn't help but imagine him sitting there, running that slippery cake of soap over his lithe, hard-muscled body. Her pulse fluttered, heat pooling in her lower belly.

They'd been through much in the past days—starting as enemies and then forging a bond of sorts during their wedding night, before the hunt had set them back once more. But during their ordeal at the hands of the Campbells, something had shifted. Their lives had all been at risk. Suddenly, the things they'd quarreled about seemed petty. When he'd been hauled from the pit to be executed, a weaker man would have pleaded for his life. But instead, Bran had held fast.

She was proud to be married to such a man, and she wished him to know it.

Her husband was as skittish as a colt around her this evening, but he didn't need to be.

She needed his closeness. Grief and anger had been her companions since they'd escaped Finlarig, but she didn't want them to consume her. Instead, she longed to forget, at least for a short while—to embrace life and reassure herself that despite the ugliness, pain, and loss, beauty existed too.

And so, as the moments slid by, and she finished combing out her hair, she gathered her courage. The truth was, she wanted Bran. Badly. Even so, she hesitated.

What are ye waiting for?

What if he rejected her?

What if he laughed at her?

Enough of this nonsense. Rising to her feet, she smoothed her suddenly damp palms upon her drying sheet.

How could they start afresh if they continued to be so awkward around each other? *Be bold. Be brave.*

And so, she moved across the bedchamber and slipped beyond the screen.

26: TAKE ON THE WORLD

SHE FOUND BRAN standing in the bathtub, reaching for the drying sheet he'd placed on a stool while he bathed. And the sight of him, naked skin gleaming, red hair dark and mussed after being washed, made Makenna halt abruptly.

She must have made a noise, for Bran turned swiftly to her, his eyes widening.

Heart pounding now, she drank him in, taking in the broad strength of his shoulders, the hard, sculpted lines of his body.

Heaven help her, he was beautiful.

And as her gaze traveled down his chest and over his flat belly to his groin, she watched his shaft, which had been at half-mast when she interrupted him, rise to greet her.

Lifting her chin—heat pulsing between her thighs now—she let her drying sheet fall.

Bran whispered an oath as he stared back at her. His gaze was hot, hungry.

And her own hunger answered its call.

There was no shyness now. Only need.

She took a step toward him, and an instant later, he was out of the bathtub and hauling her into his arms.

They kissed in a frenzy, a clash of lips, tongues, and teeth. Their hands were everywhere, but it wasn't enough. She wanted him inside her. Suddenly, she ached for him.

"Christ, Makenna," he rasped as his lips and teeth grazed along her jawline. "Do ye have any idea what ye do to me?"

She gave a breathy, shaky laugh. "No … show me."

An instant later, he was on his knees on the sheepskin before her, his wicked mouth on her breasts. He sucked each nipple hard, rolling them between his teeth and tongue until she whimpered.

Wildness throbbed inside her now. She trembled against him, panting.

He pulled her down, onto the damp sheepskin, and before Makenna knew what was happening, she was on her back, and he was kissing and licking his way down her body.

Her eyes fluttered shut. Aye, this was what she craved. Bran Mackinnon set her on fire, and she wanted to burn.

He spread her legs wide then, and an instant later, his mouth was between them.

She gasped. Pushing herself up onto her elbows, she watched him pleasure her. Good Lord, his lips. His tongue!

She started to tremble, her thighs jerking as he *devoured* her. And when he drew the sensitive bud of flesh he found into his mouth and sucked, she squealed.

Aye, *squealed*.

He gave another long, languid suck, and it was too much. She shattered, hard, against his mouth.

Panting, she watched him rise from between her thighs, his grey eyes dark now. His shaft thrust beneath them, its rounded head slick with beads of moisture.

Without thinking, for she was nothing but aching, pulsing desire now, she rolled toward him. She then pushed him onto his back and took his bone-hard rod in hand.

And when her mouth closed over its leaking tip, he cursed. Loudly.

She drew him in deep, hungry for him, letting him hit the back of her throat before she withdrew, swirled her tongue around the crown of his shaft, and repeated the action. Again and again. When she'd pleasured him like this on their wedding night, it had surprised her how much she'd enjoyed the act. Aye, she'd read the description in The Art of Coupling but had been nervous about trying it. She wasn't nervous any longer.

He'd just brought her over the edge, yet an ache started once more inside her womb. She still craved him. And each groan he gave, each strangled curse, made hunger twist and writhe in her loins.

"Stop!" Bran gasped, pulling free of her mouth.

Makenna gave a cry of protest, but he merely grabbed hold of her and rolled her away from him so she was on all fours on the sheepskin. Then, gripping her hips, he drove into her from behind in one smooth, gliding motion.

The shock of the invasion made her cry out, even as she bucked against him, bringing him deeper still. "Bran, please," she pleaded. "Now ... hard!"

He grunted a curse, tightened his grip on her hips, and rode her like a stallion.

And with each punishing thrust, Makenna arched up to meet him. Sinking down onto her elbows, she canted her hips so that every time he drove into her, the tip of him hit a place inside her and turned her liquid. "Oh, aye. There! Aye!"

And when he ground into her, thrusting deeper still, she squealed again. Pleasure churned and pulsed through her loins, tipping her over the brink. She lost any sense of where she was. Suddenly, she was spinning. And then his raw cry shattered the air, bringing her back to earth. A heartbeat later, heat flooded through her lower belly.

They collapsed together on the sheepskin, both gasping for breath. With him still buried deep inside her, Makenna welcomed the weight of him pressing her down. She wanted to stay like this forever. To think that she was wedded to this man now, and that they could tumble as often as they wished. Just the thought made her belly clench with excitement once more.

"Am I squashing ye?"

His breath tickled her ear, and Makenna giggled. "Aye … but I like it."

He huffed a laugh before shifting slightly so that he rested his weight on an elbow. His lips then grazed her neck, and she shivered. "I don't think I will get enough of ye," he said huskily. "Ever."

"And nor I, of ye," she whispered back.

His breathing hitched. Her response had surprised him.

Makenna's brow furrowed. Surely, her passionate response told him that she craved him as much as he did her? But, sometimes, words were necessary. Bran was strong and proud, yet she'd seen the insecurity he hid from the world. He needed to hear how much she wanted him.

"Just one look from ye is enough to rob me of thought," she whispered, even as her cheeks warmed. She wasn't used to being bold about her feelings, but for him, she'd do it. "Yer touch, yer kisses, set me alight … and when ye are inside me … I feel like … everything is … right."

His chest heaved against her back, emotion shuddering through his body. "I'm not used to feeling this close to anyone," he admitted roughly.

"Neither am I," she whispered.

He made a sound low in his throat. "I don't like being so … exposed."

"Ye can trust me, Bran," she replied, her tone turning fierce. She wanted him to believe her. "We MacGregors are loyal. I'm at yer side now … and I will always remain so." And as she spoke those words, she believed them wholly.

He stroked her back in response, his breathing shallow now. An instant later, he withdrew from her, in a slow slide that merely left her needing him again. Swallowing a groan, she twisted under him. Their gazes met and held, the intimacy of the moment turning the air between them heavy and charged.

"Ye'll put up with me then?" he asked softly, his lips quirking.

She smiled up at him. "Aye … if ye'll suffer me?"

Bran's hand lifted, and he caressed her face, his eyes gleaming. "Gladly."

Crouched on the bank of the River Lyon, while puddocks croaked in the nearby rushes, Makenna placed the small boat made of reeds upon the water. It carried a brooch that had belonged to Lloyd Walker, taken from his quarters in the guard tower.

His body remained at Finlarig Castle—so, instead of a burial, they were giving him one last journey.

Earlier, they'd stood in the sunny kirkyard, where Father Malcolm had spoken prayers and blessings for the souls of the fallen. The families of the warriors who'd been cut down by the Campbells wept and consoled each other. Afterward, a group gathered at a curve in the nearby River Lyon.

Craeg, Ailean, and Lyle had spent the last day making the boat. The lads had cut rushes from the riverbank and woven them tightly into a craft reminiscent of a birlinn. It was a sweet gesture, and one that Makenna appreciated.

They hadn't known Walker long, although just a couple of days after their arrival at Meggernie, they'd taken to following the Captain of the Guard around like eager puppies. Walker didn't have any bairns of his own, and he'd been delighted by the attention.

"Goodbye, Lloyd," Makenna murmured, watching the wee boat bob in the swirling current. "Have a safe journey."

She straightened up then, casting a glance over her right shoulder at where her parents stood, arms around each other, watching the boat travel downstream. Grief etched both of their faces, making them suddenly look much older. Ever since his return to Meggernie, her father's face had been uncharacteristically severe. Black Duncan's treachery would never be forgotten.

Makenna couldn't let it go either. Whenever she thought about the Campbells, her gut clenched.

Meanwhile, her sisters and their husbands and bairns stood a few feet farther back, looking silently on. Everyone gazed upon the little reed boat.

After a few moments, Makenna shifted her attention left, to where her husband stood. But Bran wasn't watching the river. Instead, his gaze was wholly upon her, and the softness, the understanding, in his eyes made her long to step into him, to let him enfold her in his embrace.

She didn't though. Aye, after the night before, things were good between them. Nonetheless, she still wasn't comfortable enough to let the last of her shields down—especially with everyone watching them.

27: VENGEANCE IS OURS

THE TIME CAME to bid her sisters farewell.

Sonia and Alma, their husbands, and brood of bairns departed a couple of days after the burials, although the Macleans of Dounarwyse and Moy had waited until a fortnight passed.

Of course, there were tears when Makenna saw Kylie and Liza off—although she promised them that she would make regular visits. She wasn't sure how Bran would react to her traveling into Maclean country, but she wouldn't be kept from her sisters. She hoped he'd understand.

Standing on the wall, watching Kylie and Liza depart alongside their husbands and bairns, she rubbed at her aching breastbone.

"Ye shall miss them greatly," Bran observed as he stood by her side.

"Aye," she whispered. "I already feel as if my heart has been ripped out."

He didn't reply to that, and when she glanced his way, she saw his gaze was shadowed. He now watched the Macleans—a party of around fifty—as they traveled across the meadows and disappeared into the woodlands beyond.

She wondered then if he was thinking about his own sister.

After their argument about her on the day of the attack, she'd avoided bringing Tara up again. She still believed he should mend things with her, but knew the subject was a raw one for him. She wasn't afraid of rousing his husband's anger—rather, she didn't want to hurt him.

"I would like to visit my sisters ... at least once a year ... if that's possible," she said after a lengthy pause.

Bran cut her a veiled look. "Aye?"

Makenna lifted her chin. "Aye."

His mouth tugged into a wry smile. "As if I'd ever be fool enough to stop ye."

"Does that mean ye shall accompany me?"

He pulled a face. "When ye go to Moy, I might be persuaded."

"And Dounarwyse?" She couldn't help it. Just a little push.

Bran looked away, his mouth pursing.

Swallowing a sigh, Makenna let the matter drop. Instead, she moved closer to him, linking her arm with his. "Can we stay on in Meggernie a little longer?"

He turned his attention to her once more. "Aye ... although the longer ye leave it, the harder it'll be. Ye know that, don't ye?"

Makenna swallowed to ease the sudden tightness in her throat. "Aye," she murmured. "But I just want to ensure Da is well ... he's not been himself since we returned from Finlarig."

Bran nodded. "He's quieter than he was, aye ... but he'll rally. Yer father is tough as weathered oak."

She snorted. "All the same, I worry."

His eyes softened, in that way of his that made her melt. He then raised his hand, brushing his knuckles across her cheek. "As ye wish, Makenna. Dùn Ara can wait."

"Isn't the pie to yer liking, mo chridhe?" Carmen's worried voice made Makenna glance her mother's way.

"It's delicious," the clan-chief replied.

"But ye have barely touched it."

"Don't fuss, my love," he growled.

Makenna's brow furrowed. Indeed, most of those at the chieftain's table had nearly finished their meal, but the MacGregor picked at his. He'd also downed twice as much wine as everyone else.

She understood exactly how he felt.

Nearly a week had passed since Kylie and Liza's departure, and restlessness within her grew with each day. They needed to act. Just the day before, she'd suggested they attack Finlarig in retribution. However, her father pointed out that such a move would likely bring the wrath of the Campbells who lived to the north of their borders upon them.

He was right, of course.

They hadn't been idle though. Her father had put more men on the Watch and doubled the patrols around Meggernie.

Makenna and Bran had led many of them. Her father no longer forbade her from carrying a longsword or doing her part to help defend the castle.

No Campbell would stray close without being spotted—and so far, none had.

Meanwhile, Carmen studied her husband's strained face. Her dark brows drew together then. She was just about to say something else when a shout cut through the smoky air.

"Black Duncan is dead!"

Jolting, Makenna's attention snapped right to where a warrior had just rushed into the hall. Breathless, he strode toward the chieftain's table.

A stunned silence fell.

Makenna watched the man's flushed face and bright eyes for a moment, until the full weight of his announcement sank in.

Dead.

Under the table, Bran put his hand on her thigh and squeezed. In response, she covered his hand with hers, gripping tightly.

"How?" the clan-chief rasped.

"The wound ye dealt him soured, MacGregor," the warrior replied, drawing near. "They say he lingered for a while ... and that his end was agonizing."

Murmurs of approval rippled through the hall at this news.

All gazes shifted to Makenna's father.

The MacGregor straightened up in his carven chair. And then, as Makenna watched, the tension he'd carried ever since their escape from Finlarig lifted.

It was like seeing a sunburst chase away storm clouds. His vision cleared, his shoulders lowered, and the deep lines that had carved themselves on either side of his mouth softened.

Likewise, something deep inside Makenna's chest unknotted. She glanced Bran's way then, to find his gaze sharp, a smile tugging at the corners of his mouth. "A fitting end for the whoreson."

Makenna nodded. She couldn't agree more.

Next to the clan-chief, Carmen shifted uneasily, her night-brown gaze flicking from husband to daughter. Although the Campbell treachery had upset her, she hadn't understood their hunger for revenge. She wasn't a warrior like Bruce or Makenna. She didn't understand the honor Black Douglas had stolen from them. Aye, they'd escaped with their lives, but not before he'd humiliated them.

Sensing his wife's discomfort, the clan-chief reached out and put a reassuring hand on her shoulder. "It's over, mo ghràdh. I can let this rest now. Vengeance is ours … finally."

The long twilight began, a gradual lengthening of the shadows while the blue sky—for it had been a bonnie day—leached of color.

Makenna, who'd spent most of the afternoon up on the walls with the Guard before taking supper with her husband and kin in the great hall, slipped away and climbed the narrow, winding stairs to the roof.

And there, she stood, leaning against the sun-warmed rock, listening to the gentle coo of the pigeons. There was a flat area on the doocot's roof, where the birds sunned themselves in the last of the light.

Her gaze traveled south, to where the outline of Ben Lawers and its brethren rose against the horizon, and her lips thinned.

Robbie Campbell would be chieftain now. The man was a swine, although not half as dangerous as his father had been. He lacked Black Duncan's cunning and malice. Even so, her clan would need to keep a close eye on their southern borders in the coming months—and years.

Every time Robbie caught a glimpse of his reflection in a looking-glass, he'd see the scar her father had dealt him.

He'd remember the MacGregors.

Makenna's gaze shifted then, sweeping across the curtain wall that surrounded the tower house. Guards stood watch there. Blair had increased their number for the moment. Just in case there was any trouble.

Sighing, Makenna murmured an oath under her breath. *It's not yer responsibility anymore ... ye need to let go.* Aye, she did, although that was easier said than done.

"That is a weary sound for such a bonnie eve."

A familiar voice made her turn, her gaze alighting upon the tall figure who moved along the narrow walkway, between the doocot and the crenelations that ran around the roof of the tower house.

"Ye found me then?" she greeted her husband with a smile, deliberately not answering his observation.

He flashed her a boyish smile, one that made her belly do a wee flip.

The more she spent time with Bran, the more she wanted him. They were both surviving on little sleep these days, as their nights were spent tumbling. They were ravenous for each other.

"I thought ye'd be in high spirits after learning of Black Duncan's demise ... I know I am," Bran continued, clearly determined not to let the matter drop. "Why the sighing?"

Makenna pulled a face. Sometimes, she wished her husband wasn't quite so observant. There was very little that got past him. "I still feel guilty about leaving Meggernie," she admitted finally. "I keep thinking I need to be here ... just in case."

Bran's gaze roamed over her face, and she braced herself for him to try and reassure her, to tell her that the Meggernie Guard had defended this castle before she served amongst it and would continue to do so after she departed.

But his response, when it came, surprised her. "Ye don't want to leave the familiar behind ... that's understandable."

"It's not that," she replied, a trifle defensively.

His lips lifted at the corners. "Isn't it?"

"No. I just worry about my clan's future."

"And yer loyalty does ye credit ... but I can't help but think ye use it as a shield." Makenna's gaze narrowed at this, yet Bran wasn't done. "Ye know every inch of this castle ... and the meadows, woodlands, and hills beyond. Ye feel comfortable here ... safe ... just as I do at Dùn Ara."

Discomfort flickered up, although Makenna masked it with a frown. How was it that Bran could see such things about her? She wanted to tell him he was wrong, but the words stuck in her throat.

"Ye understand then?" she asked finally, even as her skin prickled. Leaning up against the battlement, she placed her hands on its top, taking comfort from its solidity. Would he think her weak for wanting to remain in a place where she felt in control? She didn't like revealing a chink in her armor.

"More than ye realize," he answered, moving close. They stood side-by-side now, their shoulders touching. Bran reached out then, his finger tracing a pattern over the back of her hand atop the battlement. "It was part of the reason why I waited so long to travel to Perthshire and claim ye."

Makenna cast him a sidelong glance. "I thought it was because yer father had made ye a betrothal ye didn't want."

He huffed a rueful laugh. "There was that, aye … but there was fear too. I know Dùn Ara, even though its people don't yet respect me."

Makenna stiffened, yet Bran merely shrugged. "It stings … but it's the truth. I'm a clan-chief, but compared to the likes of yer father, who has ruled his lands for over two decades, I'm young … untested." He broke off there, his gaze shifting out to where tiny shapes flitted around them. Bats. The wee pipistrelles were stretching their wings now that dusk was nearing. "I worried I'd be mocked for my inexperience … or reminded about my failure at Dounarwyse." He shook his head, even as Makenna's chest tightened—she'd done just that once. "And ye can imagine how pleased I was to discover Rae and Alec were amongst our wedding guests."

Makenna observed him, momentarily forgetting her own defensiveness and niggling guilt. Bran's candor made something squeeze under her ribs. "Ye have the respect of both those men … ye realize that, don't ye?"

He glanced her way and nodded. "I doubt the Mackinnons and the Macleans will ever be fast friends … but at least now, there is an understanding between us."

Their gazes held then before she let out another sigh. "The devil's turds … I hate it when ye are right."

His mouth curved. "It brings me no pleasure."

"Liar." She nudged him gently in the ribs with her elbow. "What ye said struck home though ... here, I know what my role is and how others will respond to me." She paused then, swallowing. "In truth ... I struggle sometimes. My father has never really understood ... but Lloyd was always there for me." She didn't add that Tormod's attempted rape had rattled her far more than she cared to admit. In the aftermath, she'd lost confidence, and shame had dogged her ever since. She'd always thought of herself as strong, yet Tormod had taught her she wasn't invincible.

However, facing the Campbells at Finlarig healed that wound—and Tormod MacDougall was now dead.

"And now, *I* am here for ye," he reminded her softly.

Warmth rose to her cheeks. "And I will not forget it." She paused then. "I suppose Dùn Ara will be good for me. I could do with toughening up."

Bran cut her a surprised look. "What?"

"It's true."

"But ye are stronger than most *men* I've met."

She shook her head. "I can hold my nerve in battle, aye ... but on the inside, I'm far too soft. I feel things too deeply."

Bran harrumphed and lifted his arm, looping it protectively around her shoulders.

"No, ye don't," he said firmly. "And don't ever apologize for yer compassionate and gentle heart either. It's where true strength lies."

28: STRANGERS NO LONGER

RIDING AWAY FROM Meggernie, Makenna fought the urge to keep glancing over her shoulder.

Throat tight, her eyes stinging from the tears that had flowed when she'd bid her parents farewell, she stared resolutely at the tangle of branches up ahead.

She'd known leaving would be hard, but she hadn't realized just how much it would hurt.

Bran rode next to her, a silent yet reassuring presence, while the remainder of the Mackinnon company followed them. Tadhg was among them. It was now the beginning of July, and the warrior had fully recovered from the grave injury that had nearly killed him.

Even now, guilt constricted Makenna's chest every time she caught sight of him. The man was still gruff with her, although he had warmed up slightly. Nonetheless, he was a reminder of just how far she and Bran had come.

As they reached the tree line, where the dark boughs of sycamores beckoned, she gave in to the urge and glanced back at Meggernie one last time. The castle's sturdy walls glowed in the warmth of the morning sun, the MacGregor pennant—a crowned lion's head—fluttering from the top of the tower house.

"This isn't the last time ye shall see it," Bran reminded her then, his voice gentle. "With the alliance our clans have struck, we shall be back here every year or two."

A little of the pressure in Makenna's chest eased at this reassurance. "Aye," she said huskily. "I will return."

She would, but this castle would never be her home again. That wasn't what cut the deepest though. For so long, all she'd cared about was defending this fortress, and the villages, lands, and people belonging to it. But now she had to let them all go. She was crossing a threshold today—one that she'd been putting off for too long.

Gathering her reins, she turned away from the castle and favored her husband with a brittle smile. Then, she urged her courser forward.

They rode in silence through the cool green of the woods, serenaded by the languid call of song thrushes and blackbirds—and with each furlong, the wretchedness that had filled Makenna upon leaving home gradually lessened.

They'd had a bonnie summer so far, and today was another example, with a robin's egg blue sky, hot sun, and a gentle, sweet-scented breeze to take the edge off the heat. Surrounded by such beauty, it was impossible to remain heavy-hearted for long.

Presently, the road took them back to the northern shore of the River Lyon, hugging the waterway's lazy path southwest. Eventually, it would lead them to the loch by the same name, where they'd cross, but for the next day, they'd remain on this path.

Dragonflies danced in the shimmering air, and flies and midges buzzed around the horses, causing them to toss their heads and flick their tails in irritation.

Thick swathes of thistles grew by the river, their bright purple seedheads waving in the breeze. "What a sight," Makenna murmured to Bran, gesturing to the bristling carpet. "I do love thistles."

"Aye," Bran agreed before flashing her a smile. "They remind me of ye. Bonnie … but prickly."

She snorted at his teasing, her mood lightening further. "Aye, well, we both know a sweet, meek wife would bore ye."

He laughed at that, the deep sound drifting through the warm air. "How right ye are."

Bran climbed aboard the ferry and held out a hand to his wife.

And as he did so, an uneasiness quickened in his gut.

After ten days in the saddle, it felt odd to be traveling without his horse. He'd just sold them back to the horse trader he'd originally purchased the beasts from months earlier.

Nonetheless, his disquiet this morning was due to something else. The Isle of Mull lay across the water, and with it, his old life. His old identity.

"It looks as if it will be a calm enough crossing," Makenna observed as she took hold of his hand and stepped onto the ferry.

"Aye," he agreed. "We've timed things well."

"I'm looking forward to seeing Tobermory," she replied, smiling. The day before, he'd told her that the ferry would drop them there, where his birlinn had been moored for the past months. From there, it was a short journey to his castle.

"It's a pretty port," he agreed, cutting his gaze away.

"Is something amiss, Bran?"

Stiffening, he shook his head. Curse it, Makenna read him too well. "I always get a bit queasy on water," he lied.

"Ye never said."

"Aye, well … it's embarrassing."

Makenna harrumphed but thankfully let the subject drop. Instead, she made her way to the bow, where she arranged her skirts and settled herself on a wooden plank seat. Around them, his warriors also took their places, along with the other passengers who were traveling to Mull this morning.

Jaw clenched, Bran lowered himself next to his wife. Meanwhile, the ferry captain began barking orders at his crew as they untied the vessel from its mooring and prepared to cast off.

He'd been like a cat on a hot griddle since they'd arrived in Oban—ever since he'd made his way down to the docks the evening before, while Makenna soaked in a hot bath, and bought passage for their group on the morning ferry.

During the evening that followed, he'd been distracted when his wife talked to him and quieter than usual.

And now, as the ferry moved away from the docks, propelled by oars, Bran glanced back at where Oban's busy quay bustled with sailors, locals, and travelers, with the tightly packed houses lining it. A wooded hillside rose behind the port, and the sky was pale blue this morning with wispy clouds.

Bran should have been excited about returning to Mull—but he wasn't.

Old insecurities died hard, it seemed. His experiences over the past months had changed him, but everything back home would be the same. His people would expect a sullen young clan-chief to return. He remembered their smirks and whispered comments over the years. How would they respond to him now? And, more importantly, how would he conduct himself?

But that wasn't the only thing that bothered him.

The evening before, he'd made a choice, one he was already regretting. He'd told himself the past needed to be faced, but now he wasn't so sure. However, reconciling with his sister was the right thing to do.

She might not want to see me.

Aye, that was a real possibility. The last time they'd seen each other, he'd said ugly things to Tara. Words he could never take back. Regret had gnawed at him for a long while now, despite his best efforts to pretend otherwise.

As they sailed away from Oban, and Mull's dark outline etched the western sky, he started to feel lightheaded and queasy.

It wasn't long before his sharp-eyed wife noticed something amiss.

"Shouldn't we be heading north … rather than west?" she asked.

Bran didn't answer, pretending he hadn't heard.

She was silent for a short while before plucking at his sleeve. "Bran ... isn't that *Craignure*?"

Tearing his gaze from where the row of cottages lined a white-sand beach, with a long wooden jetty thrusting out into clear water, Bran nodded. "It is."

"I thought this ferry went direct to Tobermory?"

He shook his head, their gazes fusing.

Moments passed before understanding dawned in his wife's eyes. "We're going to Dounarwyse ... aren't we?"

"Aye," he replied, wishing his voice wasn't so strained. He hoped Makenna wouldn't start asking him questions. He didn't want to go into his reasons for this decision, although she was largely responsible. He'd never forgotten her words on the day the Campbells had attacked their hunting party. They'd taunted him ever since.

Tara is a good woman ... with a kind, generous soul. She wishes to be reconciled with ye. Why won't ye bury the ax?

Makenna hadn't let him blame his sister. She'd angered him at the time, but her words were like thorns that had worked their way under his skin. There was only one way to pluck the things out.

He had to see his sister, to try and put things right between them.

Wordlessly, Makenna reached out, taking his hand and entwining her fingers through his. "I'm with ye," she murmured, squeezing his hand.

Bran's heart kicked hard. This woman. "Thank ye," he answered gruffly.

Dust devils scattered across Dounarwyse's barmkin, ignored by the small crowd that had gathered there.

Rae, Kylie, and the chieftain's two sons stood on the steps before the broch, looking on from a discreet distance while Tara faced her brother. Her husband, Jack, waited a couple of feet behind his wife. A wee lassie clung to her father's leg, while he held a younger bairn in his arms.

However, Jack Maclean's attention wasn't focused on his daughters, but on his brother-by-marriage. His fern-green eyes sliced like ax blades into Bran.

Makenna had halted a few feet back, allowing her husband to face his sister without feeling crowded. And like everyone else, she waited for either Bran or Tara to speak.

The pair studied each other for a long while, each taking the other's measure.

Tara looked well. Her long bright-red hair was unbound and whipped around her. Her face, the same shape as his, with the same stubborn chin, wore a guarded expression.

It struck Bran that she was bracing herself. She expected the first words out of his mouth to be harsh ones. He couldn't blame her, for the last time they'd been face-to-face, he'd raged at her, had called her a 'traitor'.

He cleared his throat then, unclenching his hands at his sides. It would help if he didn't look as if he were about to throw himself into a fight. "I'm sorry, Tara."

The words fell heavily in the silence.

Her eyes widened. A moment later, a nerve flickered on her cheek. She didn't believe him. Of course, an apology wasn't enough.

Huffing a sigh, Bran reached up and dragged a hand through his hair. "I didn't understand what drove ye to run away ... but I do now. I shouldn't have cursed ye as I did. And I should have been there when ye needed me." He swallowed then, wishing his throat didn't sound so tight. "It's because of ye that Loch Maclean didn't have me strung up by the neck from the walls ... I've never forgotten that."

He recalled then, the way his sister had sunk to her knees before the Maclean clan-chief, how she alone had begged for his life. At first, Maclean had been unmoved, but then, when Jack had stepped up next to his wife and asked him to heed her, he'd relented.

He owed his life to them both, yet he'd been heinously ungrateful at the time. Aye, he was alive but humiliated. He'd left Dounarwyse without speaking to his sister again and vowing never to do so. But 'never' was a long time.

"I'm cursed with our father's stubborn pride, it seems," he admitted after a few moments.

Tara's throat worked. "I'm sorry too," she replied huskily. "For leaving without telling ye. I was desperate and wasn't sure I could trust ye not to betray me."

The admission made him flinch, yet she was likely right. He didn't know how he'd have reacted had she come to him in the hours before she escaped from Dùn Ara and bribed a fisherman to take her away in the dead of night.

"Life with our father wasn't easy for me either," he admitted after a brittle pause. "When ye fled, ye left me alone with the bastard."

A muscle ticked in her jaw. "I know," she whispered.

The pain in her eyes cut him to the quick. "Ye did what ye had to ... I understand now." Bran took a tentative step forward, his throat burning. "I've missed ye."

With a strangled sob, Tara threw herself at him.

The force of their collision nearly knocked him off his feet. Righting himself, Bran hugged his sister tightly. His eyes stung dangerously as she sobbed against his chest.

Christ's blood, he shouldn't have left this for so long. Tara hadn't deserved to be punished. And he'd spoken the truth. He *had* missed her. Losing her had left a chasm inside him that even Makenna couldn't quite fill. He and his sister had a shared history.

"Fear not, we will be strangers no longer," he assured Tara, stroking her back as she hiccoughed and attempted to knuckle away her tears. "Makenna plans to make regular trips here ... and, if ye wish it, I shall join her."

"Of course, I wish it!" Tara grabbed his hand, squeezing it so tightly that his bones creaked. "Ye are my *brother* ... and I have missed ye too."

29: DEEPLY, MADLY

SEATED IN DOUNARWYSE'S hall, at Bran's side, Makenna watched him talk to his sister.

They were so alike, with many of the same mannerisms. The jut of the chin when they disagreed. The narrowing of the eyes. And the same bright, playful smile when they were amused.

Tara had become a friend during her stay here the year before, and she'd marked the sadness in the woman's eyes when she'd spoken of her brother all those months ago.

Earlier in the day, it had surprised Makenna to see Craignure looming on the horizon. She'd known something was amiss though; Bran hadn't been himself ever since their arrival in Oban. She'd sensed something was gnawing at him, and had thought it had more to do with his imminent return to Dùn Ara.

However, his decision to mend things with his sister impressed her.

They'd avoided speaking about Tara over the past two months.

Aye, there had been many times when Makenna wanted to bring the subject up, to gently press him into confronting the past, but she'd choked the words down every time.

Bran knew how she felt—and she'd decided to let it lie. For the time being, at least.

But unbeknown to her, he *had* been thinking over things. And better yet, he'd made up his own mind.

Farther down the table, Kylie also observed brother and sister catching up on the years lost. A soft smile curved her lips, and her oak-colored eyes were luminous. Like Makenna, she understood what this meant to Tara. To them both.

"Uncle Bran," a sweet voice trilled then. "Can I sit on yer lap?"

Wee Grace, who was currently sitting with her father, flashed Bran a shy smile.

The lass, who was around three summers old, had been watching her uncle with wide, fascinated eyes.

"Aye," Bran replied, answering her smile with one of his own. "If yer Da permits it."

Jack gave a grunt before nodding. Throughout the meal, he'd watched his brother-by-marriage warily. He was slower to forgive and forget than his wife, yet there was warmth in his green eyes now as he let his daughter slide to the floor and clamber under the table.

A moment later, Bran picked her up and let her perch on his knee.

The lass turned to look at him. "Ye are bonnie."

Bran huffed a laugh, his smoky eyes twinkling now. "*Bonnie*, eh?"

She reached up then, her small fingers brushing his wavy hair. "It's the same color as Ma's."

"That's because she's my sister."

"Like me and Arabella?"

"Aye."

The lassie continued to look at him, in that unabashed way that bairns possessed. "Arabella is annoying."

Bran's mouth twitched at this, while Tara made a disapproving sound. Ignoring her mother, Grace went on. "She cries too much ... and pulls my hair."

"She doesn't do that on purpose, love," Jack answered with a wry shake of his head. "Ye *will* insist on treating her like one of yer poppets."

Meanwhile, the bairn in question made a gurgling sound as she chewed a piece of bread. She'd heard her name uttered and was delighted.

Grace pouted at her father's gentle reprimand.

Something tugged at Makenna as she watched softness settle over her husband's face. He'd make a wonderful father one day. Despite that they coupled regularly, her womb hadn't yet quickened. They still had plenty of time though.

"Sisters can be annoying sometimes," Bran said, pushing one of Grace's auburn curls off her forehead. He then flicked Tara a cheeky smile before focusing on his niece once more. "But life is so much sadder without them."

Bran's eyes fluttered shut as his climax barreled into him. Heat exploded in his lower back, pleasure pulsing through his loins and belly. Gasping, he arched into Makenna, spilling deep inside her.

She cried out—a sound halfway between a sob and a squeal, and one that never ceased to thrill him—her fingernails raking down his back.

They clung together in the aftermath, the rasp of their ragged breathing filling the bedchamber.

"Woman," Bran panted against her neck as he propped himself up on his elbows. "I swear, one of these days, ye shall stop my heart."

She giggled, wrapping her strong legs around his hips and pulling him close. He was still buried within her, and neither of them wanted to separate. Her mouth then found his, and she kissed him. They clung like that for a while, savoring slow, tender kisses while their pulses slowed and the sweat cooled on their bodies.

Tumbling Makenna was like riding a storm. Each time they came together, she gave herself passionately, wildly—and he answered her with equal hunger.

Tonight though, after he'd reconciled with his sister, he felt a freeness with his wife that hadn't been there before.

He was now ready to tell her the words that had been burning within him for a while.

Drawing back slightly, he cupped her face and stared down into her limpid moss-green eyes. "I love ye, Makenna," he whispered. "Deeply, madly."

Her pupils grew large, her lips—swollen from their passion—parting. "I've been longing to hear those words," she whispered. "I've been wanting to say them too ... but I was shy."

He gave a soft snort.

Her lips curved, making her cheek dimple. "Aye ... I can be demure about some things, ye know?"

He laughed, and she gave his cheek a playful slap. "Knave!"

He caught her hand and placed a kiss on her palm. "I love all that ye are, Makenna," he murmured. "Never forget it."

"And I love ye too, Bran." Her eyes gleamed with tears now, her voice husky. "I am so grateful that fate brought us together."

He smiled. "It wasn't fate, lass … but our ambitious, power-hungry fathers."

"It was," she admitted with a soft laugh. "I spent years dreading meeting ye … but now, I don't ever wish for us to be parted."

Lifting his hand, Bran swept away a tear that rolled down her cheek with his thumb. He swallowed then. Like her, his emotions boiled close to the surface tonight. For years, he'd believed happiness would never find him, but his marriage to Makenna had taught him that he did deserve it, after all.

"I have little to thank my father for," he admitted roughly. "Yet the day he made an alliance with yers, he unwittingly did something I will always be grateful for."

She nodded, staring up at him. The love in her eyes made it difficult to breathe.

However, as the moment drew out, and the joy and excitement of their tumbling faded a little, the worries that had plagued him ever since leaving Meggernie returned.

His jaw tightened.

Makenna's brow furrowed. "Ye have that look on yer face again."

He stilled. "What look?"

"The one that means ye are worrying about something ye are keeping to yerself."

Bran grimaced. She was right. He didn't want to admit his fears to her. There was a part of him—even after the trust they'd built—that worried she'd think less of him if he did.

But when her gaze narrowed, it was clear she wouldn't let this lie.

Eventually, he huffed a sigh. "Ye know the folk of Dùn Ara have never fully accepted me?"

She nodded, her green eyes shadowing. "I reminded ye of it when ye signed that agreement, remember?"

He grimaced. Aye, of course. It shouldn't have surprised him to learn that all of Mull had been gossiping about him, yet the knowledge had stung all the same.

"When we lost to the Macleans and I returned home, defeated, there were moments when I thought they'd rise up against me." Cold washed over him as he remembered those fraught days. "But luckily, many members of my Guard were loyal to my family ... and thanks to them, I remained clan-chief."

He fell silent then before raking a hand through his hair. Why was this so hard?

"With the passing of the years, things improved ... slightly ... but the fact remains that when I departed Dùn Ara, few folk bothered to see me off ... and many would prefer I didn't return."

"But if ye didn't, who would rule?"

He pulled a face. "I've got a cousin who has a holding at Croig, west of my castle, who'd be only too happy to take my place."

Her frown deepened. "Are ye worried he's tried something while ye were away?"

Bran shook his head. "I'd trust the Captain of the Guard with my life … but the fact remains, ye may find we get a lackluster welcome at Dùn Ara. I want ye to be prepared."

A steely look flared in the depths of her eyes, which was a relief, for the last thing he wanted was to see pity or scorn there. "However they respond, ye shall walk in there with yer head held high," she replied, her voice turning fierce. "And I will be at yer side." She reached up then, her hand cupping his face. "I'm proud that ye are my husband, Bran, and I dare anyone to challenge me on it."

30: FORTUNE FAVORS THE BOLD

MAKENNA'S FIRST GLIMPSE of Dùn Ara made her stifle a gasp.

The castle was more imposing than she'd expected, enough to equal the might of Duart Castle. It perched high on a crag above the water, its thick curtain wall made of stone and lime glowing white in the afternoon sun. A rocky inlet curved at its feet, with noosts, hollows in the rock where fishing boats nestled above the tideline.

Tearing her gaze from the fortress, Makenna glanced her husband's way.

Bran was staring at his home. Standing there, at the prow of the Mackinnon clan-chief's birlinn, which they'd collected from Tobermory, he looked like one of the Norsemen from the old stories: Vikings who'd raided and then settled the Western Isles centuries earlier.

A brisk breeze whipped his hair about his head, although his expression was stern.

He was readying himself to face his people.

An ache rose under Makenna's breastbone. It cut her to the quick that he'd endured so much. The Mackinnon defeat against the Macleans hadn't been his doing, but the man responsible was dead.

Would they have preferred him to have defied Loch Maclean, and have died for it? Perhaps. Common folk sometimes resented the privilege of those who ruled them, not realizing that with it came great responsibility and hard choices.

Feeling her gaze upon him, Bran tore his attention from the castle and looked her way. "What do ye think?"

Makenna smiled. "It's magnificent," she answered honestly, moving close so that he could put an arm around her waist. Arriving here with him felt right. Now that Meggernie lay far behind them, her old life had lost its hold. She was free to embrace the next chapter.

The sun shone brightly today, although the wind had a bite to it. She was glad for the fur-lined cloak she'd donned before departing from Dounarwyse. They'd lingered at the Maclean stronghold a few days—longer than anticipated. During their stay, relationships had been properly mended. Initially, Jack had been off-hand with his brother-by-marriage, but by the time he'd taken them north on Rae's birlinn, he and Bran had become friends.

They would be welcome at Dounarwyse now, whenever they wished to visit. Makenna planned to travel there again the following spring before making their way down to Moy on the southern coast.

However, in the meantime, she had the rest of the summer, autumn, and winter to settle into her new home. That was her priority now.

The men lowered the sail and rowed the birlinn in, mooring it to a thin stacked stone jetty. The Mackinnon clan-chief's galley was a fine one and held up to forty oarsmen. Taking Bran's hand, Makenna climbed up onto the dock and looked around her. Steep hills covered in scrubby woodland fell away behind the castle to the south. One glance and she could see it was easy to defend.

Turning to Bran, she met his eye. "Has Dùn Ara ever fallen to an enemy?"

"Never," he replied, pride lacing his voice. "There are few castles as hard to take as this one."

Makenna believed him.

Hand-in-hand, they walked down the jetty, followed by the company of warriors who'd accompanied them home. They then made their way up the steep path that wound its way to the gates. The entrance through the curtain wall lay on the southeastern side. Close up, Makenna could see just how thick the wall was—indeed, around five feet in places.

And as they climbed, she resisted the urge to glance Bran's way to see how he was faring. His grip on her hand was firm though, reassuring.

Guards flanked the gates ahead. Clad in leather and mail, they grasped schiltron pikes.

Makenna was pleased to note that they snapped to attention as their clan-chief approached. However, their expressions were difficult to read.

Bran nodded to them but didn't check his stride. Instead, he led her under the portcullis and into a wide barmkin.

There, he halted so she could view her new home properly for the first time. Instead of a tower house, like Meggernie, the keep resembled something much older: a beehive-shaped structure on two levels. "I've never seen the like," she murmured, gazing up at it.

"It's the oldest part of the castle," Bran replied. "There was originally a broch here ... and everything else was added on much later."

Makenna nodded, slowly turning in a circle as she took in the stacked stone outbuildings, kitchen, bakehouse, and stables surrounding her. The great hall—a rectangular building with a thatched roof—appeared to be separate from the 'broch'. Like the outer wall, the stone within was also flecked with white limestone.

"Welcome home, Mackinnon." A tall, lanky figure with a shock of greying hair that had once been auburn descended the stone steps from the walls and strode toward them.

"Finlay!" Bran stepped forward, and the two men clasped arms before the clan-chief pulled the older man into a hug. "It's good to see ye."

Clearly surprised, yet pleased, by Bran's show of affection, Finlay grinned. His attention then flicked to where Makenna stood a few feet back. She was dressed in her usual way, in a fashionable kirtle and surcote that had both been cut at the sides to allow her ease of movement. Underneath, she wore woolen leggings and high boots. She'd braided the sides of her long hair and drawn them off her face, for it was practical when traveling. At one hip hung 'Arsebiter', while at the other she wore a dirk.

Finlay's gaze lingered on her, his grey eyes widening. "And this is yer bride?"

"Aye." Bran stepped back. "Makenna … may I introduce ye to Finlay Mackinnon … Captain of the Dùn Ara Guard. He has acted as steward in my absence."

Makenna smiled. "Pleased to meet ye, Captain."

"And I ye, Lady Mackinnon," he answered.

"How have things been while I was away?" Bran asked then, his brow furrowing.

"Quiet enough," Finlay replied. His gaze glinted then. "Yer cousin came calling a week after ye departed, but I sent him away."

Bran's eyes narrowed, and when he replied, his tone was flinty. "Good."

The captain studied him curiously. "Yer last message was delivered a fortnight ago though … so we knew to expect ye. From yer letters, it sounds as if ye had an adventurous time in Perthshire."

Bran snorted. "Ye could say that. Meet me in my solar after supper later … and we can give each other full reports over a cup or two of ale."

The captain's lips tugged up into another smile before he nodded.

Makenna was aware then that the barmkin had filled up. Cooks, kitchen lads, grooms, stable hands, and others had ventured out of the broch and numerous outbuildings to catch sight of the clan-chief—and his bride. Many of them eyed her, their gazes lingering on her unusual attire and weapons. She noted the sharpness of their stares, and the way some of the men surrounding them thinned their lips. One or two even smirked.

Aye, Bran hadn't exaggerated the mood here.

Not remotely cowed, Makenna stared back boldly. She even rested her hand upon the pommel of her sword, drawing attention to it. She might as well start as she meant to go on.

They'd mind her, just as they would her husband.

"Fortune favors the bold," Bran called out, also noting that they now had an audience. His voice was loud as he used his clan motto, echoing against stone. "As ye can see, I have returned to ye safely ... as has my lady wife."

He paused then, his silvery gaze glinting as he stared the crowd down.

"Ye will also mark that she carries weapons. I shall have ye know that Makenna is a warrior of note, and that if ye don't wish to see the sharp edge of her blade ... or mine ... ye shall treat her with the respect she is owed."

Makenna drew herself up, heat igniting in her belly. Aye, he'd shocked them now. Some of the women flushed, while the men dropped their gazes. Tension rippled through the barmkin.

"We have made a strong alliance with the MacGregors of Meggernie ... one that will ensure our clan prospers," he added. "We have also healed relations with the Macleans of Dounarwyse and Moy. No longer will we fight with our neighbors."

Murmurs erupted at his admission, but Bran silenced them with a deft movement of his hand. "When I left Dùn Ara in the spring, many of ye wished I'd never return."

Faces around him grew taut at these blunt words, but he ignored their reaction.

"Ye believed a man who'd make peace with his enemies isn't fit to rule the Mackinnons … but ye don't know what real strength is … *real* honor. My father would have sacrificed the lot of ye if it meant he could rule all of Mull. He cared about only himself." Bran paused then, his gaze narrowing as it swept over the now hushed crowd. "Know this … I'm not Kendric Mackinnon and nor do I wish to be. However, if ye mistake my decency for weakness, ye do so at yer own peril."

"That was quite a speech ye gave out there."

Bran flashed Makenna a grin as he led the way up a steep spiral stairwell. "It was long overdue. Did ye enjoy it?"

"Aye."

"I wished to make myself clear."

She smiled back. "Oh, ye did that. How does it feel?"

"Like freedom," he replied. "Like I've finally laid my father's ghost to rest."

And he had. In truth, Makenna hadn't expected him to be quite so forthright, or eloquent. Pride had warmed her chest as she watched him address his people.

Afterward, they'd left the stunned crowd behind and entered the broch, and Bran was now giving her a tour. He took her upstairs before they stepped onto the landing of the second level. Moving to the nearest door, he pushed it open and led the way into an imposing, if slightly intimidating, chamber. An array of weapons decorated the stone walls, and above the wide hearth, three glowering boar heads had been mounted.

Observing them, Makenna murmured an oath under her breath.

"Quite a sight, aren't they?" Bran said with a shrug. "They're my father's trophies."

Makenna grimaced.

"He even named them," Bran went on. "The ugly one at the end, he called Loch. The middle one is Leod … and the other is Rae."

She snorted a disbelieving laugh. "He named them after the Maclean clan-chief and his chieftains?"

"Aye … he had a twisted sense of humor." Bran observed the boar heads then, as if seeing them with new eyes. "Well … Loch, Leod, and Rae have graced the hearth for long enough. I will have them taken down today."

Relief washed over Makenna at this news. The trophies were a reminder of a cruel man, and neither of them wanted his presence to linger in here.

"I'm sure after we've been stag hunting together, we will soon have something else to mount over the hearth," she replied.

He nodded, his gaze soft as he shifted his attention to her. After a moment, his lips curved. "Did I tell ye that Dùn Ara has a walled garden accessed via the southern curtain wall?"

She raised her eyebrows. "No."

His smile widened. "It's one of this fortress's many secrets. It was my mother's once … but gardeners keep it tended these days. It will be full of roses in bloom this time of year. Would ye like to see it?"

Makenna grinned. A private garden within the castle was something that Meggernie had always lacked. She was delighted to discover that Dùn Ara had one. Bran already knew she loved roses.

"Aye, husband," she replied, taking his hand and lacing her fingers through his. "Lead the way."

EPILOGUE: WINTERTHORN

Two months later ...

MAKENNA LISTENED TO the cook prattle on, barely restraining herself from tapping her toe in impatience. She was late.

"We shall have venison stew at least twice this week, Lady Mackinnon," Donald enthused, rubbing his hands together. "We have plenty of meat after yer successful hunt."

Makenna nodded, managing to keep the encouraging smile still plastered to her face.

Indeed, she and Bran had returned to the castle with five deer hinds just a couple of days earlier. It had been a chance for her to further explore the rugged hills, deep corries, and sprawling woodlands of northern Mull. She'd been here two moons, and Bran had wanted to take her out hunting before the weather turned.

They'd stayed out for three days, camping overnight in a shallow valley with the small group of warriors who'd joined them.

Sitting by a fire under the stars, listening as the men told stories and tried to outdo each other with boasts, had filled her with contentment. She could have explored the wilderness for a few days longer, but home, and the duties that awaited them there, called.

And one such duty was regular meetings with the castle cook. She liked Donald, yet he'd been talking her ear off for a while now. She had somewhere else to be.

"That's excellent," she said, taking a step backward toward the open door of the kitchen. "I'll just—"

"Can ye take a look at the spence with me, Lady Mackinnon?" he asked, eyes bright. "I'm running low on spices ... we shall need to order more."

Makenna swallowed a sigh before casting an eye over the surrounding kitchen. The large oaken table that dominated it was scrubbed clean, and kitchen assistants worked industriously at it, chopping vegetables for the noon meal. "Very well," she murmured. "The clan-chief will be putting an order in soon ... let's see what's needed."

Donald nodded eagerly before moving toward the archway at the far end of the rectangular kitchen. "This way."

It was a while later when Makenna finally stepped outside into the barmkin and heaved a deep sigh.

"By the Saints," she muttered. "The man's harder to escape than a gossiping fishwife."

The morning sun warmed her face, although the air was crisp, for it was mid-September. Life had been busy of late. The day before, they'd just sent off their first shipment of smoked herrings to Meggernie—a haul her father would receive with delight—and any day now, a cog was due with a cargo of Breadalbane wool.

As always, the barmkin was a hive of activity. Stable lads swept out soiled straw from the stables and used a fork to heap it up onto the back of a cart. One of the kitchen lasses was scattering grain for the clutch of fowl that provided eggs for the castle. The farrier was shoeing a horse, and two warriors were arguing about something by the gate.

Makenna's gaze flicked upward, and she caught sight of a flash of fiery hair. Bran was up on the walls, talking to Finlay. They were discussing something important, it seemed, and things were getting animated as they gesticulated with their hands. She smiled as she watched them. Bran and Finlay had a good rapport, one built on mutual respect.

She noted then that the sun was almost directly overhead. The noon meal was approaching. Donald had kept her even longer than she'd first thought.

Shifting her attention from her husband, Makenna looked over at the smith's forge. Bac's bulky form filled the interior as he hammered out a horseshoe for the farrier.

Anticipation quickened within her. *Finally*. He'd wonder what had kept her.

Shortly after her arrival at Dùn Ara, she'd visited the smith and made a commission—one she'd asked him to keep secret. The day before, he'd let her know it was ready. She needed to collect the item she'd asked him to make.

Keeping an eye on where Bran still spoke to Finlay, Makenna hurried across the cobbled expanse. She didn't want her husband to spot her going into the forge. Nonetheless, the stable lads working nearby turned as she walked by.

"Lady Mackinnon," they both greeted her respectfully.

She nodded back at them, reflecting that it was difficult for her to sneak up on anyone. The rattling of the heavy set of chatelaine keys that now hung from her belt warned others that Lady Mackinnon approached.

Her life was busier than ever these days. When she wasn't training with her husband or discussing the defense of the castle and the management of their lands, she was organizing servants and running the household. There was barely time to retreat to her solar or linger in her beloved rose garden in the afternoons, but she always made sure she did. It was easy to get swept away by all the things that needed to be done, but in the quiet moments, Makenna could put her thoughts in order. Spending time alone every day kept her calm, focused.

Reaching the forge, she ducked inside.

Bac glanced up from hammering yet another horseshoe as she entered, a grin splitting his sweaty red face. "Morning, Lady Mackinnon."

She flashed him a contrite smile. "Sorry I'm late."

"Och, it's nae bother." He stepped away from his anvil, rubbing a stiff muscle in his back as he did so. "I was behind on work this morning anyway." He flashed her another wide smile. "However, yer commission is ready, as promised."

Moving to the back of his forge, he picked up a sword sheathed in an embossed leather scabbard. Turning to face her, he then withdrew the blade from the case.

Steel glinted in the ruddy light of the forge, and Makenna's breathing caught. She then murmured an oath.

Bac's eyes shone with pride as he crossed to her and handed Makenna the longsword. Gripping its pommel, she tested its weight and balance. Then, stepping back, lest she catch the smith with its sharp edge, she made a few practice strikes and feints.

"What do ye think?" Bac asked eagerly. "It's been a while since I crafted anything so fine."

Grinning, she lowered the sword. "It's perfect."

When Makenna climbed up to the walls, she found her husband standing near the northern watchtower, looking out over the sea. He'd finished his discussion with Finlay. The captain had gone down to the barmkin and was now talking to the guards at the gate.

A brisk breeze had stirred the water up, white caps foaming now. Placing her hand on her rattling keys, she approached as quietly as possible before stepping up to his side.

Bran cut her a surprised look. "Where did ye come from?"

Makenna laughed, turning to face him.

He observed her for a moment, a quizzical expression flitting across his features. "What have ye got behind yer back?"

"A gift."

"For me?"

"Aye, mo chridhe … would ye like it?"

A grin tugged at his mouth. "Of course."

Smiling, she brought the sword, encased in its beautifully stitched and worked scabbard, into view.

Bran's eyes snapped wide. "Ye had a sword made?"

"Aye, Bac's been hard at work on it since I arrived here … and luckily, the smith knows how to keep a secret."

Her husband took the sword, his gaze still awed. "Bac used to forge weapons for the Mackinnons of Skye," he murmured. "But these days, he insists he's too old for such work."

"I had to do some convincing," she replied, noting the reverent way he held the blade. "Bac and I both agreed that ye needed a new sword. 'Bonestrike' doesn't suit ye."

Bran snorted. "That's why it now adorns the wall of my solar," he replied. "My father's claidheamh-mòr never sat easily in my hand."

"After watching ye fight, I knew a longsword would suit ye better," she replied softly. "Ye are quick and light on yer feet … and this blade will help ye take advantage of yer speed."

Flashing her a grin, he wrapped his fingers around the grip and drew the sword from its scabbard. The folded steel blade with its twin sharp edges gleamed in the bright noon sun. "Bac is a master," he murmured, admiring the workmanship.

"Aye," she agreed. "But now, ye must name this blade … what will it be?"

He stepped back from her and tested the sword. It whispered through the air. "It shines as if it were made of ice," he said, his voice awed now. "And it will have a cold, vicious bite." His gaze glinted then. "I shall name it 'Winterthorn'."

"Winterthorn," Makenna tested the name out for herself. "A good choice."

Bran tried out a few more moves with his new sword, and she noted how well-matched they were. Her instinct for what weapon he needed had been on the mark. Satisfied, he sheathed the blade and buckled the scabbard around his narrow hips.

He then focused his attention wholly on Makenna. "No one has ever given me something so special," he murmured.

"Ye like it then?" she asked, warmth flowing through her.

"Aye." He moved close and caught her around the waist, drawing her in for a hot, passionate kiss.

Reaching out, Makenna grabbed his gambeson, fisting the quilted material as the kiss deepened. They were in full view of everyone here, up on the walls, but neither of them cared. Once, Makenna had been embarrassed about displaying affection in public, although those days were now far behind her. She loved Bran and didn't care who witnessed it.

And over the past two months, the people of Dùn Ara had gotten used to seeing their laird and lady show each other affection.

When they finally drew apart, breathless now, heat pooled in the cradle of Makenna's hips. Suddenly, she wished to forget about the looming noon meal and instead drag her husband up to their bedchamber.

The look that burned in his grey eyes told her he was thinking along the same lines.

"The sword is fine indeed," he said roughly, reaching out and cupping her cheek, "but it is the love and thoughtfulness that prompted ye to commission the blade that touches me more."

Her throat tightened. "Ye deserve it," she whispered. "I wanted ye to finally have a weapon worthy of ye."

He swallowed, his eyes glistening now. "My fierce, bonnie wife," he whispered. "Have I told ye how much I love ye?"

Her lips tugged into a smile as she raised her hand to cover his upon her cheek. "Many times, dear husband … but go on … tell me again."

HISTORICAL NOTES

I did a deep dive into lots of fun historical facts and figures with this book!

In THE CHIEF'S WILD PROMISE, we spend most of our time in Perthshire, and Meggernie Castle.

Meggernie Castle is a square tower house with five levels. Set in a picturesque spot in the mountainous Glen Lyon, it was built by 'Mad' Colin Campbell of Glenlyon around 1585. Apparently, the laird was responsible for the kidnapping of the Countess of Errol.

The castle is reputedly haunted by the severed upper half and lower half of a woman. Her ghost has apparently been seen many times, both in the castle and in the grounds. She is said to have kissed visitors to Meggernie, waking them from sleep. The story goes that she's the ghost of the beautiful wife of one of the Menzies lords. He was a very jealous man, and in a fit murdered her and cut her in half. A grisly tale ... and not one that appears in my story though.

Instead, since my book takes place in the early 14th century, I needed to imagine what an earlier version of Meggernie Castle might have looked like, as most fortresses are built on the site of a fort or smaller stronghold.

As such, I based the layout of the tower house on the beautiful Huntingtower Castle, which is also in Perthshire. Huntingtower is well preserved and still has a 'medieval' feel to it. It's actually two tower houses side-by-side, and one of them has a 'doocot' on the roof. A 'doocot' is a Scottish term for a dovecote, a structure designed to house pigeons or doves. You usually find them in the gardens or grounds of a castle, but Huntingtower is a little different. The castle also has a colony of tiny pipistrelle bats roosting in its eaves, so I took inspiration from this as well.

The other locations that feature in this novel are:

- Finlarig Castle: Located near Loch Tay, in the village of Killin, these days it's an atmospheric ruin, but it has a dark history associated with it (see my notes below). Built in 1629 by 'Black' Duncan Campbell (Donnchadh Dubh) of Glenorchy, the castle is an L-plan tower house, formerly protected by an outer enclosure or barmkin.
- Dounarwyse Castle: known today as Aros Castle, Dounarwyse is a ruined 13th-century castle near Salen on the Isle of Mull. The castle overlooks the Sound of Mull.
- Dùn Ara Castle: a medieval ruin sited 8 km northwest of Tobermory, upon a prominent rocky outcrop. The castle had a curtain wall of stone and lime that was between 4 to 5 feet thick in places. These days, little remains, although it's best preserved on the northeast side. The entrance is on the southeast side. The medieval castle was built on an older dùn, or fort.

'Black' Duncan Campbell is based on a real historical figure. Sir Duncan Campbell, 1st Baronet of Glenorchy (1545-1631), was a powerful chieftain, landowner, courtier, and favorite of Queen Anne of Denmark. Duncan became the 7th Laird of Glenorchy, and his shrewd, ruthless dealings earned him the moniker 'Black Duncan'. He built part of Kilchurn Castle, began the construction of Finlarig Castle at the west end of Loch Tay, and improved farmland around Finlarig, Kilchurn, and Balloch. Duncan Campbell died in 1631 and was buried at Finlarig.

Duncan had three wives: Jane, Margaret, and Janet. His first wife provided him with four children: Colin, Robert, Jean, and Margaret.

Of course, I move his timeline a little in my novel, fictionalize some details, and give him a different end to the one history gave him!

The feuding between the Campbells and the MacGregors was well-known. The Campbells eventually drove the MacGregors out of Glen Lyon and seized their property, and later helped enforce the ban on the MacGregor name.

There are stories about how the Campbells bred fierce bloodhounds (suckled on the milk of MacGregor women to better sniff out their prey) to hunt MacGregors down. And at the Campbell stronghold of Finlarig Castle on the banks of Loch Tay, 'Black' Duncan Campbell of Glenorchy had a pit, where MacGregors were beheaded for the entertainment of dinner guests. There is indeed a stone-lined pit near the north wall of the now-ruined castle!

Did you know that a 'puddock' is a frog or toad in Scotland?

'The Art of Coupling' makes another appearance in this book. There is evidence to suggest that 'sex manuals' existed in the medieval period. The Voynich manuscript is one. Carbon dating shows the skins used to make its pages come from animals that died between 1404 and 1438. The book's first known owner was Holy Roman Emperor Rudolf II, who lived from 1552 and 1612, although it is likely to have had earlier, unrecorded, owners.

There are other recorded 'manuals' from Europe in the Middle Ages too, such as 'The book of intercourse by Constantine the African' (11th century, Salerno), the anonymous 'The minor book of intercourse' (12th century, Salerno) and the 'Manual to copulate' (14th–15th centuries, Catalonia), also of unknown authorship.

So, who is to say something like 'The Art of Coupling' didn't exist in Scotland?

DIVE INTO MY BACKLIST!

Check out my printable reading order list on my website:

https://www.jaynecastel.com/printable-reading-list

ABOUT THE AUTHOR

Multi-award-winning author Jayne Castel writes epic Historical and Fantasy Romance. Her vibrant characters, richly researched historical settings, and action-packed adventure romance transport readers to forgotten times and imaginary worlds.

Jayne is the author of a number of best-selling series. A hopeless romantic in love with all things Scottish, she writes romances set in both Dark Ages and Medieval Scotland, and Romantasy with a Celtic vibe.

When she's not writing, Jayne is reading (and re-reading) her favorite authors, cooking Italian feasts, and going on long walks with her husband. She's from New Zealand but now lives in Edinburgh, Scotland.

Connect with Jayne online:
www.jaynecastel.com
www.facebook.com/JayneCastelRomance
https://www.instagram.com/jaynecastelauthor/
https://www.tiktok.com/@jaynecastelauthor
Email: contact@jaynecastel.com

Printed in Dunstable, United Kingdom